The Great Scarlet Reset

Book 3
Ruin & Restoration Series
by
Simon Driscoll
and
James T. Prout

Grendelmen Publishing
Mesa, Arizona, USA

The Great Scarlet Reset
Book 3 Ruin & Restoration Series

First edition copyright
© 2021 Grendelmen Publishing
Version 1.0
Imprint Publisher:
Grendelmen Publishing
Mesa, AZ
http://grendelmen.com

All rights reserved. No part of this book may be reproduced or transmitted in any form or by any means, electronic, or mechanical, including photocopying, recording, or by any information storage or retrieval system, without written permission of the author, except for brief quotations embodied in critiques, articles or reviews referencing this book.

ISBN: 978-1-948451-48-2

1. Fiction 2. Mainstream 3. Conspiracy 4. World Religions

Printed in the United States of America

ACKNOWLEDGMENT

SPECIAL THANKS TO THE FOLLOWING

First, thanks be to God for inspiring the authors and others in writing this book.

Christie: Your love and support make all I do possible.

Lilly: Your smiles and tears give my actions purpose.

Jenny: It is a miracle to have you in my life.

Beta Readers: Your feedback and insights have always improved our works of fiction.

Dear Reader,

This book is dedicated to bringing people to Christ and preparing them for His Second Coming. This is a work of fiction based on prophecy and recent history. It is intended to show one way in which End Times Prophecy may be fulfilled in the near future.

As always, let the Spirit guide you in your quest for truth.
— Simon Driscoll

A Note about Endnotes:

The Endnotes found throughout this series are provided to give the interested reader a resource for learning more about the prophecies used to construct the main plot. There are many more references that I haven't included in the book. I would enjoy discussing any prophecies with those who want a better understanding of what is to come.

The authors can be reached in the following ways:

Simon Driscoll
Facebook: Author Simon Driscoll
email: simon@grendelmen.com
website: http://ruinandrestoration.com
Twitter: @AuthorSDriscoll

James T. Prout
Website: www.LastDaysTimeline.com
Email: author@lastdaystimeline.com

Table of Contents

The Silver Lining 1
Victory Silenced 5
The Right Questions 9
Presidential Pronouncements 12
The First Interview 16
#FreeBaldwin 20
Diverging Priorities 27
A Lifetime Vacation 32
Walking Free 34
A Very Shumway Christmas 36
Being Presidential 40
Second Chances 42
Breaking Ties 45
The New Seven 47
Taking the Reins 50
Legal Retest 54
Unwelcome Visitor 56
Farewell to Feathers 58
The First Eagle Head 61
Fortunate Misfortune 65
Clearing the Line 69
Berning Desires 72

Presidential Predictions	74
The Puppet Pope	77
Law and Order	79
Glory for Terror	82
Special Request	85
A New Angle	88
Digging In	92
Down Below	95
Connections	98
A New Score	102
While You're Waiting	104
Explosive Update	107
The Prophet and the Pope	110
Securing the Future	114
Generosity and Destruction	117
The Burden of Damascus	121
Swing and a Miss	123
The Cities of Aroer	125
Yesterday, Tomorrow	127
The Gift of Life	131
Special Delivery	133
Explosive Holy Days	135
Shadow President	138

The Last Speech	140
From Religion to Law	144
Dead Men Walking	149
The Secret Manhunt	152
A New Teacher	155
An Offer He Can't Refuse	158
A New Pope	164
The New G30	166
Friends in High Places	172
General Inspection	175
New Beginnings	179
Wedding Bells Are Ringing	182
New Pope, Old Hope	186
Visual Aid	188
New Duties	190
The Old Man and the See	192
New Foundations	196
Selection Day	198
The Middle Game	201
DCEP Forever	203
Black Thursday	205
Shadow Request	207
The First Order	211

Legal Beginnings	214
Swimming Buddies	216
Crash and Boom	219
Analyzing God's Hands	221
Universal Basic Income	223
Third Time's the Charm?	226
Painful Award	229
Godfather Gideon	232
Those Who Wait	235
Puppy Love	237
The Third Star	239
Nationality Override	243
Pioneer Day	245
The Wrong Place at the Right Time	248
Group Date	250
Islamic State Reborn	253
Failed Inspection	255
Collateral Damage	258
The Last Touchdown	260
From Land to Sea	264
Forging A New Path	266
Aggressive Recruiting	269
The Final Rejection	272

Decision Time	274
Guard Duty	277
Tomorrow Starts Today	279
Endnotes	E1
Appendix A	A1
About the Authors	B1
Other Works by James T. Prout	B6

The Silver Lining

Thanksgiving Day – Notre Dame, Indiana

Gideon Shumway turned on his computer after a less than satisfying Thanksgiving meal with his roommate, Duane, and his girlfriend, Khepri. Gideon felt like the third wheel. Still, it was better than going home and facing his father.

Karen dumped Gideon back in September after reading his book on Ezra's Eagle.[1] The subject was just too scary for her. President Towers was dead, and President Michaels had resigned. She didn't want to accept that President Ball would meet a similar fate.

Gideon picked up one of his copies and turned it over in his hands three times. *Ezra's Eagle; What Ancient Prophecy Tells Us About Today and Tomorrow.* Gideon spent three months writing the paper for his Comparative Religion class. Five months later, President Towers was assassinated, proving Gideon's analysis right.

It was still a thrill to see his name on the cover. But perhaps writing it was a mistake. So far, it had brought nothing but heartache. Losing Karen wasn't the only problem this book had caused. Gideon's father, Benjamin Sr., had enjoyed the paper on which the book was based. But quitting football and spending his summer on a book tour instead of at home had soured what little relationship he had left with Dad.

Gideon spent that summer doubling the length and depth of his analysis, guided by Professor Jenkins. Gideon thought finishing the manuscript was the last step.

Instead, he spent six weeks researching publishers and publishing methods. He finally found a hybrid publisher that allowed Gideon to maintain control of his book while still giving him access to broader distribution.

Then Gideon spent four months going back and forth with the editor, making changes, rewriting phrases, adding more citations, and approving the cover art. Two months later, Gideon's book was for sale at Christian bookstores everywhere.

Book sales were dismal. President Michaels' resignation boosted his sales from a dozen copies a month to several hundred. The ten thousand dollars he'd earned in profits wasn't enough to cover his tuition next semester. Without his football scholarship, Gideon would have to take out a student loan.

As Gideon's email loaded, he saw ninety-three emails in the last two hours. Curious about the flood of emails, he started reading through them. Amazon said his book was sold out. That was odd. That morning, Amazon had more than a hundred copies.

The next one was from Christianbook.com. They were also sold out and were requesting five hundred copies to cover their backorders. Gideon gasped. What was going on?

Five more emails had similar content. Every bookstore and online retailer carrying his book was requesting more copies. He even found a second email from Amazon, asking him to send one thousand copies to cover their backorder demand. The printer wasn't even open today.

Gideon's phone rang, showing his younger brother's face on the caller-ID. "Hello, Ben. How was your football game?"

Ben was the quarterback for BYU. "*I'm not calling about football! Turn on the television!*"

Gideon turned on the TV, and Channel 16 came up. "Which channel— Oh."

The Breaking News banner was flashing at the bottom of the screen. "*President Ball is confirmed dead,*" Beatrice Price said. "*Vice President Nicholson was rushed to the hospital in critical condition. We're all waiting anxiously to see if she pulls through. Former President Michaels and dozens of family members were pronounced dead at the scene in what appears to be the worst mass poisoning ever which didn't involve a religious cult.*"

"Ball is dead?" Gideon asked.

"*That's not the only piece of news,*" Ben said.

"Something else happened?" Gideon asked.

"*In a strange twist of fate,*" Price continued, "*a book released earlier this year predicted the death of President Ball and warns that Haley Nicholson may not live through the night. Even if she does, her Presidency is as doomed as the last three Presidents. Local author Gideon Shumway's book, Ezra's Eagle; What Ancient Prophecy Tells Us About Today and Tomorrow, officially hit the shelves on February 10th. Shumway's book shows connections between recent events and a little-known ancient prophecy from the Old Testament's apocryphal section. Shumway was unavailable for comment.*"

"Unavailable for comment?" Gideon asked. "Is that what they say when they can't find my phone number?"

3

"*Give them a break,*" Ben said. "*President Ball has been dead for less than an hour. I just thought you should be prepared.*"

"Thanks, Ben. This explains all the emails." Something about Ben's warning was out of place. It took a moment for Gideon to put his finger on it.

"*What emails?*"

"Every bookstore carrying my book is sold out. They're all demanding more copies. Hey, this is a local station talking about me. So how did you know they would mention my book?"

"*Your local station isn't the only one discussing your new book,*" Ben said. "*You're national news.*"

Gideon gasped. "I need an agent."

Victory Silenced

November 27th – Atlanta, Georgia

Scott Knox woke in his hotel room, feeling free for the first time in years. He wasn't consumed by hatred or guilt. His hatred led him to almost become a murderer. Instead, he'd accidentally caused the death of his best friend, as well as a stranger who'd invaded Scott's home. That's when he found out there was a price on his head.

All of that was in the past now that Gary Sanders was behind bars. The true mastermind behind the death of President Towers and so much more had finally been exposed and caught. Scott took his time taking a shower and turned on the TV while he dressed.

"Our top story this morning is the horrific attack at Mar-a-Lago." The name on the anchor desk read Tanique Flores. It was a local station, but it was still news. *"President Don Ball was pronounced dead upon arrival at the Good Samaritan Medical Center.[2] The cause of death has yet to be released. Among the dead are First Lady Breanna Ball, former President Spencer Michaels,*

former First-Lady Caroline Michaels, Hank Nicholson, and many other family members. Of the twenty-two grandchildren in attendance at the Thanksgiving celebration, only three survived. We stand with President Nicholson as she mourns their loss."

There were ten seconds of silence, during which time Tanique shed a tear. Scott felt moisture on his cheek and wiped away a few tears of his own. It was hard to imagine losing your spouse, children, and grandchildren, all in a single hour. Yet Gary Sanders's plans had been thwarted once more. Scott hoped Haley Nicholson would have a long and prosperous presidency, now that Sanders was behind bars.

"In local news," Tanique continued, *"media mogul Gary Sander was found dead in his penthouse suite this morning. Initial reports say he died in his sleep from a fatal heart attack."*

"What!" Scott asked the TV as he gripped his pants in one hand, forgetting for the moment that he was putting them on.

"He was found by his housekeeper and personal chef as—"

Scott shut the TV off and grabbed the phone half a second after it rang. "No time for room service," Scott said, thinking it was the kitchen calling as requested to take his breakfast order. "I need to contact a friend."

He was reaching for the hook when Maria Croix's voice cut in. "Don't bother. I'm on my way up to speak to you." She was using a fake British accent for some reason, but it was definitely her.

Scott gulped. "Give me a minute to get my pants on."

He was just buckling his belt when there was a knock on the door. He opened it, and Maria waltzed right in, followed by a bellman with a cart.

"Have a seat," Maria said, continuing to use the accent. Her poor impression of a Brit stretched out all the vowels. "Let me get you caught up on what's been happening this morning while we eat."

The bellman put enough food for three people on the table and accepted Scott's tip before leaving.

"Do you think you ordered enough food?" Scott asked with a smile.

"In the last forty-eight hours, you've been kidnapped, dragged halfway across the country, faced a mortal enemy, and brought him to justice," Maria said. "And the next forty-eight don't look very promising." She grabbed the breakfast burrito and took a bite as she flicked the TV back on and turned the volume up. They were going through the list of Gary Sanders' accomplishments.

"How did Gary get out of police custody?" Scott asked before he grabbed a fork and shoved a bite of waffle covered in strawberry syrup in his mouth. The sweet, fluffy, tangy taste distracted him for a moment.

"Gary Sanders was found dead in his cell at 1 a.m. this morning," Maria said between bites, finally speaking normally. "The guards swear Sanders was asleep at midnight when they did their rounds and that no one else entered or left. Despite my best arguments, I was ordered to have his body moved to his penthouse. I was also ordered to dispose of any evidence I've collected against him."

"What!" A piece of juicy red strawberry waffle fell back out of his mouth onto the table, looking like a half-chewed piece of flesh. "You're going to let Baldwin, an innocent man, rot in prison? So you can, what, save face with the Secret Service?"

"Officially, yes," Maria said. "This is a high-profile case, and we can't figure out what caused his heart attack. The monitors cut out for just the wrong five minutes."

"So that's it? The investigation is over because the prime suspect mysteriously died?"

Maria shook her head. "That's where you come in." The British accent was back.

"Me?" He finished off the waffles and started in on the eggs, finding he was hungrier than expected.

"Yes, you." Maria finished her burrito as she chewed on how to phrase her next sentence. "If they delete all the evidence against Gary, they'll also have to delete any evidence that you ever spoke with the Joint Terrorism Task Force. A man of your skills knows how to prepare for such eventualities, right?"

Scott nodded as he chewed his eggs. He didn't understand why she was using that poor fake accent or talking circles around subjects they'd spent hours discussing only a few weeks ago.

"Well then, I'm sure you can find a way to use what you've saved. Just be sure you don't mention ever speaking with the JTTF or Secret Service." She turned the TV off.

"What good will it do to release the data myself?" Scott asked. "People will think I've made the whole thing up."

Maria shook her head. "I'm sure you'll find everything you need to prove your point."

Scott scowled at her, confused about why she was so cryptic. "Can't you just—"

"No." Maria cut him off. She mouthed the word 'bugged.' "Always assume someone is listening." She left before Scott could ask any more questions.

Scott stared at the door as she left. When would someone have had time to bug his room? He didn't make a reservation, and he was registered under a false name. He spent several hours searching online for more ways to thwart surveillance before looking through the encrypted files stored on his remote server. There was a lot more there than he'd anticipated. Now he needed to figure out what to do with it.

The Right Questions

November 27th – Nephi, Utah

Benjamin Shumway Jr. returned home from Church completely drained. After a football game, flying home always left him exhausted on Sunday morning, even when the flight was short.

He pulled off his tie as he entered his room and flopped down on the bed, trying to decide if he had enough energy to remove his shoes before taking a nap.

Ben's phone buzzed. Gideon's name appeared on the screen. "Hello, brother."

"*Hi, Ben. Is this a good time to talk?*"

"Depends on the subject," Ben said, suppressing a sigh. "If you're going to ask me what the giant letter 'G' stands for, I don't have a clue."

"*Giant G?*" Gideon asked.

"You don't know about that?" Ben asked. "I thought you followed all those conspiracy theories."

"No," Gideon replied. *"Only the ones found in the Bible."*

Ben chuckled. "The day after Gary Sanders died, someone posted a large letter G on his Twitter account. No one has taken responsibility for it, and no one knows what it means."

"Very strange," Gideon concluded. *"But that's not why I called. Do you remember what the angel told me?"*

Ben sat up, all weariness forgotten. "The part where your sins were forgiven, or the part where you'll get a front-row seat to major changes both political and spiritual?"

"The second part. I may be on the verge of getting that front-row seat the angel told me about."

"Is this because of your book?" Ben asked. "Half a dozen friends and most of the football team asked me about it."

"Have you read it yet?"

"No," Ben admitted. "I read the paper that started it all, of course."

"Right," Gideon said. *"There is a lot more in the book, but it is mostly more supporting material, with only a few new conclusions."*

"You didn't call to ask if I've read your book." Ben's weariness started creeping back.

"No," Gideon confirmed. *"I've received several offers to appear on national talk shows. I've also received two death threats."*

"Neither of those is surprising," Ben said.

"True. The question is, should I put myself even further into the spotlight?"

Ben thought about that question for a moment. "Not many talk show hosts are going to agree with your conclusions."

"No kidding!"

"But that doesn't mean you should ignore every offer. The world as a whole will never love you."

"What do you mean?"

"You're not a worldly person, are you?"

"No."

"The world only loves its own." [3]

"But you still think I should do the talk show circuit?"

Ben nodded, then remembered Gideon couldn't see him. "Yes, I do. Just don't expect to be treated like an A-list celebrity."

Gideon sighed into the phone. *"So, you're saying this is going to be a difficult journey."*

"Yes. But, you feel this is the next step in getting closer to the changes that are already rocking our world?"

"Exactly."

"Then how can you possibly say no?" Ben waited for a reply. When none came, he added, "Have you prayed about this?"

"Yes," Gideon said slowly. *"I haven't gotten an answer."*

"Then, you're asking the wrong questions."

"What are the right questions?" Gideon asked.

"I don't know," Ben said. "Perhaps that *is* the right question."

"Wow. That's deep."

"Glad I could help."

Presidential Pronouncements

November 29th – Washington, D.C.

President Haley Nicholson marched into the conference room, her head buzzing with anger. "You cut out every part of my speech relating to the group who killed the President! Not to mention my family!"

"I understand your anger, Madame President," Lee Barker said. He was the lead legal advisor overseeing Presidential speeches. "But as President, there are certain things you simply cannot say, even with more proof than we now have."

"How much more proof do you need?" Haley shouted back. "President Towers was assassinated." [4]

"And the man responsible is dead."

"I'm not convinced he was acting alone," Haley retorted.

"But you need proof," Lee insisted.

"President Michaels was forced to resign," Haley shot back. [5]

"Due to his own actions, of course," Lee pointed out.

"But that wasn't enough for these people," Haley continued. "He was killed, along with President Ball and dozens of family members. *My* family members were among them."

"I'm well aware of the body count, Madame President," Lee said. "It's not enough to prove your allegations."

"It's proof enough for me," Haley said.

Lee nodded. "I understand that, and the investigation will continue. But this is your first speech as President. It is a historic moment. Do not taint it with accusations that we cannot yet prove beyond a reasonable doubt. Please read the speech we've approved, and avoid any impromptu statements."

"I'm the President of the United States," Haley said, pounding her fist on the table. "I should be able to deliver whatever speech I want."

"You have much power as President, it's true," Lee replied calmly, speaking slowly and carefully. "However, this is still a nation governed by laws which even you cannot violate. Suppose you begin your Presidency by making accusations that are difficult or impossible to prove. In that case, you will only invite attacks upon your character and state of mind. Anything else you hope to achieve as President will be stunted or prevented."

"Madame President, it is time," an aide said as he came in.

Haley heaved a huge sigh, then turned to follow the aide without replying to Lee.

As she walked down the hallway, she pondered the advice she'd just received. Was she willing to risk her entire Presidency on her first speech?

Haley Nicholson was mindful of this moment's historic nature as she walked to the podium. She looked out at the assembled press corps, eagerly waiting to hear the first words spoken by a female President.

"I stand before you through a series of most unfortunate events," Haley began. "The deaths of President Ball and the others in attendance at our Thanksgiving feast appear to be the work of one person."

Haley gripped the podium, trying to grab the courage to say what she had to say next. There was so much she wanted to say. But there was even more she wanted to do. "Miss Schott is being held on suspicion of treason. After my remarks, Press Secretary Thomas will address the details of the events on Thanksgiving. But first, I want to focus on the larger issues."

Now that the hard part was over, Haley settled into the heart of her prepared speech. "I know the events of the last few years have been chaotic and confusing. I am, after all, the fourth President in less than two years. Such a rapid change in leadership has never been experienced by this country. That is why I will be keeping nearly all of the current staff. In these times of uncertainty, we must retain continuity to ensure prosperity."

Haley walked away from the podium, ignoring the dozens of overlapping questions she wished she could answer.

Janet Thomas walked to the podium and opened her portfolio, filled with notes. "At this point, we know that the shrimp was marinated in pure Fentanyl, which caused the death of nearly everyone who ate it. The source of the Fentanyl and who administered it are still under investigation."

"Miss Thomas!" Victor Barton shouted. "Who has resigned from the administration?"

"We are also investigating the connection between this poisoning and the so-called protests around the country," Janet continued, ignoring the question. "These riots are now classified as terrorist acts and will be investigated and prosecuted as such."

"And the resignations?" Barton tried again.

Janet scowled at Barton. "If you cannot maintain decorum, you will be removed from this hall, and your press pass revoked. Do I make myself clear?"

"You don't have the authority to—" Barton began.

Janet waved to the guards who closed in from both sides and escorted Victor from the room, removing his press badge as they did so.

"I see the rest of you have learned to save your questions until the proper time," Janet said. "The Secretary of Health and Human Services, Xander Xing, has resigned to spend more time with his family. The Secretary of Homeland Security, Geoffrey Tanner, has resigned over what he sees as a personal failure to stop these riots. Now, are there any questions?"

Every reporter either raised their hand or shot to their feet.

The First Interview

November 30th – Irving, Texas

Gideon Shumway walked into the studios for The Blaze, looking everywhere, trying to take it all in. He'd seen this room through the camera hundreds of times. But to actually be here gave him a thrill he could feel from his head to his toes.

"Gideon?" Gregg Burke asked, offering his hand. He looked like a younger version of Colonel Sanders.

Gideon shook the offered hand. "Gregg Burke! Wow. It is an honor to meet you!"

Gregg smiled. "That's always great to hear. I got the list of questions from your agent. I just thought I would warn you, I don't always stick to those questions."

Gideon laughed. "That doesn't surprise me. I think it will be okay."

"Okay. Zalina will get you set up." Gregg motioned toward a woman with bright purple hair holding three different headsets.

Gideon walked over to her. "Hello."

"Hello, Mr. Shumway," Zalina replied with a smile. "You'll need a headset for the show. Let's find you a good fit."

The second pair Gideon tried on was perfect. Zalina motioned for him to sit at one of the desks. The logo behind the chair showed Gideon was sitting where co-host Mike Steno usually sat.

"Welcome back to the Gregg Burke program," Gregg said. "I have in studio with me today, the author of Ezra's Eagle, Gideon Shumway. Gideon, for those few listeners who haven't already read your book, can you tell us what Ezra's Eagle is about?"

"Thank you, Geoff." Gideon's agent coached him for two hours on how to do a live interview. "Ezra's Eagle refers to a prophecy from the Old Testament prophet, Ezra. Around 400 A.D., the prophecy's authenticity came into question. Unfortunately, that meant the text was excluded from most Bible printings in the last two hundred years. But, as my book shows, this is a true prophecy. In fact, it's being fulfilled right now."

"What does the prophecy say?" Burke asked.

"There isn't time to go through all five chapters of the prophecy," Gideon replied. "The part everyone is interested in today talks about a political kingdom in the last days represented by an eagle. The details in Ezra's prophecy about each of the last twenty-three leaders of this eagle kingdom match up perfectly with the Presidents of the last ninety-four years."

"The New York Times quoted you as saying, 'There are two Presidents after President Michaels before a new and terrible leader takes over.' Are you saying President Nicholson is the last U.S. President?" Gregg asked.

"No, no," Gideon replied. "Not at all. Haley Nicholson matches up with the eighteenth leader of the eagle kingdom of Ezra's prophecy."

"So, we have six Presidents before the fall of America?" Gregg clarified.

Gideon nodded. "Pretty much. During the reign of the twenty-third leader, there is a civil war before America is restored to its original glory."

"Was it a coincidence that your book was released the same day as President Michael's resignation?" Gregg asked.

"Completely," Gideon said. "I worked on the book for over two years before it was released."

"Then, your book wasn't inspired by the death of President Towers?" Burke pressed.

"Only partially," Gideon confirmed. "I wrote a college paper months before Towers was assassinated. It was Towers' death that encouraged me to expand the paper into a book. I sent the first draft to my publisher for review months before President Michaels resigned."

"That explains why you don't mention President Nicholson by name."

Gideon nodded. "Exactly. Michaels took over and named Ball as VP before I published the book. But predicting who the fourth short feather would be—"

"Short feather?" Gregg interrupted.

"Yes," Gideon confirmed. "Ezra used the feathers of the eagle to represent the leaders. One feather was twice as long as any other. Short feathers represent Presidents who left office before their term officially ended."

"So, is Haley Nicholson a long feather or a short feather?" Gregg asked.

"Definitely a short feather," Gideon said. "In fact, in the book, I wasn't even sure whether the fourth short feather would actually take office. Based on the prophecy, President Nicholson will have less time in office than President Ball."

"You're claiming that you not only predicted the death of President Towers," Gregg replied, "but also the resignation of President Michaels and the death of President Ball? You're also claiming President Nicholson's life is in just as much danger?"

"Not quite," Gideon said. "My book shows that before Kevin Smith assassinated President Towers, there were two examples of short feathers, Presidents Kennedy and Nixon. So I can't say for sure whether President Nicholson will be assassinated or forced to resign, or forced out of office by some other means. But if my interpretation of Ezra's Eagle is correct, one of those will happen before Spring."

"That's quite a bold prediction," Gregg said.

"I know," Gideon replied. "But it's already in print. It's been in print for two years."

"What about after President Nicholson?" Gregg pressed.

Gideon gave a big smile. "You'll have to read the book to find out."

#FreeBaldwin

December 1st – San Francisco, California

Scott Knox rang Tonya's doorbell, then took a step back. He wasn't sure how he'd be received by his ex-wife, mainly because Scott had been declared dead more than eighteen months ago. Having a price on his head hadn't been an easy life, but it had given him time to get his priorities straight.

The door opened.

Tonya screamed.

Scott cleared his throat as she went silent. "Hello, Tonya. May I come in?"

"Scott! I thought you were dead! I cried at your funeral. How are you alive? What are you doing here?"

Scott raised his hand to stem the flood of questions. "If you'll permit me to come inside, I'll happily explain everything."

Tonya stepped out and pulled him into a long, hard hug. Scott gently hugged her back, thinking this was going far better than expected.

After a long moment, Tonya whispered, "I've missed you."

Scott wasn't sure that she'd actually spoken but replied anyway. "I've missed you, too," he whispered back.

"Come inside," Tonya said softly, pulling him in by the hand.

Scott allowed himself a small smile as he was pulled into the living room where a toddler was sitting on the carpet, surrounded by a dozen toys.

"This is our son, Samuel," Tonya said as she picked up the boy. "Sam, this is your father, Scott."

Sam took one look at Scott and started crying, hiding his face in Tonya's chest.

Tonya smiled and put Sam down on the carpet. "He's a little afraid of strangers. Don't worry, he'll warm up to you."

Scott frowned briefly and nodded slightly. "I'm a stranger to him. That's among the things I regret the most." He took a seat on the couch.

Tonya sat in an armchair and studied Scott carefully. "You've lost weight."

Scott nodded. "A lot has happened in the last two years."

Her expression turned serious. "It certainly has. Sam has sort of consumed my life."

Scott looked down at his son, who looked back with a wary expression. There was so much Scott wished he could tell Sam but knew anything he said today would be forgotten.

"Why don't you start with how you're not dead," Tonya said, drawing Scott's attention away from Sam.

Scott looked up at her. "I'm really sorry about that whole mess," he began. "I got in far deeper than I'd ever intended, and when I tried to pull back—"

"Into what?" Tonya interrupted.

Scott took a deep breath and started from the beginning, a few months before their divorce. He explained how he began earning money for illegal actions, leading to Kevin and Scott preparing to kill President Towers and V.P. Michaels. Scott described his attempt to stop Kevin and the disastrous result. Then when he returned home, someone was there, waiting for him, plotting to kill him.

Tonya didn't interrupt except with the occasional gasp. Sam spoke to his toys in a broken toddler speech, which made no sense to Scott. Once in a while, Sam said a word Scott recognized, but nothing more than that.

Scott didn't try to hide any of his mistakes or poor choices. He explained as quickly as he could about the brief struggle he had with his would-be killer and the man's latex allergy. Once the man was clearly dead, Scott turned on the stove to start the fire and went on the run. He told her about the year he spent in Phoenix before trying to turn himself in. That led to his attempt to find the man behind everything and the arrest of Gary Sanders.

"Since I can't leave an innocent man in prison," Scott concluded, "I released everything about Gary Sanders's involvement in the assassination of President Towers onto the internet. Frank Baldwin should be a free man within a month."

Tonya studied him for a long time, neither of them saying anything. She tried several times to start speaking, but no words came out. Eventually, she said, "Scott, I'm so sorry."

Scott frowned. "I'm the one who's sorry. You were right all along. I just hope God will forgive me."

Tonya nodded. "I'm sure He will."

"But, I killed a man."

"In self-defense," Tonya shot back. "Even man's law allows that." She paused before adding, "And you clearly feel terrible about it. That's a good sign."

Scott sighed deeply, letting go of tension he'd held bottled up for a year and a half. At last, he'd found someone he trusted, telling him that man's death wasn't Scott's fault. After two hours of talking, he stood up, preparing to leave. "I've set up a trust fund for Samuel—"

"Scott, please don't leave," Tonya said, rising from her chair and standing between him and the door.

He looked at her, puzzled by this reaction. "You want me to stay?"

Tonya nodded. "If you walk out that door, I'm worried you'll never come back. I'm not ready to lose you again."

Scott blinked several times, trying to understand her words. She was the one who kicked him out and asked for a divorce. He had prepared himself for a complete rejection, thinking she never wanted to see him again. But he never thought he'd be invited to stay. "It's not that simple," Scott said, remembering why he had to go.

"Then make it simple."

"I'm legally dead," Scott said. "If I suddenly declare I'm alive, they're going to ask about the man who died in my apartment."

"You said you turned yourself in," Tonya replied. "You fixed all that."

Scott shook his head. "I thought I fixed all that. But when Gary Sanders died in that cell, Agent Croix was forced to delete everything about me from her records. It was a clandestine operation from the beginning. She can't protect me from prosecution."

Tonya's eyes darted from Scott's face to his hands, to his feet, and back again, as if looking for an answer. "We can figure it out. As long as we do it together."

"What do you mean?"

She took his hand and gently pulled him back onto the couch, sitting next to him. "I kicked you out because I was afraid. I'd just found out I was pregnant, and I was feeling overly protective of our child. I should have stuck by your side. I should have helped you through those rough times. If I had, maybe you wouldn't have been pulled in so deep. Maybe becoming a father would have refocused your priorities."

Scott took a breath, but no words came out. Here was something he hadn't considered. If Tonya had told him that day that she was pregnant, would Scott have reevaluated his life? Would he still have been willing to risk attending violent protests if he knew there was a child on the way?

Everything he'd done was still his own responsibility. He'd made his own choices and had already come to terms with that. Yet could all that have been avoided by Tonya speaking those two words which change so many lives forever? All she had to say was 'I'm pregnant,' and who knows what might have happened.

Scott looked deep into her eyes and found the fear and anguish of someone living with great regret. It was something he'd seen in the mirror for far too long. "It's not your fault, Tonya. And I don't need you to fix me."

Tonya nodded. "I know I can't fix you. But maybe we can anchor each other to prevent us from flying off into strange roads again. I've had Sam to keep me grounded. But who did you have?"

"First Kevin, then Agent Croix," Scott said. "But that didn't really help."

Tonya nodded, tears forming in her eyes. "Scott, whatever it takes, we can work through or around any problems. But please, promise me we'll do it together."

Scott nodded slowly. "Okay. Together."

They hugged and kissed until Sam started fussing. Tonya picked up the toddler and changed his diaper. "So what exactly did you mean when you said you released all the information onto the internet? Did you issue a press release or something?"

The Great Scarlet Reset

Scott shook his head as he tried to find words to explain. "No, I don't know how to issue a press release. I used the tools Agent Croix loaded on the laptop. I hacked into Gary Sanders's Twitter account and posted the letter 'G' with a link embedded in the image."

"That was you?" Tonya asked.

Scott nodded. "I guess no one has found the link yet, because no one is talking about it on the news."

"Did you really expect people to find such an obscure clue and track it down?"

Scott shook his head. "Not really. That is why I've also uploaded all the information to Wikileaks."

"Wikileaks?" Tonya asked. "I thought that site was shut down. They arrested everyone connected with that site eight months ago after they published classified evidence about an old disaster scenario.[6] What was it called again?"

"The Adam and Eve Story,"[7] Scott said. "Yes, I read that report. It claims the real reason for the moon landing was to verify that the Sun explodes every six thousand years. Most of it was already public knowledge, but they released the redacted part."

Tonya nodded as she finished buttoning up Sam's pants. "Yes, that's the one. A very different sort of story for them."

"Yeah. This one will leave people wondering, though." He followed her into the kitchen, where Tonya put Sam in a highchair and gave him carrots and cucumber slices from the fridge.

When she sat at the kitchen table, Scott took the seat next to her. "Won't people think it's a hoax if new files show up on a site that's supposed to be dead?"

"Maybe," Scott said. "But Wikileaks was just a tool to get the information on the web. The real plan starts tomorrow. I've scheduled a series of posts on Facebook and Twitter with links to the juicier bits of the story. I've made it look like an editor at

Wikileaks found the link I embedded in the letter 'G' and decrypted all the data."

"Won't people figure out you posted it?"

Scott shook his head. "I used a laptop built by the CIA for the Secret Service to perform clandestine operations. Even then, I used a Virtual Private Network to access files stored on a highly encrypted cloud server and move them to a website server. Most people won't even know any of that was done in the United States."

Tonya got a dazed look on her face, showing she only understood half of what Scott had just said. When she rallied her thoughts, she asked, "Doesn't the CIA track their computers? Won't they know everything you've been doing?"

"Agent Croix already looked into that," Scott said. "The machine was built to avoid any kind of detection. It doesn't send updates to the CIA or any other organization. That would defeat the purpose."

"Won't they notice that all the files were uploaded in the last week? Or that you hacked into their servers?"

Scott shook his head. "I backdated my admin access by five years and changed the dates on all the files, so it looks like they've been on the servers since November 29th. The first post will go out in about an hour, and another post will hit every twelve hours for the next two months. By the time it's all done, I expect every news agency will be discussing the hashtag #FreeBaldwin."

"Does this mean you're done?" Tonya asked. "Can we just disappear?"

Scott nodded. "I believe we can. We have enough money to go anywhere you want."

"Let's start with Paris."

Scott nodded. "Let's start there."

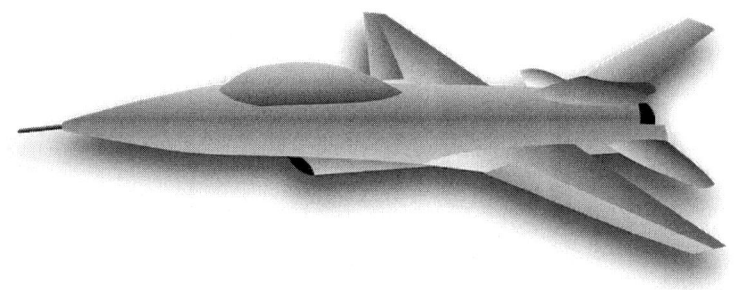

Diverging Priorities

December 2nd – McLean, Virginia

Jonathon Shumway shoved his phone back in his pocket as he flopped back down on the couch next to his wife, Elizabeth. His long, deep sigh was almost a groan.

"Was that your dad?" Liz asked.

"The files speak for themselves," James Jones said on the television. He was sitting at the small table they used to wrap up and review the most important news of the day on The Blaze. *"Mark my words. The FBI will find those same files on one of Gary's computers."*

"Yeah," Jon said, barely diverting his gaze from the TV. "My parents aren't coming."

"We can't know that," Patty Parker shot back. *"All we have is a series of documents which was mysteriously released on WikiLeaks, even though everyone authorized to post there is in prison."*

Liz frowned. "Did he say why?"

"Everyone we know of," Gregg Berk said. *"Someone is clearly still running the site. And let's not forget the giant G posted on Sanders's Twitter account the day after he died."*

"Yeah," Jon said, failing to keep the bitterness out of his voice. "Grandma Tulley can't travel, and they can't afford to hire someone to watch her."

"And we have yet to have a single WikiLeaks document proven wrong," James added. *"Everything you can find on Wikileaks can also be found by following the link in that giant G. Did Gary Sanders get hacked, or did he set all this up before he died?"*

"I thought the Briggs's agreed to watch her for the weekend," Liz said.

"Even so," Patty said, *"It's not enough to get Frank Baldwin released, no matter how much proof they uncover."*

"That was before Grandma wandered out of the house," Jon said. "It took a twenty-man search party twelve hours to find her. They were on the verge of issuing a Silver Alert."[8]

"It'll have to be verified, of course," Gregg said.

"Wow," Liz said. "So delaying won't help."

"But if our justice system can't admit when it makes a mistake," Gregg continued, *"then we really do need more criminal justice reform."*

Jon shook his head. "I'm afraid not. Besides, my brothers are both flying in tonight."

"First, the FBI or Secret Service will have to investigate," Patty said. *"Even then, Frank has a better chance at a Presidential pardon than getting his trial verdict reversed."*

Liz nodded. "You're right. We'll just have to do Jaime's baby blessing without them."

"How can you say that?" James asked. *"Surely you don't still think he's guilty."*

The Great Scarlet Reset

Jon felt a knot in his gut. He wanted to talk about this, to tell Liz how disappointed he was that Ben Sr. wasn't coming to the blessing of his first grandchild. Jon wasn't sure how to explain himself adequately. He only knew there was a lot of emotion wrapped around this issue. More emotion than he could handle right now.

"He was given a proper trial," Patty said. *"I'm not ready to jump on the Free Baldwin bandwagon just yet."*

"What was that about Baldwin getting released?" Jon asked.

"It's a shame Sanders isn't here to explain himself," James said.

"Apparently, WikiLeaks had one more surprise for us," Liz summarized. "It's been inactive for over a year, but yesterday someone released a bunch of documents showing how all the evidence against Baldwin was faked."

"That's a little too convenient for me," Patty said. *"I don't care whether The Gateway Pundit claims the documents are already verified. I'll wait for the FBI investigation."*

"WikiLeaks?" Jon asked, finally focusing on the news. "Really?"

"Well, nothing convenient about it," Gregg said. *"Info Wars explained the whole sordid conspiracy."*

The three of them laughed.

Liz nodded. "I know. There must still be one of their admins that no one has identified yet."

"Do tell," Patty said. *"What explanation did they come up with this time?"*

"They claim Gary was behind the whole thing," Gregg explained. *"According to Info Wars, the giant G was a posthumous confession."*

"Gary Sanders hired Kevin Smith?" Liz asked. "That's impossible!"

"Sure," James said. *"Blame the dead guy."*

Gregg nodded. *"If the President and former Vice-President had died on the same day, Frank Baldwin would have stepped in as President under the control of Gary Sanders. But when Michaels survived and became President, Gary needed a fall guy."*

"There's not one shred of evidence that Frank Baldwin and Gary Sanders ever communicated," James shot back.

"So, Gary manufactured all that evidence against Baldwin?" Patty asked. *"Why would anyone go to that much trouble?"*

"More important than why is how," Liz said. "Those voice recordings and phone records fooled the experts and convinced a jury."

"Because Gary isn't at the top of the food chain," James said.

"Of course not," Patty said. *"You can't have the whole ball of wax rolled up that neatly. One question we haven't asked is how Gary Sanders did this."*

"I've been telling you for years the deepfakes[9] are coming," Gregg said. *"A man with Gary's resources certainly had the technology to produce a fake voice recording good enough to fool a jury. Even our best experts at the FBI thought they were really listening to a conversation between Kevin Smith and Frank Baldwin. The WikiLeaks documents included voice profiles for both Frank and Kevin from dozens of recordings stored on Gary Sanders's home computer, as well as the software required to fake a phone conversation between them."*

"There you go," Jon said. "It's almost like they heard your question."

"And let's not forget that Xander Johnson showed how this was all orchestrated by the globalists!" James added.

"I'm sure Patty had the same question," Liz said. "Great minds think alike."

"Please don't tell me Johnson tied this whole thing to that secret group he claims meets in old underground tunnels," Patty said.

"So do conspiracy theorists," Jon said with a smirk.

"Why give up a good theory?" Gregg asked. *"Xander Johnson has been ranting for years against the globalist conspiracy. It's only recently that he's added the underground meetings and decided that everything wrong with the world is being orchestrated by them. Towers' assassination, the Halo Virus, vaccination mandates, the string of bankrupt businesses, the strange and severe weather, the increase in earthquake frequency, the weakening of the Earth's magnetic field, the Mar-A-Lago poisoning, even the death of Gary Sanders. To him, they are behind it all."*

Liz grabbed the remote and turned off the TV. "There's no way the globalists are affecting the Earth's magnetic field. Even if they *do* exist."

Jon shook his head. "Of course not. But the magnetic field really is weakening. And the Book of Mormon tells us the globalists are real." [10]

"Just another sign of the times," Liz concluded. "Besides, it looks like your brothers shared an Uber from the airport."

"How could you possibly know that?" Jon asked.

The doorbell rang.

"Because they're both standing on our porch." Liz held up her phone, displaying the feed from their doorbell camera.

A Lifetime Vacation

December 14th – Paris, France

Scott Knox looked out the window from the restaurant in the Eiffel Tower.

"Is there something wrong with the food?" Tonya asked.

Scott turned back to Tonya with a smile. "Of course not. It's delicious."

"Then what's on your mind?" Tonya asked.

"I was just enjoying the scenery," Scott said. He looked from his wife to his son, deciding the scenery at the table was far better than the city outside the window.

Tonya turned and looked out the window. "A lovely and romantic setting … if you ignore the smoke from the fires."

Scott scowled. "All too common a sight these days." [11]

Little Samuel glared back, clearly unhappy with his chicken and vegetables.

"We have more money than I ever dreamed possible," Tonya said as she picked up Samuel. "More importantly, I have you back from the dead."

Scott's smile faded. "I'm sorry for—"

"Stop apologizing," Tonya interrupted. "I've already accepted your apology. Let's put it behind us."

Scott nodded. "As you wish."

"Are you quoting The Princess Bride to me?" Tonya asked.

Scott smiled and nodded again. "Where do you want to go next?"

"Next?" Tonya repeated. "I thought we'd be going back to America for Christmas."

"What for?" Scott asked. "Our family is all here."

"What about my mother?" Tonya shot back.

"We can pay to fly her wherever we're going to be," Scott suggested. "Or simply set up a video call, if she'd prefer that."

Tonya started to respond but realized she had no other reasons to return right away. "I guess this vacation isn't over yet."

Scott shook his head. "Not even close."

Walking Free

December 23rd – Washington, D.C.

Frank Baldwin stood as Judge Morris entered the courtroom. The judge looked like he'd lost twenty pounds in the last ten months. Meanwhile, Frank had put on muscle, having little else to do with his free time than workout, study, and meditate. Ten months of solitary confinement wasn't easy, but it was better than a life sentence.

"You may be seated," Morris said as he sat. "I've reviewed the motion put forward by the defense. Does the state have anything to say on this matter?"

"Yes, your honor," a woman in a power suit said.

Frank looked over at the District Attorney in surprise. Every seat in the gallery was filled with reporters. Apparently, the previous prosecutor was too embarrassed to show his face. The proceedings were being broadcast on the major news networks and dozens of online blogs and self-proclaimed news sites.

The Great Scarlet Reset

"We have reviewed the evidence provided by Mr. Baldwin's defense team," the female prosecutor said, "and we support the motion to have the verdict reversed."

"Very well," Morris said. "Since both parties are in agreement, the motion is granted. Mr. Baldwin, you are free to go." The judge banged his gavel and stood up to leave.

The gallery erupted with applause.

Frank let out a sigh of relief. He'd lost everything he'd worked for his whole life, but he had his freedom. He'd completely missed the election, but in two years, he'd have all this behind him and take back what was lost.

He stood up and turned around. Betty, his wife, and Hannah, his daughter, sat in the gallery's front row with tears running down both of their faces. Neither of them had visited him in prison or come to a single day of his hearing.

"I'm so sorry," Betty said, pulling him into a hug. "I shouldn't have given up on you."

"Hush," Frank said. "I'm free now. Merry Christmas."

A Very Shumway Christmas

Christmas Day - Nephi, Utah

Gideon Shumway got up on Christmas morning, feeling less joy than ever before on this day. The last two days had been a combination of cold stares and cold shoulders from Dad, mixed with warm hugs from Mom. Unsurprisingly, the combination left Gideon twisting in a tornado of emotion.

Between the death of President Ball and Gideon's appearance on five talk shows in the last month, book sales had shot up from two thousand to two hundred thousand. Gideon was officially a millionaire, making any presents his parents could afford paltry compared with what he could buy for himself.

Gideon got showered and headed downstairs. Dad looked up at him and grunted before returning his attention to a plate with three cinnamon rolls.

The Great Scarlet Reset

The smell of cinnamon and sugar brought a brief smile to Gideon's face, and he dished up three of his own. Mom's homemade cinnamon rolls were a Shumway Christmas tradition.

Halfway through Gideon's second roll, Ben Jr. sat down with four rolls on his plate.

"Merry Christmas, Ben," Dad said.

"Merry Christmas, Dad," Ben Jr. replied.

Dad got up from the table with half a roll still on his plate. "We'll be opening presents in half an hour."

"I'll be ready," Ben Jr. said with a mouth full of roll.

"Sounds good," Gideon said.

Dad grunted as he left the room, plate in hand.

"Still getting the cold shoulder?" Ben Jr. asked.

Gideon nodded. "I thought he'd be excited to talk about my book. Instead, all he cares about is football."

"That's not entirely true," Ben Jr. said. "He's had a lot on his mind lately."

"Like what?" Gideon turned to face his brother.

As if in answer, Mom led Grandma Tulley into the kitchen. "Have a seat, Mom," Ruth said. "I'll get you a cinnamon roll."

Grandma smiled up at her daughter after she sat down. "You've been so wonderful these last few months."

"Merry Christmas, Mom," Ruth said.

"Merry Christmas, Mom," Ben Jr. echoed. "Merry Christmas, Grandma."

"Merry Christmas," Gideon repeated flatly.

Ruth brought two plates of rolls to the table and sat next to Grandma Tulley. Mom looked from Ben Jr. to Gideon and said, "Merry Christmas, boys. Gid, I know Dad will come around eventually. He's just been swamped lately. The extra stress isn't a good environment for—" Ruth trailed off, as if she couldn't find the right word.

"Forgiveness?" Ben Jr. offered.

Mom shook her head. "Grieving is a better word. He still can't accept that you'd throw away your football career to write a book."

"That's not why I quit football!" Gideon shot back.

Mom just smiled.

"I'm not even sure why I came back for Christmas!" Gideon blurted out.

"Because you love your mother," Ben Jr. said. "Plus, I begged you to come."

"You did?" Grandma asked. "Why would you have to beg your brother to come home for Christmas?"

Ben patted Grandma's shoulder gently. "Because I couldn't get Jon to come."

"Where is Jon?" Grandma asked. "I wanted to make my cookies. I know how much he loves them."

"Jon's baby is only two months old," Mom said. "Liz didn't want to fly with a child that young, and driving was out of the question."

Grandma shook her head. "That's too bad. I was hoping to make a few more Christmas memories before I forget them all."

"Grandma," Ben Jr. shot back. "You shouldn't talk like that."

"Why not?" Grandma asked. "I know I'm losing my memories. By dinner time, I probably won't remember this conversation. Do you think I don't know it was my fault your parents couldn't make it to little Jaime's baby blessing? Do you think I don't see what a burden I've become for my only daughter?"

"Uncle Timothy's daughter moved back in with him to raise her child," Mom said. "We all agreed you're better off here."

Gideon dropped his fork. "Veronica had a baby?"

Mom nodded. "Almost. She's due in March."

"But she's in high school!" Ben Jr. said.

"Not anymore," Mom said. "She graduated a semester early."

The Great Scarlet Reset

"Who's the father?" Gideon asked.

Mom's lips pursed. "Either she won't say, or she doesn't know."

"So she's raising the baby on her own?" Gideon asked.

Mom nodded.

A thought buzzed around in Gideon's mind. Uncle Timothy wasn't exactly rich. If Veronica put the baby up for adoption, the adoptive parents would pay for her medical bills. But Gideon was now in a position to help. He whipped out his phone and sent a text to Uncle Timothy.

Hey, I just heard about Veronica. Congratulations! I want to help cover her medical bills. Don't tell her it's from me.

Gideon put his phone back in his pocket. Suddenly his heart was much lighter. Perhaps this would be a Merry Christmas after all.

Being Presidential

December 26th – Washington, D.C.

President Haley Nicholson shuffled through a mountain of paperwork in the Oval Office, trying to read every document before signing it.

"You'll never survive as President that way," Howard Markowitz said as he entered. "Your Chief of Staff is supposed to tell you what they say."

"I know." Haley nodded without looking up. "But, it's my signature on these things."

"That's why you have to trust your Chief of Staff implicitly," Howard said. "I've got the list of candidates for Secretary of Homeland Security you asked for. You know, Presidential Cabinet positions are more important than reading every line of those documents. But if you want to tackle it yourself, I could just tear up this list."

Haley sighed, finally looking up. "I don't have the time or resources to compile a list of candidates for every position and vet each one. That's why I have you and the team of people who—"

She paused, realizing she'd just made Howard's point for him. Her staff had already reviewed these documents, and she had to trust them to do their jobs following the directions she'd given them. She signed the document. "I see your point. Who is at the top of your list?"

"General Becker," Howard said, "but he's not likely to come out of retirement. The second choice is Frank Baldwin."

"The mastermind behind President Towers's assassination?" Haley asked.

Howard shook his head. "He was acquitted of all charges after files appeared on Wikileaks, proving he was framed by Gary Sanders. The judge released him a few days ago."

"Why is the former Speaker of the House an excellent choice for Secretary of Homeland Security?" Haley asked.

"He has close ties to the members of the Council on Foreign Relations, plenty of experience in administration and delegation, and a keen understanding of our legal system."

"You don't think spending a year in prison for a crime he didn't commit would make him biased in his thinking?" Haley shot back. Something about Frank Baldwin bothered her. She didn't want to have anything to do with him. But maybe that was because he'd been accused of killing President Towers. Or because he never supported Towers or the new direction for the Republican Party.

"If it did, wouldn't it be in favor of making sure only the guilty go to prison?" Howard offered. "I assure you, he's been thoroughly vetted for this position, and it will improve your relationship with the establishment Republicans. You need to show them the party isn't divided. This is a small gesture, but it will go a long way toward healing the rift in the party." [12]

Haley sighed. Her gut told her it was a mistake, but she couldn't think of a single concrete reason not to. "Sounds good. Let's move forward."

Second Chances

January 1st – Orleans, France

Scott Knox took off his shoes after a long day of walking through the museum dedicated to Joan of Arc. His head was buzzing from the facts and guesses related to a woman who died almost six hundred years earlier. He flicked on the TV, hoping for a distraction.

Tonya pulled Samuel out of the stroller and set him on the bed while she prepared to change his diaper.

President Nicholson came on the screen, standing next to Frank Baldwin and someone Scott didn't recognize.

"With the new year upon us, the administration needs to be whole. Therefore, I urge Congress to move swiftly in approving the two appointments I am announcing today. First, after much consideration, I have asked Dr. Winslow Park to take over as the Secretary of Health and Human Services. His long career in

medicine and hospital administration makes him an excellent candidate for this position.

"Secondly, in addition to long years of service in the House of Representatives, this next candidate has extensive experience with managing large organizations. As such, I am convinced he is the best man for this job. I have named Frank Baldwin as the Secretary of Homeland Security."

"Do you have to watch the news?" Tonya asked.

Scott quickly changed the channel, and the image of the President was replaced by Dr. Strange with a dubbed audio track in French. But the idea of Frank Baldwin standing next to the new President stuck in his mind.

Why should it bother me? Scott thought. *I was the one who exonerated his name.* Yet, he couldn't shake the feeling that Baldwin was up to something.

"Why do you need to watch that at all?" Tonya asked. "You don't even speak French."

Scott shrugged. "I needed something to distract my mind from information overload."

Tonya smiled at him as she finished changing Samuel and started redressing him. "Thank you for going with us. I know history isn't your favorite subject."

The door opened again, and Veronica, Tonya's mother, came into the room. "There's a decent looking restaurant downstairs, but the maître d' says there are three much better places to eat less than a block away. He also told me there is a Temple in Paris. Did you two get to tour it while you were there?"

Scott shook his head. He hadn't been to the Temple in years. His recommend had expired, and his activities lately hadn't lent themselves to paying tithing or attending Church. The last month had been amazing, but he was a long way from feeling worthy of reentering the Temple.

"Can we go there before we leave France?" Tonya asked.

"I ... don't have a recommend," Scott said.

Tonya nodded in understanding. "We should at least visit the grounds. Or, you could watch Samuel while Mom and I take in a session."

Scott nodded at this. His wife's spirituality meant more to him now than it had during their marriage. In fact, this mention of the Temple was the closest they'd come to discussing getting remarried.

Breaking Ties

January 1st – Nephi, Utah

Gideon Shumway went downstairs to join his parents for dinner. His father had continued giving him the silent treatment over the last two weeks, making Gideon wonder why he was still here. When Gideon sat down, Mom's smile was almost enough to endure another week of Dad's icy stares.

Halfway through dinner, Ben Jr. said, "Gregg Burke is predicting a very turbulent year."

"Based on what?" Dad asked.

"Mostly on my book," Gideon said.

"So you go on a few talk shows," Dad shot back as he stood up, "and now even Burke is relying on your book. Is that enough for you?"

"What do you mean?" Gideon was confused.

"Well, you made your splash in the pan," Dad said. "You took a year off, so now you can get back to football at Notre Dame this fall."

Gideon shook his head. "That's not going to happen."

"Bernelli had a horrible season!" Dad shot back. He took one step toward Gideon. "I'm sure Coach Harper will take you back."

"No, Father," Gideon replied slowly. "I am done with football. I'm keeping up with my physical fitness, but I'm taking the LSAT in three—"

"Done with football?" Dad repeated loudly, cutting Gideon off. Now he was standing over Gideon, glaring down at him. "One more year, and you'll be drafted into the NFL! That's got to be more important than this book."

"It's not just the book, Dad!" Gideon shouted back as he stood. "I'm on a new path now! I'm graduating this year. Why can't you accept that?"

"I worked with you for fifteen years," Dad said through gritted teeth. "You never complained. You never once indicated there was anything you ever wanted more than an NFL contract. I think those fifteen years mean something."

"It means you love me," Gideon said as the tears started to flow. "But if you can't respect my choices, then perhaps they were meaningless."

Dad glared back, raised one hand in the air as if he were about to strike. The hand lowered slowly, and he turned away before saying, "Perhaps they were meaningless after all." Then Dad walked out of the room before Gideon could say anything.

The New Seven

January 2nd – New York City

Edwin Torres took his seat in the underground conference room, the first person to arrive, as usual. Such was his lot as Thirteen, the lowest ranking man of the Shadow Council.[13] Today that would officially change. He waited patiently as the others filed in. Seven's seat remained empty as One sat at the head of the table.

"The first order of business is, of course," One said, "The promotion of Thirteen to the position of Seven."

Edwin stood up as the others cheered. He moved to his new seat, already planning how he would advance to Six or even Five in the coming year.

"Yes, yes," One said. "Congratulations on your promotion. You executed the elimination of the last Seven perfectly. Do you have a recommendation for who will replace you as Thirteen?"

"I do," Edwin said.

"Has he endured the trials?" One asked.

Edwin nodded. "I have spoken to the witnesses myself. This man did not hesitate."

One nodded, accepting the report. "What is this man's proficiency level?"

"Sixty-two," Edwin replied.

"Very well," One said. "Arrange a face-to-face. I want to interview this man well in advance of the next council meeting. Now, what can you tell me of your predecessor's plans to secure us the Presidency?"

Edwin sighed. "His efforts have been splashed across the news for the last month. My research hasn't uncovered anything which hasn't already been publicly revealed."

"Were you able to terminate the bounty on Haley Nicholson?" One asked.

Edwin shook his head. "The Dark Augur [14] site he used does not permit the retraction of funds. Once a price is placed on someone's head, the smart contract will pay whoever owns the token corresponding to the week of their death. There is no way to recall the bounty."

"A bunch of crazy inexperienced amateurs going after the President could spoil everything," One said.

"Not likely," Three said with a smile. "My plan won't be affected by added security."

"Don't be so cocky," One said. "You can't control every security guard."

Three smiled. "I'm still confident no amount of failed attempts on the President's life will affect my plan."

"And the massive data dump," One redirected. "Was that done with a smart contract as well?"

Edwin cringed. "I don't believe Sanders set up that data release. He was hacked by the CIA the night he was arrested. Given the level of intrusion, the CIA probably took control of his Twitter account and made it look like a deathbed confession."

"No one in the CIA was involved," Two shot back. "I would have heard."

Edwin cleared his throat. "I apologize. I should have said someone with CIA resources hacked into Sanders's accounts. Their digital fingerprints were all over his servers."

Two nodded, apparently satisfied by the correction.

"Is there any cause for concern?" One asked.

Edwin shook his head. "I've reviewed the breach. Sanders did not keep any recognizable notes about this council or the meetings he attended."

"Further evidence he kept his oaths," One said. "Very well."

Taking the Reins

January 8th – Atlanta, Georgia

Edwin Torres marched past Marge and into the boardroom.

"Can I help you?" Marge asked as the doors closed behind Edwin.

"Good morning, gentlemen."

"This is a private meeting!" Jim Valance shouted back. "Marge! Call security!" Jim was as tall as he was broad, making him a threat to most chairs.

"That won't be necessary," Edwin said. "I own this building."

"You—" Jim started.

"Security is on the way," Marge said, poking her large head in. Her hair added a full four inches to her height.

Edwin smiled and stood there, twiddling his thumbs.

Fifteen seconds later, two burly men came into the boardroom. "What seems to be the problem, Mr. Torres?"

Half the room gasped.

Edwin turned to the guards, smiling more broadly than ever. "Just a slight misunderstanding. It appears not everyone got the memo. I'll call if anyone becomes unreasonable."

"You're Mr. Torres?" Jim asked.

The security guards nodded and left.

Edwin turned to him. "Yes. Were you expecting someone else?"

"Well, no," Jim said. "I just thought you'd be from Texas, like Gary."

"I grew up in Texas," Edwin said. "Nothing more Texan than the grandson of a real vaquero."

Half the room laughed at that.

"Now that the introductions are out of the way," Edwin said, "why don't we get down to business. It has come to my attention that a certain internet blogger is talking about these meetings. Does anyone know where he is getting his information?"

"Are you speaking about Xander Johnson? Or Gideon Shumway?" Harold Weissman asked. He ran the newsroom at MSNBC.

"Xander Johnson," Edwin replied.

"I hardly think that man's rantings are a threat to us," Harold said as he stroked his long beard.

"Why is that, Harold?" Edwin intentionally used his name to show he knew everyone in the room.

"Well, he's been wrong so many times before." Harold didn't react to his name. "His rants about Pizzagate [15] and Sandy Hook Elementary [16] have discredited him, even to his greatest admirers."

"Still," Edwin said. "I don't like people talking about these meetings. It's better if the American public doesn't know all the major news networks work together."

"Only a few of the details are accurate," Jim offered. "He claims we meet in underground caves and that hundreds of people attend our annual meetings."

"He even blames us for the Earth's failing magnetic field,"[17] Harold added.

"Seriously?" Edwin asked. "How would we have anything to do with that? Why would we do that?"

No one answered.

"Apparently, I need to hear this man's rantings for myself instead of just reading reports," Edwin concluded. "Then, I can decide if he should be silenced."

"I recommend against it," Harold said. "Making Johnson a martyr will only rally people to the cause and convince them that he got too close to the truth. We would be better off feeding him more lies."

Edwin nodded at this idea. "Excellent thinking. Harold, I'm assigning this to you as your first official task. Get Xander Johnson to discredit himself further. I don't want anyone to believe a word he says."

"Of course, Mr. Torres," Harold said.

"Now, who is this Gideon Shumway?" Edwin asked.

"He is an author who's recently appeared on many talk shows," Mark, the editor of The National Enquirer, chimed in. "Gideon doesn't talk about these meetings. He just claims we're all owned by a larger organization that's been killing Presidents."

"What exactly did he write?" Edwin asked.

"An analysis of Ezra's Eagle," Mark said. "He concludes that some grand conspiracy has controlled every President from Herbert Hoover to Barack Obama. Shumway's book also says once the great conspiracy eliminates Nicholson, they will finally get their man in place as President. Then the conspiracy will rule the United States for three Presidencies. During the reign of those three Presidents, the U.S. will spread the power and influence of the great conspiracy through a single world government. This new world government will unite the former British Empire, the European Union, and the Russian Empire."

The silence that followed clearly made Mark uncomfortable. Edwin had never heard of this Shumway person before. Perhaps hardly anyone here had.

"Shumway's book really says all that?" Edwin asked at last.

Mark nodded. "All based on an Apocryphal prophecy. I'm preparing an article on him."

"And is Shumway the only one writing about this prophecy?" Edwin pressed further.

"No," Harold jumped back in. "He's just the most accurate. And it helps that his book came out before Michaels resigned. It's been the number one bestseller every week since Thanksgiving."

"So we face the same problem as with Johnson," Edwin concluded. "If we kill him, it will only draw more attention to his book."

Everyone nodded.

"But we can't simply discredit Shumway," Harold objected. "He's never spoken about any other topic."

Edwin's smile broadened. "Then we should give Shumway every possible opportunity to slip up. Make sure he is a live guest on the news during the next three or four major news stories," he said to Jim. "An inexperienced person will say something to incriminate or discredit himself when he has no time to prepare."

Jim nodded. "I believe I can arrange that. But how will I know when a major news story is about to break?"

"I'll send you a schedule," Edwin replied. "Like my predecessor, I don't just control the narrative. I create the news."

Legal Retest

January 21st – Notre Dame, Indiana

Gideon Shumway walked into the testing center with a thousand thoughts circulating through his head. His September test results weren't good enough to get into any law schools to which he applied. Six of them suggested he take a few more months to prepare and retake the test.

Today was that day. If he failed again, he'd have to find a new path. His father would say it was a sign Gideon had chosen wrong, that football was Gideon's true destiny.

Gideon shook his head, casting those thoughts out. An angel told him he would have a front-row seat to major world events. Gideon felt he needed to put his life on a path to help make that happen. No NFL player ever became an important political figure. But a lawyer with an emphasis on religious analysis? That felt right.

The Great Scarlet Reset

He scanned his student ID at the desk and received his test. He sat at one of the desks and pulled out his pencils before looking at the LSAT.

Something inside held him back from diving into the test. There was something he was forgetting.

"Of course," Gideon whispered to himself as he bowed his head. "Heavenly Father, I have done my best to prepare. I need to do well on this test to follow the path I believe you've asked me to walk. Please help me remember what I have studied. In the name of Jesus Christ, Amen."

Gideon opened his eyes and was instantly filled with confidence. He opened the test, and the answers came quickly to his mind. When he didn't know an answer, he took a guess and moved on.

When he'd marked every answer and double-checked every question, he handed in the test, knowing he'd done his best. The Spirit hadn't given him answers, only helped him remember what he'd studied.

Unwelcome Visitor

January 22nd – Springfield, Missouri

Pope Ferdinand walked into the American headquarters for the Assemblies of God. He was more than a little put out that they wouldn't meet with him in their main offices in Brazil. Still, they did agree to meet.

"I must say, I was surprised to get your call," Superintendent Gray said. He oversaw the American assemblies.

"It was actually I who received the call," Superintendent Cruz said. "But I was concerned he wouldn't be welcome in Brazil right now."

"Why shouldn't I be welcome in Brazil?" Pope Ferdinand asked as he took a seat.

"A world leader like yourself is surely aware of current events, even in Brazil," Cruz said.

"What do you mean?" Gray asked.

"Pope Ferdinand here has taken quite a progressive stance on gay rights," Cruz said.[18]

"I thought I was rather restrained," Ferdinand said. "Do you really think those so-called Evangelical gangs would mark me as an enemy in their holy war?"[19]

Cruz nodded. "Word got out that you'd asked to visit us in Brazil. We heard little more than rumors of an attack, but that was enough for me."

"You ask us here to speak of resolving our differences," Gray began. "But your views on homosexuality alone are enough to keep us from ever agreeing with you."

"I never advocated for gay marriage," Pope Ferdinand said. "Just for giving the same legal protections that other couples already enjoy. Tax benefits, rights of survivorship, and medical decisions for spouses aren't too much to ask for, are they?"

Cruz shook his head. "In America, perhaps not. But the Protestants of Brazil are already up in arms over churches accepting gays into their congregations. None of them are pleased with the current views of the Catholic Church on the subject. Any agreement we make with you would only bring their anger to bear."

"And the American Assemblies of God have not forgotten the ongoing sex abuse scandals," Gray added.

"All of those events are in the past," Pope Ferdinand argued.

"Hardly," Gray shot back. "Even the old cases where a single Bishop or Cardinal was defrocked have cracked open again. People are asking questions about the support network that allowed such scandals to take place."[20]

Pope Ferdinand sighed. "I had hoped we could heal old wounds. Perhaps now is not the time."

Cruz shook his head. "Not even close."

Farewell to Feathers

January 24th – Washington, D.C.

President Haley Nicholson waited in the prep room as both the House and the Senate gathered in the House chambers. Eight of the nine Supreme Court Justices had also arrived, along with most of her cabinet. Frank Baldwin's appointment as Secretary of Homeland Security was her way of bridging the gap between the new face of the Republican Party and the old establishment. Yet despite her best efforts, Frank would not be in attendance.

Frank was randomly chosen as the designated survivor.[21] The Secret Service had reminded Haley multiple times that the entire Presidential Line of Succession could not be in one place simultaneously. No matter how beneficial Baldwin's attendance would be, this was one rule they couldn't bend.

Shrugging off her frustrations, Haley calmed her mind and steeled her emotions. At last count, fifty-three million people were tuned in to hear the first State of the Union Address delivered by a female President. This was always a big speech, and this year was more significant than usual. Of course, everything she did was the first time a female President did it.

A sudden pang of grief swept over her. Haley wished her husband Hank could be here with her. Or one of her children, or even her grandchildren. Two-year-old Michaela was the only one of her five grandchildren to survive. Michaela now lived with her maternal grandparents in California.

Haley heaved a huge sigh and pushed back the tears. She could not afford to break down now and undo the thirty minutes of facial prep she'd already endured. She was on in less than five minutes.

"Madame President," a suit said as he entered. "It's time."

The earpiece was enough for her to know this man was a Secret Service agent. Haley hadn't had time to learn all their names yet.

"Thank you." Haley followed the suit out of the room. She was quickly surrounded by agents for the short walk to the podium.

A gavel banged twice before a booming voice declared, "Mr. Speaker! The President of the United States!"

Hail to the Chief began playing as soon as Haley stepped into the room. Thunderous cheers and applause echoed around the chamber. Haley waved like a queen and shook hands as she slowly walked up to the podium.

Haley looked out at all the people who'd come to see her deliver this speech in person. Everyone was standing on their feet and clapping or cheering. This was a day to celebrate for both parties. No matter how it had come about or which party she belonged to, Haley Nicholson was the first female President. Everyone wanted to show their approval.

The teleprompter turned on, and the first line of her speech came on the screen. Haley gripped the podium and took in a deep breath.

A blinding light drowned out the teleprompter. No, not just the teleprompter, but everything in the room.[2]

Haley blinked for a moment. Something wasn't right. What happened?

"It's okay, Haley," Hank said. "You're home now."

The First Eagle Head

January 24th – Hauvers, Maryland

Secretary Frank Baldwin watched the preamble to the State of the Union from inside a secure bunker under Camp David. The shelter was so top secret that he didn't know it existed until he was escorted inside by Secret Service agents.

The entire room shook.

Frank jumped to his feet.

President Nicholson opened her mouth to begin her speech when a bright flash and loud boom came through the television half a second before the picture and sound cut off.

"What just happened?" Frank asked.

The blank screen was replaced by a stunned white-haired man. *"What just happened?"* Gregg Burke asked. Someone must have answered him through an earpiece. *"I can't say that without confirmation."* Another brief pause. *"You have confirmation? Okay, here goes. The feed from the U.S. Capitol building was cut off due to a bomb of unknown size and origin. We don't yet know if there are any casualties or survivors. Please stay tuned."*

The station switched to a commercial break.

"Confirmed," Agent Jenkins said. "Sidewinder is secure."

Sidewinder? Did that refer to me or the bunker? Frank thought.

Jenkins changed the channel to some sort of action film. A small mushroom cloud was slowly expanding. Buildings were ripped apart, grass and roads alike were torn up or just gone. Strangely, there were no flames.

"What is this?" Frank asked.

"Live feed from our drone over Washington, D.C.," Agent Jenkins said. "Directly over the Capitol Building."

"Are you saying—" Frank choked on the words.

"I'm afraid so. Someone has detonated a bomb large enough to destroy everything from the Supreme Court building to the reflecting pool." Jenkins demonstrated by drawing a circle in the air with his finger. "The Capitol Building was directly in the center of the blast zone."

"I'm the designated survivor—" [21] Frank's heart tried to leap out of his throat. He knew who had done this, but he never thought they would go this far. Many members of Congress were owned by the Shadow Council, either directly or indirectly. They'd just sacrificed at least 150 members of their organization to make him President. And they hadn't even bothered to let him know.

"Before we declare you President, we have to determine the status of the other eighteen people," [22] Jenkins said. "Until then, you'll have to stay here."

Frank sat down and started thinking about his next moves. The Shadow Council would have a playbook for him to follow. Most of the federally elected officials had just died, along with the Supreme Court and the rest of the President's cabinet. He had a clean slate to reshape the government any way he saw fit. And if anyone disagreed, they'd have to appeal to the people he would appoint.

He couldn't rewrite the Constitution, at least not yet. But who would stop him from ignoring the more annoying articles and amendments? There would probably be open rebellion if he tossed the dusty old document aside entirely. But he could definitely lay the groundwork for ignoring it in the future.[23]

Frank flicked the TV back on and switched to MSNBC.

"Joining us in the studio tonight, we have Gideon Shumway, author of Ezra's Eagle; What Ancient Prophecy Tells Us About Today and Tomorrow," Leroy Parker said. *"Mr. Shumway, we brought you in tonight to get your perspective on President Nicholson's speech. However, I think we'd all like to hear how tonight's events relate to your book."*

The image shifted to a freckled red-head who couldn't be more than twenty-five. *"Thank you, Leroy. First, I'd like to say I'm as stunned as everyone by this bombing. Ezra's Eagle did predict President Nicholson would have less time in office than President Ball. However, it said nothing about how it would happen."*

"Do you maintain that a great underground conspiracy is to blame for this?" Leroy asked.

Gideon shook his head. *"It's too early to lay blame. Besides, if the great conspiracy were behind this bombing, they probably acted through a third party. Even an act of this magnitude isn't enough for them to reveal themselves to take credit."*

Leroy Jones looked confused. *"You're saying that even if this bombing is proven to be the work of a serial killer, a terrorist organization, or just a large gas explosion, it won't prove or disprove the claims in your book?"*

"I'm sure whoever is named President tomorrow will appoint a commission to investigate this bombing," Gideon said. *"We'll*

probably have more details before summer. Even then, if the great conspiracy is behind all this, we won't know for years or even decades."

"Who is this Shumway person?" Baldwin asked, muting the television.

"That's outside my area of expertise, Sir," Agent Jenkins said.

"I intend to find out," Baldwin replied.

Fortunate Misfortune

January 24th – Washington, D.C.

Nancy Garrett sat in her luxury apartment, fuming over the phone call she'd gotten the night before. She was supposed to be at work, protecting the Capitol Building during the State of the Union Address. Today they needed the highest level of security, and Nancy was stuck at home because she tested positive for the Halo virus. Her last test was six weeks ago, and she was told that it came back negative.

Pacing in front of the TV, she watched as eight of the nine Supreme Court Justices entered the hall, followed by nearly every member of the President's cabinet. She'd dedicated her life to protecting these people, and today she was sidelined by a clerical error.

President Nicholson entered the hall and walked to the podium.

The entire apartment shook briefly, and a second later, a bright flash and boom on the screen erased the image.

Nancy grabbed the kitchen island for support as her mind tried to process what had just happened. She had to know for sure.

She grabbed her keys and ran up the final flight of stairs to the roof. Looking up Pennsylvania Avenue, there was smoke rising slowly above the trees and buildings. Sure enough, even from two miles away, in the dark of night, she could see a small mushroom cloud where the Capitol Building had been only moments before.

Others from her apartment complex started appearing on the roof.

"It's true!" Victor said. "They bombed the State of the Union Address!"

"How?" Nichole, his wife, shot back. "There's no way a plane would get through security!"

Nancy knew the answer. She'd been there on Thanksgiving weekend when a leading member of the Shadow Council had moved the bomb into place. Two months that bomb sat there undetected. And she was one of the few surviving witnesses.

"Was it a nuke?" Barry asked.

"Naw," Victor said. "The cloud isn't big enough."

"Of course it is," Barry shot back. "They make those backpack nukes now.[24] Someone could have walked into the Capitol Building with it and blown themselves up."

"Come on," Peter chimed in. "If it was a nuke, we'd all be dead from radiation."

"It takes time to die from radiation poisoning," Barry said.

Nancy left them on the roof, debating what kind of bomb was used and how it got there. She needed to think.

The Shadow Council knew she was a witness. But someone arranged for her to not be at work today. The question was, did that make her a loose end or a faithful servant?

The Great Scarlet Reset

Knowing now that her Halo virus results were faked, she grabbed the burner phone she kept for such occasions and headed out the door on foot. She didn't bother turning it on until she was across the Anacostia River. She walked past the pirate ship play area and into the open field of Anacostia Park.

Dialing her designated contact, she waited for three rings, then hung up. Two seconds later, per protocol, her phone rang. "Agent 4210 checking in."

"What do you have to report?" the garbled voice asked.

"That's what I want to know," Nancy said. "Were there any instructions left for me?"

"Just a moment."

Nancy looked around to make sure she was alone. Everyone else was too busy either trying to get into downtown D.C. or away from it.

"Yes, Agent 4210. I do have instructions for you," the voice said at last. *"Protocol Clean Sweep. Report to Station Bravo."*

Nancy swallowed hard before saying, "Understood." She hung up the phone, walked to the river, and threw it in.

The mile-long walk back to her apartment gave her plenty of time to think. Clean Sweep protocol meant the world would think she died in the blast. It would be months, if not longer before anyone could sort out whether she had gone to work today or not. Perhaps they never would know.

Once she got home, she grabbed only the essentials. Items she carried to work would go with her. Everything else must stay put. It must appear that she went to work and never came home.

With her backpack less than half full, she got on her bicycle and headed south.

The ride to Station Bravo took an hour and a half, but she didn't care. What did time matter to her now?

As she rode up to the World Refuge Church, she was surprised to see the gates were open. There was a white van in the parking lot. As soon as she got off her bike, a man exited the van.

"Agent 4210?" the man asked.

Nancy nodded.

"I'm Agent 34." He offered his hand to shake.

Nancy took a moment to catch her breath before shaking his hand using the secret codes and gestures to verify the man's identity. "Nice to meet you."

The man's number wasn't lost on Nancy. A two-digit number meant this man may have had direct contact with the Shadow Council. But since his number was in the thirties, there might be an intermediary. Still, it meant Three hadn't forgotten about her.

"Put your bike in the back," Agent 34 said.

Nancy did as told, adding her bicycle to the four others already there. She climbed into the passenger seat. Looking behind her, Nancy saw four strangers. She held all her questions as Agent 34 drove out of the parking lot, locked the gate behind them, and drove off into the night.

Clearing the Line

January 25th – Bethesda, Maryland

Director Hank Janson sat next to Winslow Park's bed. Unless something could be done, Winslow would be made President by the end of the day. "Dr. Park, we have a grave matter to discuss."

Dr. Park sat up, coughed several times, blinked twice, and finally said, "Can't you see I'm ill? This Halo virus is a serious matter."

Hank nodded. "I'm well aware of your medical condition. It's part of the reason I'm here. President Nicholson was killed last night."

This news sent Dr. Park into another fit of coughing. Once he'd taken a large drink of water, he said, "The only reason that could relate to me is if a dozen other people died at the same time."

"Hundreds, actually," Hank confirmed. "You are next in line to become President. Your present medical condition and your past ties with Planned Parenthood will cause people to question your fitness for duty. I'm asking you to refuse the Presidency with the promise that you will be given another opportunity to take office."[25]

"Another opportunity?" Winslow asked. "You mean, if I let myself be bypassed, you'll support me in a future Presidential election?"

Hank nodded. "Something like that. I have the authority of some very influential campaign contributors who can work with you to groom you for the position at a future date. But if you were named as President in your present condition, it would send the wrong signal to the world."

Winslow launched into another fit of coughing. When he could speak again, he said, "You'll be able to take care of that old Planned Parenthood problem?"

Hank nodded. "Absolutely. Given time, we can make sure you never hear about it again."

Winslow nodded. "Deal."

"Sign here." Hank held out the form which had existed for decades but had never been used. No one had ever passed up the position, and the Line of Succession[22] had never been tested beyond the office of Vice President.

Winslow signed it before launching into another fit of coughing.

Hank signed as a witness and had another Secret Service Agent witness as well.

Perfect, Hank thought as he left. *Just one more stop to make.*

An hour later, Hank had the second copy of the same form signed by the wife of Leon Robertson, the Secretary for Veterans Affairs. Leon was found amidst the rubble of the U.S. Capitol Building about an hour after the bombing. By some miracle, he was the only survivor.

The Great Scarlet Reset

Leon was alive, though his chances of surviving the week were only ten percent. The Advanced Medical Directive gave his wife Power of Attorney for all such decisions. It was easy to convince her that her husband was not fit to be appointed President today.

Once Hank was back in his limousine, he made two phone calls. The first was to Camp David, where Frank Baldwin waited to hear the status of the Line of Succession.

The second was to his contact in the Circle of Lu. "Mission successful," Hank said.

"Excellent," Agent 9 replied. *"Agent 4210 has arrived. She'd better live up to your expectations."*

The line disconnected before Hank could reply. "Yes. She'd better." Hank had stuck his neck out to save Nancy's life, knowing she could be a significant liability if her loyalty ever waivered.

Thousands of years ago, the first Circle of Lu was betrayed by the wives of Cain's great-grandson.[26] His disgrace and the betrayal of his wives continued to echo down through the centuries.

To this day, the top leadership didn't trust women, but Hank had managed to convince them Nancy had value. If she proved him wrong, both she and Hank would pay the price.

Berning Desires

January 25th – Bern, Switzerland

Scott Knox stared at the television with his jaw hanging open. Frank Baldwin was being sworn in as President of the United States.[27] The bombing of the U.S. Capitol Building was all over the news. Despite Tonya's objections, Scott refused to turn it off.

He knew a group had tried to kill the President and VP. If that had happened, their chosen man could take over. Now, Frank Baldwin was President, the same as if Scott had fired his gun in the other direction almost two years earlier.

How many people had died because Scott had fired on his best friend instead of the Vice President? Or would Frank have been the third casualty of this war?

Tonya turned the TV off. "You've got to make a choice," she said. "I know you're thinking about heading back to the United States and trying to figure out who was behind all this. But if you leave now, you'll get so involved in that world that it won't be safe to ever see Samuel or me again."

Scott looked up at her, swallowing hard. She was right. A large part of him wanted to call Maria Croix and track down the source of this bomb. But that world had almost cost him everything. How could he return to a life of espionage after he'd regained so much?

He stood up and pulled Tonya into a big hug and a long kiss. "The only place I'm going is wherever you are."

"Good choice," Tonya said. "It's time to get going. You and I are headed to the Swiss Temple. Get dressed."

"As you wish." Scott spent the last three weeks working with a local Stake President on getting back his Temple Recommend. Today that same Stake President was remarrying them. Then they would go to the Temple and do sealings as a way of renewing their eternal marriage covenant. No matter what was going on back in the United States, he was needed here.

Presidential Predictions

January 25th – Irving, Texas

Gideon Shumway sat once more in Gregg Burke's studio, preparing to go live on The Blaze. He thought sales of his book were high right after Thanksgiving. Every retailer stocked up. But today, they all sold out again. The printer was already working on the largest print run yet.

"I have back in studio with me the man who foretold our doom," Gregg Burke said. "Gideon Shumway, author of the best-selling book, Ezra's Eagle; What Ancient Prophecy Tells Us About Today and Tomorrow."

"Thank you, Gregg," Gideon said. "It's great to be back here, though I wish the circumstances were better."

"Gideon, can you walk us through where we are now in the timeline of the prophecy?" Gregg asked.

"Of course," Gideon replied. "We've now gone through the first eighteen feathers of Ezra's Eagle, leaving only the three eagle heads and two small feathers reserved for the end." [27]

"Are you saying President Baldwin is the first eagle head?" Gregg asked.

Gideon shook his head. "Prophecy can be interpreted in many ways. Only Baldwin's actions will show us whether he is the first Eagle Head or whether the prophecy needs to be reinterpreted. Everything about the prophecy has fit perfectly so far. We may have finally entered the period of the heads."

"What does that mean for Baldwin's Presidency?" Gregg asked. "Will he serve a full term or be eliminated as quickly as our last three Presidents?"

"There is nothing in the prophecy stating how long each of the three eagle heads will be in office," Gideon explained. "We can infer from what they will accomplish that each head will be in office for several years.[28] Perhaps even a whole decade."

"Well, that's a relief," Gregg said. "This constant changing of the President has tanked an already failing economy and the stock market."

"Investors don't like chaos," Gideon agreed. "But the three eagle heads won't be good for investors either."

"Why not?" Gregg asked.

"The European Union has fallen," [29] Gideon said. "Sometime between now and the end of the third eagle head's time in office, the United States will expand her borders. We will swallow up the European Union, the lands once controlled by the British Empire, and the Russian Empire.[30] Even if that happens via treaties, it's still a lot of change. Chaotic change."

"I see," Gregg said. "And if all these mergers don't happen through treaties?"

"The best way for any government to expand its borders and control over its people is through war," Gideon said. "The United States could form treaties with the former E.U. countries as well as the former British colonies to stave off or fight a war against Russian and China. But that's not all. This won't merely be a merger of nations, but of religions as well."

"You're saying President Baldwin wants to merge the world's religions into one?" Gregg asked.

Gideon knew Gregg had all these answers. These were softball questions to allow Gideon to put forth the ideas of his book. "Not necessarily. It might be the second or third eagle head. What is clear is that at some point during the reign of the three heads, the United States will be transformed into the Scarlet Beast Kingdom of the Book of Revelation."

"You mean Babylon?" Gregg asked.

"No, that's a common misconception," Gideon replied. "Just like calling the monster Frankenstein. Babylon is the name of the Church that sits atop the Scarlet Beast Kingdom." [31]

"What exactly does that mean?" Gregg asked.

"It means a state-sponsored religion in a state that controls most of the world's population," Gideon explained. "All religions who refuse to conform will be made illegal."

"When, exactly, will that take place?" Gregg asked.

"Some time in the next twenty to thirty years," Gideon said. "Perhaps sooner."

"You can't narrow it down more than that?" Gregg asked. "I mean, how is the country supposed to survive another couple of years, let alone thirty?"

"Very carefully," Gideon said. "And it won't be easy."

"The book, Ezra's Eagle," Gregg said. "The author, Gideon Shumway. Get your copy now."

The Puppet Pope

January 28th – The Vatican

Pope Ferdinand scowled as five men entered his private study. This was his meditation hour, and those entering never brought good news or wise counsel. "Not today. Please, not today."

"You do not dictate times or terms to us," Cardinal Torchon shot back. "Not when we are here on official business."

"I thought I made myself clear the last time you barged in," Pope Ferdinand shot back. "I don't actually answer to you."

The heavy-set Russian with bushy eyebrows pushed his way to the front. "In fact, you do." He stroked his long beard as he glared down at Pope Ferdinand. The man never gave his name.

"Well, I don't want to anymore." Pope Ferdinand turned his gaze back to the painting of Pope Peter on the wall. This portrait reminded him that the office of the Pope should not answer to any higher authority than to God Himself.

"You dare to break your oaths?" The Russian boomed back. "You have achieved your goals, and now you wish to ignore the path you took to get here?"

Pope Ferdinand sensed a challenge and a threat, and he leaped to his feet to meet the Russian eye to eye. "I haven't forgotten the oaths I've taken or the things I've done. They haunt me every night. That is why I must do as my conscience tells me. I must unite the body of Christ under His true banner."

The Russian growled. "Then you insist on this farce of ignoring our counsel?"

"Yes," Pope Ferdinand declared.

"So be it," the Russian concluded. "You will face the consequences."

"I welcome them," Pope Ferdinand shot back. He watched the men as they left, hoping he'd done the right thing.

Law and Order

January 30th – New York City

Bryan Benson poured over his books while the news played in the background. Four weeks into the new semester and he was struggling to keep up with the course load. Bryan had a decent handle on College Writing. However, Macroeconomics and Business Statistics were so far beyond the math he'd done in High School that he was drowning in numbers.

As if that weren't enough, he had to keep up with Business Management and Project Planning. It would all be worth it when he graduated and followed his father into the family business.

War.

Military leadership was all his father talked about through Bryan's childhood. Martial arts, games of strategy, and military history were the only ways Bryan knew how to connect with his father.

Bryan had dedicated enough of his young life to his future military career to earn him an ROTC scholarship to NYU. Bryan wasn't prepared for the heavy workload and complex subjects a Project Management major required.

President Baldwin came on the screen. Bryan unmuted the television.

"The events of last Tuesday have raised many questions, many of which have no answers yet." President Baldwin said. *"Here is what we know so far. A non-nuclear forty-four kiloton blast destroyed the U.S. Capitol Building at 9:03 pm Eastern Time as President Nicholson began the State of the Union Address."* [32]

President Baldwin took a breath before continuing. *"All but four House members and one Senator were killed in the blast, along with eight of the nine Supreme Court Justices and most of the Presidential Cabinet. It will take some time for new elections to replace the duly elected representatives of this republic. In the interim, I will use the powers granted to me as President to focus on restoring Law and Order. My first executive order deals directly with the chaos in the streets. Effective immediately, any protestors taking violent action will be shot on sight.*

"If these protests do not end in less than three days, martial law will be declared in any city where violent protests break out. Martial law will continue until such time as those responsible are brought to justice. The end of these destructive protests will allow us to focus on finding who is responsible for this unprovoked attack on our Republic."

Bryan sighed. He wanted to be out in the field, hunting down the people who did this. Instead, he was stuck in college for the next three and a half years studying. Without this degree, Bryan would be a grunt on the front lines. But once he graduated, he'd be far more effective as a military leader.

Shaking off those thoughts, Bryan shut off the television and refocused on his macroeconomics lesson. Five minutes later, his phone beeped, indicating a calendar event. Frowning, Bryan looked down at it.

Date with Claire

"Crap!" Bryan slammed the book shut and ran to get changed.

Glory for Terror

January 31st – Kasur, Pakistan

Mohammad Ali Malik flipped through the various news channels. None of them showed scenes of the bloodshed he'd caused in Warsaw. The bombing in Washington, D.C., was almost a week old. Yet, the news cycle didn't leave any room for a new story.

"You have a visitor, Mahdi," Karim said.

"Th-thank you," Ali replied. While his stutter frustrated him, it was also a sign of his destiny as Mohammad Al-Mahdi, the Muslim Messiah.[33]

"Good morning." A skinny man in simple robes walked into the underground bunker Ali called home. The lack of accent suggested he was a local. He held out his hand.

Ali took the man's hand, surprised to find it was no ordinary handshake. This was one of the secret signs he'd known since he was eight. Ali quickly offered the countersign and key phrases in his halting speech.

"I am Twelve," the man said. "We have work to do."

Ali raised one eyebrow. The man's voice was familiar. "A m-member of the Sh-shadow Council coming here in p-person? It m-must be imp-portant. Wh-what can I d-do for you?"

Twelve smiled. "Pope Ferdinand has become a threat to our goals. You will eliminate him."

"Are we t-talking s-suicide b-bombing?" Ali asked. "Or s-something more s-spectacular?"

"It doesn't have to be quiet," Twelve said. "It just needs to get done."

Ali saw an opportunity. "How much t-time do I have?" Six months ago, Alamgir had proposed killing Pope Ferdinand by concentrating attacks in Warsaw, where the Pope had grown up. Patience would be the key to drawing the Pope into the crosshairs.

"However long it takes to guarantee success," Twelve replied. His beady eyes studied Ali, searching for something.

"Guaranteed s-success is a s-slow p-process for s-so prominent a t-target," Ali offered back. "Would t-three y-years be t-too long?"

Twelve shook his head. "This isn't a negotiation for more funding. This is an assignment."

"N-no, no," Ali said, smiling back. "I'm n-not trying to s-squeeze more m-money from you. I have a p-plan in place. But it r-requires t-time."

Twelve frowned. "You're already working on a plan to kill Pope Ferdinand?"

Ali nodded.

"Without consulting me?"

Ali shrugged. "I have to t-target p-prominent p-people if I'm going to p-prove myself worthy. Besides, y-you're here n-now. D-do you approve?"

Twelve nodded. "Take three years if you must. I will let you know if the timetable accelerates."

"Th-thank you," Ali said. "By the w-way, c-congratulations on your p-promotion."

Twelve smiled again. "Thank you. When this job is done, I'll probably get another."

As Twelve left, Ali smiled. News coverage of his attack in Warsaw no longer mattered. Only one person needed to know about it, and Ali was sure Pope Ferdinand already knew.

Special Request

January 31st – Washington, D.C.

Maria Croix walked into the Oval Office, feeling a little like a tourist. The office had changed so much since her last visit here under President Towers. She'd never seen how Michaels, Ball, or Nicholson had redecorated. Come to think of it, President Nicholson hadn't been in office long enough to redecorate the Presidential Bedroom, let alone the Oval Office.

"Ah, Special Agent Croix," President Baldwin said as he looked up from the usual stack of papers. "Please, have a seat."

Maria nodded and sat down. "What can I do for you, Mr. President?"

"Word around the White House is that you headed the investigation that got me released from prison last month." Baldwin's smile was broad, but his eyes warned of danger.

"I'm not sure what you've heard, Mr. President," Maria said carefully. "The information that got you released came from Wikileaks, not my office."

Baldwin's smile became a smirk. "Come now, Maria. No need to be modest with me. I know you arrested Gary Sanders a few hours before his unfortunate demise."

Maria gave a slight nod. She couldn't fathom why the President brought up a classified report that Maria hadn't even read herself.

"Good," Baldwin said as if this confirmed everything. "Then you're just the person I need to figure out what happened at the Capitol Building. Put together whatever kind of team you need. You'll have the full cooperation of every law enforcement agency, of course."

Maria squirmed in her chair a moment. She still wasn't sure whether this President was involved in that plot, and now he was asking her to lead the investigation?

"What's the matter?" Baldwin asked in answer to her hesitation. "You *are* up to the task, aren't you?"

"Yes," Maria said slowly. "Don't you think that Director Janson—"

"Janson has other duties to attend to," Baldwin interrupted. "If he's going to stay the Director of the Secret Service, he's got a lot to answer for. No, I need someone who knew about the plot against President Towers and risked her career trying to stop it. Someone who was hot on the trail of the man behind the poisoning of President Ball as it was happening. A woman like that should have no problem figuring out how the Capitol Building was destroyed and where the bomb came from. I know you're up for this task, so tell me, why are you hesitating?"

Maria swallowed her objections and her hesitation in one gulp. "I'm honored, Mr. President. I'll be happy to take on this task. Just tell me who gave you the information you shared in last night's briefing, and I'll get started right away."

Baldwin smiled. "That's more like it. I want weekly reports on your progress. Janson will give you the file on what we know so far."

Maria stood as Baldwin did the same, shaking his offered hand before turning and heading down the hall to Director Janson's office.

Janson sat behind his desk with a scowl affixed to his face. He glanced up as she entered but quickly refocused on his work. "The file is there," Janson said brusquely.

Maria nodded and took the three-inch-thick envelope. She could feel a thumb drive inside. Without bothering to open it, she left the room and the White House, anxious to dig into this new assignment. Either this was connected to the riots around the country, or this was a massive distraction.

A New Angle

February 1st – Washington, D.C.

President Frank Baldwin poured over the reports on the rise in terrorist attacks around the world. There was a disturbing rise in Islamic Extremist actions. Larger and larger attacks kept happening. Yet small groups kept taking credit for them.

"You wanted to see me?" Senator Ryan Morgan asked. He was the one Senator who couldn't make it to the State of the Union address.

"Yes, come in." Frank motioned to one of the couches as he came out from behind the Resolute Desk and sat on the other couch. "With only one Senator at the moment, we need to reevaluate the committees."

"You have some you want to get rid of?" Ryan asked. "Or some you want to form?"

"Both," Frank said. "The Finance Committee, Appropriations Committee, and the Budget Committee all do the same thing. They should be one committee."

Ryan laughed and shook his head. "They don't do the same thing, but you're right. They do all affect how much the government spends. If you tried to merge them last year, you'd have endured endless debate and pandering from the committee members. Each one would tell you why their particular committee is the most important and must remain separate."

"Which is exactly why I'm doing it now," Frank said. "You're the only surviving member of all three committees."

Ryan nodded. "Very true. We can merge those three committees into the Budget Committee. What committees do you want to form?"

"Other nations have a committee on religious affairs," Frank began.

"Hold on," Ryan interrupted. "You can't form a committee on religion. Our government cannot dictate what religions will do."

"But we do that all the time," Frank said. "The members of the various religions are citizens of our country. They have to follow our laws, no matter what their religion says."

"Sure," Ryan said. "But that's not how a committee on religion will look to the Christians of our nation. They'll see it as you telling them what to believe."

"But I need to know more about the religions of the world," Frank said. "Why do these Islamist groups keep blowing things up?"

Ryan studied Frank for a moment. "If that's all you want, I can hire a few research analysts. They can explain things in terms you'll understand."

Frank shook his head. "It has to be more than that. Some of these religions preach things that are completely antithetical to everything I'm trying to achieve. Most Muslims don't believe in blowing up people or places that have offended them. We will have to set some kind of limits on what religions can preach."

"You're talking about an attack on the First Amendment," Ryan said.

Frank rolled his eyes. "The entire bill of rights has been under constant attack for the last hundred years. People will be free to live their religion, as long as their religion doesn't violate public safety."

"And you want this committee on religion to define that?" Ryan asked.

Frank nodded.

Ryan paused, considering this. "The FBI and Homeland Security won't support this kind of restriction. So we should make it a sub-committee of the Committee on Foreign Relations."

"Foreign Relations?" Frank repeated. "That puts it under the purview of the CIA. They can't operate on American soil."

Ryan nodded. "Most of the religions you're talking about are international and not based in America."

Frank shook his head. "That won't go far enough."

"But it is the right place to start," Ryan explained. "When the CIA finds a threat but is prevented from acting, the other agencies will be drafted into enforcing the restrictions. Then you can expand the restrictions to those few religions which formed in America."

Frank thought through Ryan's explanation. The more he thought about it, the more sense it made. "Let's do it. Just make sure you get that Shumway author on our analysis team."

"Shumway?" Ryan asked. "He's a flash in the pan. Why should I hire him?"

"Because if he's working for us, he won't be able to give any public analysis without getting permission first. It will all be part of his work product."

The Great Scarlet Reset

"So you don't care how good or bad his analysis is," Ryan clarified. "You just don't want him calling you the first eagle head."

Frank nodded. "By forming this committee, I will be confirming his theories. A best-selling author could turn the will of the American people against me. I can't let that happen. You must prevent Shumway from publishing a second book."

Ryan smiled. "I can do that."

Digging In

February 2nd – Washington, D.C.

Maria Croix studied what was left of the U.S. Capitol Building. The building itself was in pieces, scattered in every direction for half a mile or more. A hole marked the site where the building once stood tall and proud. A fence marked off the majority of the blast zone with dozens of agents combing over every detail.

"You're the one who got stuck with this task?" a bald, middle-aged man asked from the other side of the fence.

Maria nodded as she flashed her badge. "Special Agent Croix. I'm here to speak with Allen Barton."

"I'm Dr. Barton. Welcome to my mess. What can I do for you?"

"Have you found conclusive proof of what caused the blast?" Maria asked.

Barton nodded. "Absolutely. A forty-four-megaton bomb exploded in the tunnel beneath the Capitol Building."

"Any idea where the bomb came from?" Maria asked.

"Russia."

"Russia?" Maria repeated. "You're sure?"

Barton nodded. "I have no idea how it got here, but there is no doubt this was a Russian bomb. They only make one bomb this big, other than their nukes. This was the Father Of All Bombs."[32]

"You mean the Mother Of All Bombs," Maria corrected.

Barton shook his head. "The MOAB is an American invention. The Russian version is the FOAB. It left its signature on the remnants of the building. This bomb was hotter and more powerful than the MOAB, and the chemical signature matches what we know of the FOAB."

"You're confident enough in your findings to swear to it in a court of law?" Maria pressed.

"If I have to," Barton said. "But everything I just said is top secret. You know that."

"Until such time as the President feels it is in our best interest to be transparent in our findings," Maria corrected. "If I can wrap up this investigation quickly, that day will be here sooner than you think. After all, how many of those monsters could there be?"

"Not many," Barton said immediately. "To-date, America has only made seventeen MOABs. If it had been one of those, I expect you'd have the specific bomb and its movement history by the end of the day. But I doubt there's any American who knows exactly how many FOABs have been constructed. I don't think the Russian government is going to cooperate in your investigation. Still, if Russia made more than five of these beasts, I'd be surprised."

"Can you think of anyone who might know?" Maria pressed.

"Start with Trey Watkins," Barton said.

"The CIA recruiter?" Maria asked automatically.

"You've met the man?" Barton's question was almost a statement. "Yes, Agent Watkins will know who in the CIA has the information you're looking for. Given the scope of this investigation, I doubt he'll stonewall you."

"No one stonewalls my investigations," Maria said proudly.

Barton laughed. "Sounds about right. The two of you should get along just fine then."

"Thank you for your time," Maria said. Walking back to her car, she pulled out her phone and searched for Watkins's number. She'd programmed it into her phone almost two years earlier when she'd first met Agent Watkins. After all, if the JTTF no longer valued her services, Watkins had promised the CIA would welcome her with open arms.

Down Below

February 3rd – Washington, D.C.

President Frank Baldwin woke with a start. He sat up in bed, trying to find the source of the noise that woke him.

All was quiet.

Betty was still asleep next to him. The clock read 4:12 A.M.

The noise came again, but this time Frank could tell it wasn't an audible noise. Someone was calling to him, someone who knew how to reach out without making a sound.

Frank climbed out of bed, careful not to wake Betty. He walked slowly and silently across the bedroom. Two Secret Service agents stood in the hallway and didn't say a word until Frank shut the door behind him.

"Something we can get you, Sir?" Agent Bellows asked.

Frank shook his head. "I just need to stretch my legs."

"Sidewinder is on the move," Agent Hadley said softly.

Agent Bellows followed Frank while Frank followed the voice. They made it twenty paces before Agent Zidan joined them. Frank had made a special effort to memorize the names of every agent assigned to the White House. He didn't want any surprises.

Frank turned one more corner and stopped. The man standing before him was dressed as a Secret Service agent but definitely did not belong here. If Frank hadn't recognized him—

"Good morning, Agent Torres," Frank said.

"Morning, Mr. President," Edwin Torres said. He was holding a suit, complete with a shirt, tie, and shoes.

Agent Zidan nodded and turned back while Torres led Frank and Agent Bellows around one more corner. Torres stopped in front of a blank wall. He reached up and touched a spot on the light fixture.

The wall opened to reveal a hidden elevator. Frank did his best not to react to this surprise. Agent Bellows's lack of reaction showed he'd seen this before.

Torres stepped in and waited for Frank to do the same before pushing a button. When the doors closed, Torres said, "Get changed."

Frank quickly obeyed. He knew Edwin Torres was no man to cross. Down in the underground city to which they were descending, Torres outranked Baldwin.

The doors opened while Baldwin was still putting on his shoes, and Torres waited until Frank was fully dressed before moving forward. Frank suspected what this was about, and he appreciated the opportunity to make himself presentable.

Artwork lined the walls of this underground fortress, making it more ornate than the White House above. Frank didn't know how long these halls had been here, but he did know they'd gotten a lot of use in the last hundred years.

Torres walked into a large conference room where a man sat, drinking coffee. He looked British with a receding hairline and pronounced widow's peak.

The Great Scarlet Reset

"Good morning, Mr. President." The man's accent confirmed his British heritage. "You may call me One."

"A title only One may claim," Frank replied. He offered his hand, and One obliged him with the proper handshake and signs.

"Cautious, even before your superiors," One said. "I like that." He motioned for Frank to sit next to him.

Frank sat, noticing for the first time the carafe of coffee and cups. "These are turbulent times. It pays to be cautious." He pointed to the carafe, and One nodded.

"Yes, please," One said. "You're probably wondering why we've called you down here."

Frank poured himself a cup of coffee. "I suspect you have instructions for me. You've waited two weeks longer than I expected."

"Yes," One confirmed. "Seven could have relayed those without the additional risk of having the President of the United States disappear from the White House. But that's not the only reason. No, we have a much greater purpose for meeting in person. I'm here to evaluate you."

They talked while One probed Frank's mind. Frank blocked him without batting an eye or missing a beat in their banter. The probe became more intense until it was a full-on attack. Still, Frank showed no outward signs and prevented One from learning anything.

"I was told to expect a level sixty-two," One said. "You're closer to a seventy-five."

Frank set down his cup. "Nine months of solitary confinement offers plenty of time for meditation and practice."

One smiled for the first time. "You're right, Seven. This man will make a fine choice for Thirteen. Schedule a full evaluation of his proficiency before the next meeting. Now, let's get down to business."

Connections

February 3rd – Langley, Virginia

Maria Croix followed Agent Watkins through the upper floors of CIA Headquarters, searching for the world's leading expert on Russian conventional bombs. The typical cubical farm was interspersed with offices. She'd already passed four SCIFs along the way, each time thinking Watkins would lead her inside.

Each SCIF, or Sensitive Compartmented Information Facility, was dedicated to information so sensitive that even inside CIA Headquarters, a different badge was required for each SCIF. Information flow in and out of these facilities was tightly controlled. Surely the information about this bombing already had its own SCIF.

Watkins stopped so suddenly that Maria almost walked right into him. He knocked on the door of a nondescript office. A nameplate on the door showed it was the office of Dr. Peter Utkin.

"Trey! How's it going?" Dr. Utkin stood two inches taller than Watkins and a whole foot taller than Maria. His broad shoulders and slight accent weren't the only things that spoke of being born in Russia.

"Peter, this is Special Agent Croix," Watkins replied. "She has a few questions for you."

"Oooh, Special Agent, is it?" Peter turned to Maria. "Are you here about my missing bomb?"

"Not unless that bomb is an ATBIP,"[32] Maria shot back.

"Come in," Peter said.

Maria followed him into the office while Watkins turned back to his regular duties.

"Yes, I was referring to an Aviation Thermobaric Bomb of Increased Power," Peter confirmed once the door was closed. "Commonly referred to as the Father Of All Bombs. Only seven of those monsters have ever been built, and one was detonated as a demonstration. So, did you recover a bomb?"

"Not exactly," Maria said. "Your missing bomb exploded two weeks ago in Washington, D.C. I need you to tell me how it got there."

"That can't be right," Peter said. "The FOAB is designed to detonate above ground. The only possible way it could produce the same blast strength is—"

Maria tried to wait for him to finish, but impatience won out. "Is what?"

"They must have included a tank of liquid oxygen near the bomb," Peter finally said. "Otherwise, the metals would have sucked all the oxygen out of the tunnel too quickly."

"I'm more interested in how it got there than in how they detonated it," Maria said.

"Probably towed in by a medium-duty truck, like the Ram 5500 or the Ford F-550." Peter shuffled through some of the papers on a shelf. He pulled two photos out and set them on the edge of his desk.

Maria sat down and looked at the photos. The first one showed six different bombs, each of similar size. The second photo showed a crate being loaded onto a flatbed trailer attached to an average-looking silver truck. "Where was this photo taken?" Maria held up the second one.

"Ensenada, Mexico," Peter said. "We snapped that shot six months ago, and it's the last suspected location of FOAB 4."

"You're telling me you can't even confirm this is a photo of the missing bomb?"

Peter shook his head. "There isn't as much budget or manpower to track non-nuclear weapons. I know FOAB 4 was on the ship that docked at that port. But hundreds of crates came off that ship and moved in every direction after leaving the port. This photo is one of five crates that were loaded into trucks or flatbed trailers. Still, I believe this crate actually contains FOAB 4."

"Six months?" Maria shot to her feet. "You've known there was a forty-four-megaton bomb loose in North America for the last six months, and this is the first I hear of it?"

"Calm down," Peter said. He sighed loudly. "I brought all this to my superiors the day after these photos were taken. I was told there was no actionable intel. I tried to track the truck via satellite data, but it went to a warehouse in Tijuana and, as far as I know, never came out."

"Did you check with the DEA?" Maria asked.

"Why would I do that?" Peter looked genuinely confused.

"Because Tijuana is well known as the source of tunnels that go under the border. If that warehouse is one of the suspected tunnels, the DEA might be able to tell you where it comes out."

Peter sat there, just blinking at her. Something finally clicked in his brain, and he blurted out, "Tunnels! Why didn't I think about tunnels!"

Maria heaved a huge sigh. "As of right now, you work for me and report to me directly. I need to know who moved that bomb into the United States."

"You don't have the authority to—"

Maria cut him off. "I've been appointed by the President himself. I have the full authority to recruit whoever I need, no matter what agency of law enforcement they work for. I'll get started on the paperwork. You get started on tracking this bomb. Whatever else you've been working on can be handled by someone else until I get the answers I need. Is that clear?"

Peter swallowed hard. "Perfectly."

A New Score

February 3rd – Notre Dame, Indiana

Gideon Shumway got home after a long day of classes and studying. He was exhausted physically and emotionally. The last thing he wanted to deal with was Duane's enormous smile.

"What did the email say?" Duane asked.

"Email? What email?" Gideon asked as he stifled a yawn.

Duane frowned. "Your LSAT retest scores, of course. You know, the test your whole future is riding on."

"Oh, that email." Gideon pulled out his phone. "I haven't checked yet."

"What did you get last time?" Khepri asked.

"159." Gideon found the correct email and clicked on it.

"What are you hoping for?" Khepri pressed.

"I need at least a 165 to qualify for a decent law school," Gideon said. His eyes scanned the email. "Yes! 169!"

"169?" Duane repeated. "That's fantastic!"

"It's not high enough for Harvard," Gideon explained, "but it's enough for BYU and maybe a few others."

"Combined with your 3.85 GPA, it might be enough, even for Harvard," Duane said.

Gideon shook his head. "If I'd gotten this score back in September, Harvard might have accepted me. But the best I could hope for now is being waitlisted."

"Still, 169 is a good score, isn't it?" Khepri asked.

Gideon nodded. "It should be good enough."

"I'll say," Duane replied. "Ice cream is on me."

"Such a big spender," Khepri replied. "You sure Gideon doesn't want a real celebration?"

Gideon laughed and shook his head. "Like Duane, I've made a religious commitment to avoid alcohol completely."

Khepri's eyebrows raised. "Then you are a devout Muslim?"

"Latter-day Saint," Gideon corrected. "But just as devout as Duane."

"You two are full of surprises," Khepri said. "Tell me more over the ice cream."

"Gladly," Duane said, taking her arm.

While You're Waiting

February 13th – Langley, Virginia

Maria Croix paced in her office inside CIA Headquarters. Two weeks had already passed with very little progress on tracking the bomb.

"Here's the report on the leadership of the Global Islamic State." Agent Michael Collins placed a thick folder on Maria's desk.

"Give me the highlights," Maria said. Most of her day now consisted of managing a team of CIA analysts researching a new group of Islamic extremists calling themselves the Global Islamic State.

"Their leader goes by Mohammad Al-Mahdi," [34] Collins said. "He was born Zakaria Nicator in southern Syria."

"So why is he calling himself Mohammad?" Maria shot back.

"No idea," Collins replied. "But most people call him Mahdi or Al-Mahdi."

Maria sighed. "Thank you." She picked up the file, preparing to place it on the bookcase behind her. Managing this team of analysts was a temporary position. She had to stay busy while waiting for Agent Utkin to find evidence of who moved FOAB 4 into the D.C. area.

Agent Trey Watkins had been very accommodating at first. He gave Maria an empty office and made no demands of her. But after three days of sitting there, Maria was going stir crazy. That's when Watkins suggested she could oversee a few of the analysts, keeping them on task.

Since she'd been trained to manage agents, she agreed. But these people often handed in reports with lots of holes. They cared more about what was happening than why. Still, she'd been told all the best analysts on Islamic extremists were busy on other projects. The GIS was a low-priority group.

Maria wondered how long ISIS was a low-priority group before they expanded into a high-value target. Out of sheer curiosity she opened the folder and started looking through the photographs. One face stuck out, but she couldn't remember where she'd seen it. She picked up the phone.

"Collins, get back in here," Maria said.

"*Right away,*" Collins shot back.

Maria looked from the photo of GIS leadership to the photos of the bomb being driven across Mexico. There he was. The same man.

"What is it, Agent Croix?" Collins blurted out as he entered.

"Who is this?" Maria showed him the photo of the leaders and pointed to the man.

"Jamil Noury," Collins explained. "The right-hand man of the leader of the GIS."

"And is this the same man?" Maria slapped down the photo of the truck driver.

Collins picked it up and examined it closely. "Yes, I believe it is. I've never seen this photo before. Where did it come from?"

"Get me every photo of Jamil Noury you have in the last six months!"

"That will take hours," Collins said. "It's almost 4:30."

"No excuses! No one on your team goes home until I have every photo of Jamil Noury on my desk with timestamp and location showing me his movements over the last six months!"

"Yes, Agent Croix. Right away!" Collins ran out of the room, shouting to his coworkers.

Maria stared at the photo again, wondering whether Agent Watkins knew more than he was letting on about the connection with the GIS. She didn't believe in coincidence.

Explosive Update

February 15th – Washington, D.C.

Maria Croix walked into the Oval Office, carrying a small envelope filled with surveillance photos and a tablet loaded with in-depth reports. "Thank you for seeing me, President Baldwin."

"Of course, Maria. Of course," President Baldwin replied. "Come in and have a seat. What did you find?"

Maria sat and pulled out the first photo, setting it on the desk. "This is Jamil Noury, driving a truck hauling the bomb on a trailer as it passed through Virginia on its way to D.C."

"What kind of bomb are we talking about?" Baldwin asked.

"A Russian-made Aviation Thermobaric Bomb of Increased Power which they have nick-named the Father Of All Bombs, or FOAB, for short," Maria explained.

"So it was the Russians?" Baldwin concluded. "This man doesn't look Russian." He pointed at the photo of Jamil.

Maria shook her head. "The bomb was Russian made, but it was passed through Hezbollah to a small Islamic group in Syria known as the Global Islamic State." She tapped on the photo. "This man, Jamil, is the right-hand man of the leader of the GIS."

"When was this photo taken?" Baldwin asked.

"October 30th."

"October?" Baldwin repeated. "Why didn't we catch him then?"

"This photo took two months of research to correlate and establish its context. No one was looking for Jamil, not even me. I was tracing the path of the bomb. When I finally found it, Jamil was the one driving the truck."

"If this man is a known Islamic extremist leader," Baldwin asked, "how did he get into the United States?"

"Through a tunnel in Tijuana that came out in southern San Diego," Maria said. "That tunnel is also how they got the bomb into the United States. Because it isn't a nuclear bomb, it didn't trip any of the radioactivity sensors we have around D.C."

"It took you two months to find this one photo that put everything together?" Baldwin asked.

Maria nodded. "FOAB 4 had already been traced to the GIS, and we suspected it was in Mexico in early October of last year. But there was no confirmation until I insisted that the CIA complete their analysis. Only then did we find proof that this truck was hauling FOAB 4. That's when we were able to track the bomb on its slow journey across the United States."

"Slow journey?" Baldwin repeated. "Why was it a slow journey?"

Maria frowned. "If the journey had taken place over a single week, it would have been easier to track them. Somehow they knew this. They drove this bomb from one small town to another, taking a day off here and there. Instead of a single week, the bomb spent four weeks crossing the United States from California to D.C."

"Who is the head of the team tracking the GIS?" Baldwin asked. "I want them in my office to explain their failure."

Maria cleared her throat. "That person was transferred to a higher value target at the beginning of February. I've been managing the group of analysts since then."

Baldwin stared at Maria, blinking. "Did you know the GIS had the FOAB when you agreed to take on that task?"

Maria shook her head. "No. I spent weeks waiting for confirmation of who brought FOAB 4 into the United States. While I was waiting, I offered my help where I could."

"Why is the GIS a low-value target if they have the connections with Russia to obtain such a powerful bomb?"

"We didn't know those connections existed until we saw Jamil's photo with the bomb." Maria heaved a huge sigh. "Once we connected the bomb to Jamil, two days ago, we were able to establish FOAB 4 and FOAB 5 were shipped into Syria in March of last year. It was easy from there to track the deliveries through Hezbollah back to a splinter group of the Russian military."

"You have each step documented?" Baldwin asked.

Maria nodded, pulling out more photographs.

Baldwin put his hands on hers. "I don't need to see it myself. I just need to know you have the information. You need to show this to the joint chiefs so we can round up these GIS leaders."

"Of course," Maria said. "Just tell me when."

"Tomorrow, 7 A.M.," Baldwin said. "Can you be ready by then?"

Maria nodded. "Absolutely."

The Prophet and the Pope

February 19th – Salt Lake City, Utah

Joseph Warr was halfway through writing his main address for the April General Conference when his phone buzzed.

"President Warr, Pope Ferdinand is here to see you." Matthew's voice remained pleasant, but there was a hint of strain to it.

Joseph pressed the button to respond. "Thank you, Matthew. Please show him to the small conference room."

"Of course," Matthew replied.

Joseph sighed deeply before saving his work and standing up. Pope Ferdinand had requested an audience, but President Warr had declined. He didn't want to be part of the Pope's world tour to unite all Christians. Yet the Pope had come anyway.

Before leaving his office, Joseph knelt down and said a brief prayer, asking for patience and wisdom for this visit. He felt the calm reassurance that this meeting was the Lord's will. Only then did he stand back up and walk to the conference room.

"President Warr!" Pope Ferdinand said warmly as they shook hands. "I'm not accustomed to being kept waiting."

Joseph smiled down at him. "For some reason, I didn't have you on my calendar today. Apparently, my assistant wasn't aware that we had confirmed your arrival today. But here we are."

"I'm not keeping you from anything, am I?" Ferdinand asked.

Joseph shook his head. "I was preparing a speech I will deliver in April. There is plenty of time for me to complete it."

Ferdinand nodded. "You have some wonderful artwork here. Very inspiring."

"Thank you," Joseph said. "But I don't think you're here to admire the artwork."

Ferdinand gave a slight chuckle. "No, I'm here on much weightier matters."

"Such as a world tour to unite the Christian faiths?" Joseph supplied.

"In a manner of speaking." Ferdinand's face betrayed his uncertainty.

"As I told your secretary when she called," Joseph replied, "we are not a Protestant religion. Ending the five-hundred-year protest would do nothing to change our relationship."

"Come now, President Warr," Ferdinand shot back. "There are only two types of Christian religions. The Catholic Church from whence they all sprang, and the many offshoots from various breaks in the past."

Joseph shook his head. "We are a church of restoration. Our founder was never a member of any other religion. Our claim to authority is completely independent of the Papal line of succession."

"The goal of Restorationism, as I understand it," Pope Ferdinand replied, "is to tear down the walls between the various denominations and return to a purer form of Christianity.[35] That's exactly what I'm seeking to do by ending the Great Protest."

"Once more, the definitions of others obscure our words," Joseph said.

"What do you mean?"

Joseph cleared his throat and motioned for the Pope to have a seat. Once they were both seated, Joseph said, "We are not following the so-called Christian primitivism you speak of. Instead, our Church has been guided by direct revelation since before its foundation. Even the name of our Church was assigned by our Lord and Savior, Jesus Christ.[36] The Priesthood itself was restored through the laying on of hands by resurrected or translated beings. We do not seek to simply mirror or copy the organization set forth by Peter, James, and John. Instead, those very Apostles have appeared in our day to give the keys they carry to mortals once more.[37] We use the restored Priesthood to build the Church the people need today."

"I see," Ferdinand said. "Then you are truly alone. Still, surely you must understand the need for unity among the Christian faiths in the face of so much opposition and hatred from other religions."

Joseph sighed. "Our core beliefs prevent us from entering into any such agreements. It would be an infringement of a person's right to worship who, what, and how they choose." [38]

"I'm not talking about restricting a person's choices or even suggesting our group create guidelines," Pope Ferdinand protested. "All I want is to show unity between the faiths."

Joseph shook his head. "Your declaration to end the great protest shows that simply isn't the case. Your past actions tell me you are an agent of those who seek to unite the world in one single government."

"What are you talking about?" Pope Ferdinand asked. "The only one I answer to is God."

"If only that were true," Joseph said. "You accept bribes from the Chinese government and ignore their attacks on religious freedom."[39]

"Those aren't bribes," Ferdinand protested. "They're compensation for our upkeep of Catholic churches inside China's borders."

"Even if that were true," Joseph said, "it doesn't solve the larger problem. The Catholic Church is the center of an organization trying to unite under a single world church.[40] Your churches in America took money meant for small businesses.[41] And you champion their current prized threat that we must unite against man's manipulation of the environment.[42] These are issues which cannot be overlooked."

"You've had good relationships with past Popes," Ferdinand offered. "Can we at least retain that level of civility?"

"We can definitely be civil," Joseph replied. "However, we cannot come to the kind of agreement you're seeking."

Pope Ferdinand sighed. "I knew this meeting was unlikely to end in success. Yet I had to come. I had to extend the offer."

Joseph nodded. "Next time you decide to visit, I hope to have a much warmer reception for you."

Ferdinand smiled. "I'll be sure to let you know."

Securing the Future

February 20th – Washington, D.C.

President Frank Baldwin read over his latest executive order before signing it. This order would direct all states to use the new voting machines. There was just one thing he had to do before signing it into law.

"Mr. President." Peter Vanco said as he opened the door of the Oval Office. "Gabriel Bandor, President of Lectus Voting Systems, as requested."

Baldwin's assistant stepped aside to reveal a tall, rotund, bald man. "It's a pleasure to meet you, Mr. President." He offered the secret handshake, which Baldwin returned.

Peter nodded, closing the door behind him.

Edwin Torres stepped out of the shadows, causing Gabriel to take a step back.

"I thought this was a private meeting," Gabriel said.

"It still is," Edwin said, offering the secret signs.

Gabriel nodded and gave the countersign. "And who are you?"

Edwin smiled. "You may call me Seven."

Gabriel gasped. "It is truly an honor."

"Honors aside," Baldwin said. "we called you here for a report."

Gabriel nodded. "Of course, of course. We've completely rewritten the algorithms and embedded them behind a firewall, protected by Artificial Intelligence.[44] No one will ever know it is there."

Edwin raised one eyebrow. "If the algorithm is powered by an A.I., the machines must be expensive."

Gabriel nodded. "We kept it within the budget outlined in your executive order on voting rules by ensuring only one machine is needed per polling place. The machine is capable of processing ten thousand votes per hour."

"Ten thousand?" Baldwin repeated. "How can anyone feed them in that fast?"

"There are eight slots for feeding in the votes, all around the machine," Gabriel explained.

"They sound massive," Baldwin said. "How can the smaller districts ever afford that?"

"There is a half-size version for the smaller districts," Gabriel said.

"But I thought you needed the larger size to house the AI," Baldwin clarified.

Gabriel nodded. "The Muta Junior has just as powerful an AI as its big brother, at half the size. The last two years of R&D have been very effective."

Torres smiled. "How soon can you deploy?"

"We have 750 Muta units in place now," Gabriel declared, "with five hundred more, ready to ship tomorrow. We can have a thousand Muta Jr.'s ready one month after receiving confirmation of the funding promised. That's enough for eighty percent of the voting districts."

"You have your funding," Torres said. "The current members of Congress and the Senate have unanimously agreed. Get started. And we're going for full coverage. How soon can you do that?"

"It'll take another month," Gabriel said

"We'll schedule the primaries for late May," Baldwin said. "Can you be ready by then?"

Gabriel nodded.

"Good," Torres said. "Make sure you are."

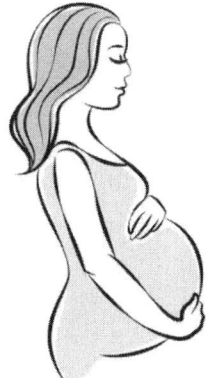

Generosity and Destruction

February 20th – Tempe, Arizona

Timothy Tulley hung up the phone and couldn't stop the tears from pouring down his cheeks. His sister's son had recently come into a small fortune and, without being asked, was willing to share in a time of extreme need.

"Papa, what's wrong?" Veronica asked. This was her second visit to the hospital in two weeks, and this time she wasn't going home until the baby was born.

"I'm just so relieved," Tim said. "I wasn't sure he was willing to help out this much."

"Who?" Veronica asked.

Tim shook his head. "I promised I wouldn't say. But he's covering all your medical expenses."

Veronica sat up, making the monitors squawk. "Dad, who do you know that can afford to pay for me to sit in the hospital for a month or two?"

Tim just shook his head.

"You didn't put the baby up for adoption, did you?"

"No!" Tim shot back. "Of course not."

"Then why would anyone care enough about me to cover a hospital bill that I know will be more money than you make in a year?"

Tim sighed. "He's a family member."

Veronica laid back down. "Are you telling me I have a rich uncle I don't know about?"

Tim shook his head. "Not an uncle. And he wants to stay anonymous."

Veronica's thoughts drifted as she tried to figure out who was related to her that could afford to cover all these costs. The baby wasn't doing well. Words like preeclampsia and toxemia entered the conversation and took over.

The doctors insisted the baby needed at least two more weeks of development. Yet they didn't want to let her out of the hospital because she could go into premature labor at any moment or worse. The fetal heart rate monitor would have to stay in place the whole time.

Veronica looked up at the television. There was some big announcement going on, and they were streaming live from the White House.

President Baldwin stepped to the podium. *"After a thorough investigation, we now have proof that a small band of Islamic extremists bombed the U.S. Capitol Building. I want you to know that no power on Earth will stop us from punishing those responsible for this devastating tragedy. Our actions will be swift and decisive. As there aren't enough members of Congress to approve our military actions, this war will be fought on the authority of my executive orders."*

A Hispanic man standing on Baldwin's left caught Veronica's attention. "Who is the man behind the President?"

"*I will be meeting with the world leaders next week,*" Baldwin continued. "*We will discuss how to deal with this small band of extremists currently hiding in the hills of Syria. I'd like to present Special Agent Maria Croix, who led this investigation.*"

Baldwin stepped away, standing next to the unknown Hispanic. The man smiled at Baldwin as if approving his speech.

"I'm not sure," Tim said. "I've never seen him before."

A short woman walked to the podium. Her dark hair brushed against her shoulders, framing her face. "*First of all, I want to reassure you that, despite theories and claims to the contrary, the bomb was not a nuclear weapon. I know Press Secretary Porlock already stated this in previous briefings. Yet, the narrative on Social Media continues to portray this as a nuclear attack. The D.C. Beltway is not radioactive.*

"*As to the identities of those who carried out this cowardly attack, we have conclusive proof of who and where they are. I can assure you, our retaliation will be devastating and immediate.*" Maria cleared her throat. She took a drink of water, then continued. "*I can now confirm that we have destroyed the headquarters of the group responsible for this horrific attack. Further details will be available as soon as we confirm that the targets were eliminated. Thank you.*"

The image shifted back to the anchor desk at CNN. "*A very confident President Baldwin,*" Patty Parker said. "*We're still awaiting word on what Ms. Croix meant by 'immediate attack'— Wait. What?*" Patty's face went white. "*We've just received word that a small nuclear bomb was detonated moments ago in Damascus, Syria. We're going live now to Gideon Shumway, author of the best-selling book, Ezra's Eagle; What Ancient Prophecy Tells Us About Today and Tomorrow. Gideon, what do you make of this attack on Syria? Does it further confirm your predictions?*"

Gideon Shumway's face appeared on the screen. Recognition shot like a bolt through Veronica's mind. That was her cousin! Her cousin, who now had a best-selling book.

"Unfortunately, Ezra wasn't precise on this period, Patty," Gideon replied. *"While a retaliation of this magnitude is shocking, it isn't out of character with the first eagle head."*

"Your book makes the first eagle head sound like a villain," Patty said. *"But you have yet to call President Baldwin evil or even confirm that he's tied to some massive conspiracy."*

"As with all analysis and predictions, such things are best understood with hindsight," Gideon said. *"The attack on Washington D.C. last month was horrific and unprecedented. It makes 9-11 look like a fistfight. Anyone who claims to be surprised by President Baldwin's response is either lying or doesn't understand the first thing about American politics. Even the most virtuous President we've had in the last hundred years would have reacted the same way. If anything, Baldwin is showing restraint."*

"It's Gideon, isn't it?" Veronica asked her dad as she hit the mute button.

"Yes, that's your cousin," Tim said.

"No," Veronica shot back. "I mean, Gideon is paying my medical bills. Isn't he?"

Timothy sighed, then nodded.

Veronica smiled. "I always liked him."

Timothy relaxed. Then it occurred to him. Gideon was minutes away from going live on CNN, yet he took Timothy's call. He didn't even hesitate to agree to cover the costs. Gideon was willing to cover whatever the insurance wouldn't, whether this was a two-week hospital stay or a two-month stay.

Timothy sighed and smiled down at his daughter, realizing that she was the only thing he had to worry about right now.

The Burden of Damascus

February 20th – Damascus, Syria

Piotr Bednarz drove a first-generation Honda Accord through the streets of Damascus, searching for the target address.[43] It was a bit of a risk driving such a new car through the streets of Damascus. Here new cars were a rarity. Vehicles were typically older than the drivers.

Still, anything older than the 1980 Honda Accord would create a greater risk of the car breaking down. Operation Oracle was one mission where the getaway vehicle was critical.

The GPS on his phone directed Piotr to drive into an alley between two buildings. One of them probably housed the terrorists he was here to eliminate. But for all he knew, their dwelling was two blocks away. After all, close always counts in horseshoes, hand grenades, and nuclear bombs.

Piotr parked the car in the alley, squeezed out, and popped the trunk. He heaved the hundred-pound bomb out and stashed it in an empty dumpster. He knew every detail of this mission was carefully timed. Close just wouldn't cut it.

Without haste, Piotr shut the trunk, climbed back into the car, and drove away. Three minutes later, he was on the highway. The techs told him the blast radius was three miles. Piotr wanted to get as far away as possible before he detonated the bomb.

He turned on the radio and found President Baldwin's speech being carried live. He listened for his cue while checking his odometer. He'd only gone twenty-five miles, but he was still making good time.

Maria Croix's voice replaced that of President Baldwin just as the odometer clicked over to thirty miles. As Maria said, "*Our retaliation will be devastating and immediate*," Piotr pressed the trigger.

One second later, a bright flash lit up the rear-view mirror. There was a long two-minute delay before the sound of the explosion reached him.

Nearly every car pulled over or stopped in the middle of the road so the drivers could get out and gawk.

Piotr kept driving. He had to dodge a few cars, but he wasn't the only one who didn't stop. He needed to get out of the country as soon as possible.

Swing and a Miss

February 23rd - Camp Snake Pit, Iraq

"You missed?" Major General Matthew Benson roared. He sat behind his desk, reviewing the daily briefing.

Colonel Perry nodded; his head hung low.

"We just set off a tactical nuke in a populated city," Benson shouted, "and you're telling me the targets weren't even there?!"

"N-no," Perry stammered. "We had hard and soft intel, placing Jamil Noury and five other HVT's at their compound in the city as of Tuesday morning, two hours before the bomb went off. There is no evidence that they left that building before the explosion."

"But Jamil's photo was flagged entering Jordan this morning!" Benson pounded his fist on the table. "If he was vaporized on Tuesday, along with the building he never left, how could he enter Jordan today?"

Colonel Perry took several slow breaths. On the third breath, Benson did the same. When his anger had dropped from a nine to a four, Benson said, "Give me an action plan in an hour. We have to fix this."

"Is the nuclear option still on the table?" Perry asked.

Benson groaned. "I'll call the Commander-In-Chief and find out."

Perry blanched. "I thought you reported to General Vickers."

Benson shook his head. "Normally, I do. But for this operation, I was appointed by the President himself. He requested all updates go directly to him." He picked up the phone. "I want a plan of action by the time I'm off the phone."

The Cities of Aroer

February 28th – Wadi Mujib, Jordan

"Settle down, settle down," Mohammad Al-Mahdi said.

The leadership of the Global Islamic State filled the second-story room. Everyone in this room believed and trusted that this man was the true Muslim Messiah. Jamil Noury was the only one here who knew Al-Mahdi as Zakaria Nicator.

When the group was all sitting and quiet, Al-Mahdi continued. "We all know that we are only alive today because we held our meeting in an underground bunker designed to resist a one-megaton blast." [45]

The men nodded and muttered their agreement.

"The lesser devil known as the United States," Al-Mahdi continued, "killed half a million proud and righteous Muslims in an attempt to murder the people in this room." He paused, looking around to gauge their reactions.

Satisfied with their tiny nods, Al-Mahdi went on. "The problem is, the lesser devil still searches for us. In fact, I've just received word that they are sending an attack here as we speak. We have one hour to leave this building and get away from here. We must scatter for now, but we must stay strong. We will be reunited when the time is right. For now, we must hide. I was warned that we must leave this building without being noticed, or they will know that we have fled. Go now, without delay."

Jamil was as stunned as everyone else, unsure what to do. Then the gravity of Al-Mahdi's words finally sunk in, and he followed his old friend down the stairs and through the alley into the adjacent building. They went right through that building and climbed into a car.

Jamil watched as the other leaders scattered, going out in twos and threes. He wondered how long it would be before they could gather again.

Half an hour later, a bright flash, followed a few minutes later by a loud boom, confirmed that once again, the little devil thought they were all dead.[46]

This time, Jamil would have to work harder to keep it that way.

Yesterday, Tomorrow

March 1st – Notre Dame, Indiana

Gideon Shumway was slogging through his studies in Christianity, Capitalism, and Consumerism, The Last 1000 years. He regretted signing up for the course after the first two weeks. Unfortunately, he couldn't drop the class without taking a fail. Plus, there were no other courses that would meet his graduation requirements.

Now he was steeped in post-modern drivel about the supposed conflict between Christianity and capitalist consumerism created by an interpretation of the New Testament as espousing poverty as a virtue.[47]

Duane came in and turned on the television.

"Hey, I'm trying to study here," Gideon complained.

"You need to hear this," Duane insisted. "The President is going to explain why they just dropped a second nuke."

"A second one?" Gideon asked. "Destroying Damascus wasn't enough? What did they flatten this time?"

"Some town in Jordan," Duane said. President Baldwin came on the screen. Gideon and Duane both stopped talking. A Hispanic man stood behind Baldwin with a somber look on his face.

"Good evening, America," Baldwin began. *"A little less than twenty-four hours ago, our operatives executed a second strategic nuclear strike. We destroyed the compound where the terrorists known as the Global Islamic State were meeting to discuss their next move. Thankfully, we made our move first."*

"You call a nuclear bomb a move?" Duane said.

President Baldwin paused as if for cheers or applause, but the room was silent. *"Now that we've dealt with the past, it is time to look to the future. Plans for a new Capitol Building are already being drawn up. We are evaluating what, if any, of the old building can be saved. While construction will take years to complete, we cannot wait that long to replace the duly elected representatives who gave their lives five weeks ago.*

"That is why I'm directing all fifty states to hold special elections in June to fill every vacant seat, at both a State and Federal level. Primaries will be held in May, giving all eligible candidates a few weeks to gather the signatures necessary to run for office." Baldwin paused again, taking a deep breath. *"I urge every concerned citizen to support and participate in this gathering of signatures."*

"Three weeks?" Gideon repeated. "It should only take a couple days to gather a thousand signatures."

"A thousand?" Duane asked. "In New York, it's fifteen thousand."

"Rest assured, I am already working with the President of Lectus Voting Systems. Their latest model has eliminated all the flaws experienced in previous elections. Twenty-two states relied on this system during the mid-term elections last year without a single incident. Lectus is on schedule to provide these machines to all fifty states before the June 27th special election."

"Why is he rushing this?" Duane asked.

"Rushing?" Gideon repeated. "I'd say five months without a legislature is enough."

"I get that," Duane said. "I mean, why is he rushing us back to using counting machines after the disaster in 2020?"

"I don't know," Gideon replied. "But those new machines are three steps above what Dominion was using."

"That's what I'm afraid of," Duane said.

"Who was the man behind the President?" Gideon asked.

"Torres?" Duane asked. "He took over the media empire from Gary Sanders."

"And now he is the left-hand man of the President?" Gideon asked.

"Or," Duane said slowly, "is President Baldwin the right-hand man of Torres?"

"What? President Baldwin is the most powerful man in the world," Gideon declared. "How can he be anyone's right-hand man?"

"What about the people who put him there?" Duane asked.

"Meaning?"

"A bomb killed everyone else in the line of succession," Duane explained. "Do you think that was an accident?"

"No, it was a terrorist plot."

"Oh, it was a plot, alright. But who says everyone involved is part of the Global Islamic State?"

Gideon considered that a moment. "Where did you hear all this?"

Duane smiled. "Remember those websites I pointed to when you were working on that paper?"

Gideon nodded. "They were full of all kinds of conspiracy theories."

"Not all of them were just theories."

The Gift of Life

March 10th – Tempe, Arizona

Veronica Tulley felt the first pangs of labor as she woke from a terrifying dream. Realizing she was still in the hospital, her dream of being poked with a thousand needles quickly faded.

Five minutes later, the next wave of labor hit. Veronica's screams brought in two nurses and woke her father.

"Today is the day!" the cheerful nurse said. "How long has it been since your last contraction?"

Veronica breathed through the pain, ignoring the nurse until the contraction passed. "What was the question?" she finally managed to say.

"How long since the last contraction?" the nurse repeated.

"I don't know," Veronica shot back. "Stick around and find out."

The nurse's smile vanished only briefly. She tapped on her tablet and then took a seat. "Did the contraction wake you?"

Veronica nodded. "The first one did."

"But it's still three weeks till the due date," Timothy objected. "Shouldn't we stop the labor?"

The nurse shook her head. "The baby's far enough along. He's got a better chance of survival if we deliver him now instead of trying to delay labor." When Veronica screamed in pain again, the nurse clicked on her tablet again. "Five minutes apart."

"Where's that epidural!" Veronica screamed back at her.

The nurse shook her head. "You agreed not to use an epidural. Don't worry. The doctor is on his way."

"It's four o'clock in the morning!" Timothy said. "Is the doctor even awake?"

The nurse nodded. "There is always a doctor on duty. He's just finishing up with a C-section."

The next four hours were a blur. The doctor arrived at 5 a.m., and a baby boy arrived at 8.

Veronica held her son with a big smile on her face. Joy filled her body from head to toe.

"What is his name?" the doctor asked.

Only one name came to mind. "Gideon Timothy Tulley."

Special Delivery

March 26th – Edirne, Turkey

Jamil Noury frowned as Al-Mahdi walked into the room. They'd been friends since Jamil was eight, so Al-Mahdi's moods were easy to interpret. "What is wrong, my friend."

Al-Mahdi scowled back. "I have word from the Council."

"What do they want?" Jamil asked.

"They want us to deliver the second package," Al-Mahdi said.

"They do know we're in hiding, right?" Jamil asked.

Al-Mahdi nodded. "There's no need to expose ourselves to American surveillance. We just need to get the package delivered."

Jamil breathed a sigh of relief. When the Council made a request, Al-Mahdi and his men obeyed. Even if it was a suicide mission. "When?"

"It has to be in place before Passover begins."

"Passover?" Jamil asked. "What is that?"

Al-Mahdi sighed. "Your studies have been too narrow, my friend. Passover is a week of holy days for the Jews. Families gather to celebrate their deliverance from Egypt. The angel of death killed the Egyptians and left the Jews alive. But this year, the angel of death will finish what he started."

"An ambitious plan," Jamil replied. "When does Passover begin?"

"The fourteenth of Ramadan."

"That's only ten days from now," Jamil said. "Ramadan has already begun. They want us to launch an attack during Ramadan?"

Al-Mahdi shook his head. "It doesn't require a battle. All we have to do is get the package into Jerusalem."

Jamil considered that a moment. Was it really waging war if they were only transporting a bomb? "What's the target?"

"The City of David," Al-Mahdi said.

"The City of—" Jamil repeated. "You can't be serious."

Al-Mahdi just nodded.

"But the range on this package will take out the Dome of the Rock!" Jamil complained.

Al-Mahdi shook his head. "If we position it properly, the Dome of the Rock will survive. But it will eliminate any chance they will complete their new temple. Now, or ever."

Jamil smiled. Removing hope from Israel would be quite a victory. "Do they insist the delivery be made in person, like last time?"

Al-Mahdi shook his head. "Just get the package delivered. They will take care of the rest."

Explosive Holy Days

March 30th – Jerusalem, Israel

Officer Paul Jacobson flipped on his blue lights and siren as the truck passed. He burned a little rubber as he pulled onto the highway. "Car 91 to base. We have the suspect in my sight, traveling south on 60. He's pulling off."

The truck pulled off at the next exit and stopped on the exit ramp. Jacobson pulled his patrol car behind and slowly exited. Officer Schiff was right behind him, approaching the passenger side of the truck.

"Easy now, Rookie," Schiff said. "This could be a trap."

"I know," Jacobson said, fingering the release on his pistol holder. "Backup is already on the way."

"Is there a problem, sir?" the driver asked.

"You've entered a secure sector," Jacobson said. "We need to check your cargo."

"The manifest is right here," the driver said, handing over a clipboard. "Check anything you want. It's all construction materials."

"Step out of the vehicle, sir," Schiff said.

The man nodded and stepped out. As he did so, three more patrol cars drove up.

"This feels too easy," Jacobson said to Schiff. "Are you sure we got the right truck?"

"We'll know soon enough," Schiff replied. "But our job here is to keep an eye on the driver while the others search the cargo."

"We've found it," Officer Gutmann called ten minutes later. "Arrest him."

Jacobson nodded. "What's your name?"

"Jonas Simons," the driver said. "I'm an Israeli citizen."

"Israeli or not, you're under arrest, Mr. Simons." Jacobson slapped the cuffs on him.

"What? What did I do?" Jonas asked. "I'm just a delivery driver."

"Transportation of military-grade explosives," Schiff said. "Don't worry. If you really are just a delivery driver, this won't take too long. Otherwise, you'll never see the sunlight again."

Paul Jacobson booked Jonas at the police station, then headed home to his wife and young son. The smell of fresh bread filled the house. "That smells amazing! Is dinner ready?"

Jennifer nodded as she greeted Paul with a kiss. "Welcome home. How was work?"

Paul sighed. "I think I arrested a man for doing his job today." He bent down and kissed little David on the forehead. "But even if that's true, we stopped a major tragedy."

The Great Scarlet Reset

"Major tragedy, you say," Jennifer said as she sat at the table. "The American President also spoke about averting a major tragedy."

"He did? When?" Paul sat at the table across from her.

"Let's say grace," Jennifer said. "Then, I can replay it for you so we can discuss it."

Paul nodded, then thanked God for the food. As he dished up, Jennifer loaded the speech on YouTube, then cast it to the TV.

"As we close the first quarter, the preliminary reports on the economy are incredibly troubling," President Baldwin said. *"The end of the European Union did nothing to slow the collapse of the economies of Europe. This is why I have reached out to the G20 and called for an expanded meeting. Some will call it G20 plus ten, while I prefer to call it the new G30. We must discuss how to prevent a major worldwide economic tragedy."*

Paul shook his head. "No. I just stopped a repeat of January."

"January? What happened in—" Jennifer gasped and nearly dropped her glass. "The bombing."

Paul nodded. "No need to worry. We got the bomb."

"How?"

Paul shook his head. "That's above my paygrade. All I know is we got the bomb before they could set it off."

Shadow President

April 2nd – Washington, D.C.

President Frank Baldwin took the hidden elevator in the White House's east wing down into the underground city. A guard met him as he exited the elevator, but not a member of the Secret Service. The guard waved a security wand to ensure Baldwin wasn't carrying any weapons before escorting him to the conference room.

Frank was the first to arrive, and he waited patiently for the rest of the Shadow Council. Everywhere else, Frank was the most powerful man in the world. But in this room, he was the lowest man on the totem pole.

"This meeting of the Shadow Council will now come to order," One declared. "I especially want to welcome our newest member, Thirteen."

Baldwin gave a slight nod.

The Great Scarlet Reset

"Three, as you can tell by your new seat," One declared, "in honor of your success, you've been officially promoted to Two. Which means your report comes first."

"Thank you, One," Two said as he stood. "The collapse of the European Union was unavoidable. But from its ashes, we have an opportunity. We have control over the leaders of five of the six most powerful nations on Earth. We can use them to force the rest of the first-world countries to follow whatever financial plan we create. The time has come to restart the Great Reset."[48]

"The world isn't ready to accept a global currency," Three said. "Europe, in particular, will be hesitant to accept any system which threatens their newly reacquired autonomy."

"I know," Two replied. "I didn't say it was time to create a new financial order. I said it was time to restart the Great Reset. It will likely be rejected at first, as it was before. However, when troubled times come around, they'll remember the plan more fondly. Eventually, it will be the only choice."

The Last Speech

April 9th - Warsaw, Poland

"We have to abort," Colonel Daniel Ross, head of the Swiss Guard, said as he walked in. Pope Ferdinand was busy making last-minute revisions to his speech. They were the same offices he'd used when he was Bishop in this very church. The latest assessment of security did nothing to reduce the Commandant's concerns. There were simply too many unknowns.

"No," the Pope replied as he got to his feet. "We go live in two hours, and you want to cancel? What kind of message will that send?"

"As long as you're alive, I don't care. You know these recent attacks are designed to draw you out. Why did we have to do the speech here in Poland?" Of course, Daniel knew the answer to this, but he was frustrated enough to ask it again.

"This is where I grew up. These people have suffered for decades. They deserve to see me in person. It will strengthen their faith. Besides, I want to show them I am not afraid."

"I wish you were. At least a little," Daniel said softly. They'd had this conversation before, and he had to work at controlling his temper, especially today.

"No." Ferdinand pounded his fist on the desk. "We cannot give in to fear."

The Commandant knew the Pope well enough to know he would not be easily persuaded. Daniel let out a long sigh. "I didn't want to do this, but you've left me no choice. If you insist on going through with this speech, then I will have to resign my post."

"What? No. I can't let you do that." Ferdinand stared into Daniel's eyes.

Daniel straightened up, preparing to disappoint the man who'd raised him from a young age. Ferdinand had watched over him, helped him find direction in life when his parents were killed. Pope Ferdinand had made Daniel the man he was today, and now he couldn't let that get in the way of doing his job. "I cannot guarantee your safety today. If I cannot do that, I cannot do my job."

The Pope sat down hard. "Daniel, my boy, I can't let you do that. You've done your job well. I know there is some risk today, but I believe the risk is worth taking."

Daniel swallowed hard and said, "Yes, Your Holiness." Without waiting for a reply, he turned and left the room.

Two hours later, Pope Ferdinand scanned the faces of those given the honor of sitting in the front rows as he began the short walk from his seat to the pulpit. He was pleased to see how many faces he recognized. Sadly, those faces showed the desperation everyone in the room felt. It was clear something more than faith was needed here to change this loss of hope. This speech, given to this Parish, might become the most important sermon he'd ever delivered and possibly the most crucial speech by a Pope in the last hundred years.

Suicide bombings, brutal public attacks, and honor killings by Muslim extremists, targeting Christians and Muslims, increased worldwide. Warsaw suffered more violence than any other city. But this was his home. This was the parish where he grew to love 'the people' more than he loved himself. This is where he learned to love all God's children, no matter their station in life or past sins. Without that love, he never would have become Pontiff. Many of the people in the audience tonight had been instrumental in teaching Ferdinand how to love unconditionally. That was why tonight's speech was worth the risk.

Ferdinand scanned the room briefly, looking for any sign of trouble, then caught himself. There were dozens of people doing that for him right now. He needed to concentrate on why he was here.

Those who worshipped at St. John's Archcathedral were no strangers to attacks of this kind. Even before Pope Ferdinand became a Bishop decades ago, Poland had been through more than its share of violence. These latest attacks were worse. Every week around Poland, at least one parish endured an attack, if not more. Increased security wasn't even close enough to stop them all. No one knew where, when, or what kind of attack was coming next. The heartache and fear were ever-growing inside his people. Daniel had explained plenty of times how these attacks were designed to force him to come here to address the problem.

Pope Ferdinand knew the risks, but these terrorists were killing people he'd personally known for decades. He had to do *something* to help, even at the risk of his own life.

He reached the pulpit, the teleprompter clicked on, and the opening of his speech appeared. The noise within the cathedral dropped to a respectful murmur, far quieter than most places he'd spoken. The little indicator light told him the camera feed had gone live. As usual, he silently counted to three before speaking.

"Dear Brothers and Sisters, I was compelled by the Holy Spirit to accept your invitation to visit you today. I know of the sacrifices forced upon you by those who believe in a god of vengeance. I am mindful that many of you wish to retaliate. However, I must urge you to—" His statement was cut short as something physically struck him.

Then a loud bang echoed through the room.

Pain exploded from his chest. He breathed in, despite the difficulty of doing so.

Pope Ferdinand saw people scatter as his vision clouded. Soon, Daniel, running toward him, was all he could see. Another bang, and his world went dark.

He wondered how many people would read his speech on enduring complex trials. Would the risk he took in attempting to deliver this address drive home the message? Or would his death tax their faith too much?

His last breath left his body.

His last mortal thoughts were, 'Daniel. How heavily will this weigh on you, my Brother, whom I loved as a son? You must know you took every measure possible to prevent this. Please remember that none of us can fight the will of God.'

From Religion to Law

April 15th - Notre Dame, Indiana

Gideon Shumway stared at the half dozen letters in his hands. Responses from all the law schools to which he'd applied; Harvard, Yale, Stanford, Brigham Young University, Columbia, and Arizona State University. Several letters arrived on Monday, while the last one arrived yesterday from BYU.

His friend James had arranged a party where he and others would open their letters and tell their friends which schools they'd gotten into and which one they chose.

He was tempted, once more, to open them all before he went to the party. Many of his friends received letters months ago and had already sent in their replies. But Gideon had to wait for his Law School Admission Test scores from the January test because he hadn't done so well in September.

Waiting to open his letters at the party would add a bit of fun and excitement to the evening. Everyone who said they were coming to the party had at least one letter left to open. Some had several, like Gideon. No one else had applied to Law School.

It wasn't a large party, and Gideon almost thought he had the wrong apartment when there was no noise coming from inside. Most students were busy studying for their final exams, which were three weeks away. This get-together provided a break from all that.

A cake covered in Notre Dame gold and blue with a sad imitation of a leprechaun lay untouched on the table when Gideon arrived. Half a dozen Comparative Religion majors littered the living room of the small apartment. Duane was among them, and they spent a few minutes catching up while waiting for others to arrive. Their friendship had formed over the surprising number of things they had in common. Three others showed up after Gideon, bearing various forms of sugar or liquid refreshments. The ten of them had studied together for the past two years. In a way, this was an early farewell party.

"Okay," James said. "We're all here. Organize your letters according to your top picks. For each rejection letter, you have to take a drink. The first person to get accepted gets to cut the cake." He turned to Gideon. "As usual, Gideon and Duane will be drinking grape soda instead of wine."

Gideon had already sorted his. Harvard lay on top.

"Now, who has more than five letters?"

Three people, including Gideon, raised their hands.

"More than seven?"

Only Betsy still had a hand up.

"Alright," James said. "Betsy, you start."

"I've applied for medical school, and my first pick is North Carolina." She ripped open the envelope and glanced over the letter. The disappointment on her face said it all.

"That's okay," James said. "Several more to go. Take a drink."

Betsy took a long swig of wine. Her glass was nearly empty, and she refilled it.

"Gideon, you next."

Gideon opened the letter from Harvard, then realized he'd forgotten the pre-amble. "I've applied for law school, and my first choice is Harvard."

"Law School," James repeated. "I didn't think you were serious about that."

Gideon ignored James and pulled out the letter. He quickly scanned the content, which read, *'sorry to inform you, your application has been rejected.'* Gideon was only partially disappointed. He took a swig of the grape soda he brought.

Thanks to his book sales, Gideon could afford Harvard, but it was still expensive. The biggest surprise from the first round was George declaring he'd applied for the Seminary at Notre Dame. He was turned down.

The first round went by, and no one had gotten into their top pick. Round two yielded the first winner as Betsy, who got into Indiana University Medical School. She got to cut the cake and take the first piece. The next slice of cake waited until round four when Gideon discovered he'd gotten into BYU Law School. He was mainly thrilled he got into any law school, but to go to the school where his father coached football? At least Gideon wouldn't be on the team.

Football was what brought Gideon to Notre Dame. At first, Comparative Religion was merely something to do while he was there. BYU had offered him a scholarship, but that was too close to home. Gideon had wanted to get away.

In the last five years, Gideon had reconciled with his father, but his trip home over the Christmas break ended in another big fight, and Gideon hadn't spoken to his dad since.

When Gideon realized football was clearly a dead end, he searched for a career. Duane mentioned how law schools and medical schools were always looking to admit a diversity of undergraduate degrees. Comparative Religion certainly wasn't a typical degree for their applicants, which should give him an edge in applying for entrance and scholarships. Gideon quickly discovered he had an aptitude and a desire for the study of law.

Thankfully, Gideon had just proven he was good enough for law school. Based on the letters, only BYU and ASU thought he was good enough.

As the Comparative Religion majors sat around eating cake while congratulating and consoling each other, James asked, "Any ideas on who the next Pope will be?"

Gideon laughed. "As if you didn't know. There are only two cardinals who could possibly obtain a supermajority vote in the conclave."

"Listen to you," Betsy said, "sounding like you're a Catholic."

"Oh, come off it, Betsy," James chided. "You've always been too severe on Gideon here for not being Catholic."

"That's only because he knows Catholicism better than she does," Fred said with a laugh.

"He does not!" Betsy frowned at him and took another long drink.

"I heard they doubled the mourning period this time." Fred became serious. "Almost three whole weeks before they can enter Conclave."

"Pope Ferdinand deserves that much respect," James said. "Especially because he was assassinated."

"How long do they wait before electing a new Prophet?" Fred asked Gideon.

"Prophets aren't elected in my church," Gideon said. "For us, the one who's been an Apostle longest has always become the next

Prophet. But he's not officially voted in until the next General Conference, and that could be as long as six months."

"So, Gideon." James jumped back into the conversation. "You're going from a Catholic university to a Mormon college. Isn't that weird?"

Gideon laughed and shook his head. "BYU isn't a college. It's a university. And I thought of all the people on campus, this group would understand. We've all been studying multiple religions. I thought the knowledge we're all supposed to be experts on would breed empathy."

"Ha!" Betsy's outburst showed she'd already had more than enough wine. "Empathy! I don't feel empathy for the Muslims or the Jews. Misguided religions, if you ask me. Neither of them accepts Jesus as the Savior."

"But both of them are waiting for a Messiah, of one sort or another," Gideon said. "The Jews expect him to only come once, while the Muslims are waiting for the return, the same as we are."

"Except the 12th Imam is a myth," James said. "No one could ever hope to fulfill all those prophecies. It's impossible."

"Are you sure?" Duane asked. "How many prophecies were written about the Savior in the Old Testament?"

"And how many more in all the documents excluded by the council at Nicaea?" Gideon added.

"You know, Gideon," Betsy slurred, "for a football player, you sure do study well. Top of our class, I'd expect."

"Thanks, I think." Gideon knew his stats. Three others might edge ahead of him during the finals. He really didn't care at this point. His GPA was already good enough for BYU, and right now, that's all that mattered to him.

Dead Men Walking

April 15th – Phoenix, Arizona

Maria Croix stared at the ten photos on her desk, absolutely stunned. "How old are these photos?"

"These two here are three hours old," Agent Burnam said, pointing to the two on the right. "These three are five hours old, and these three are about eighteen hours old."

"But, you're only bringing them to me now?" Maria didn't finish her question.

"Well, it took three hours for the computer to positively identify Jamil Noury," Burnam pointed to the photo on the far right. Once that happened, these other photos were quickly identified."

"No," Maria corrected. "All twelve of these people are dead, killed by not one, but two nuclear bombs. If any one of them is alive, it means all of them could be alive. You should have brought me these photos yesterday." She pointed to the oldest photos.

"They weren't marked as a high priority," Burnam complained. "I wasn't aware they existed until I requested all related files. That was fifteen minutes ago. I got them here as soon as I could."

Maria heaved a huge sigh. This disaster wasn't Burnam's fault, and he wouldn't be part of the team assigned to correct it. "All these photos, and related photos, are now classified above your clearance level. Understood?"

Burnam nodded and left.

As soon as the door was closed behind him, Maria picked up the phone and dialed the White House.

"How may I direct your call?"

"This is CIA analyst Maria Croix. I need to speak to President Baldwin's Chief of Staff."

"I'll connect you."

Maria only had to wait a few seconds before another female voice said, *"Chief of Staff's office, Marcy Jones speaking."*

"I need to schedule a priority meeting with President Baldwin."

"I can pencil you in for the 23rd of May—"

"No," Maria said firmly. "Tell him Agent Croix needs to discuss the leaders of the Global Islamic State. He'll make time for me."

"Please hold."

Maria tapped her fingers on the desk while she waited. It was about three minutes before Marcy came back on the line.

"Priority flight has been approved. They are prepping now for your flight out of Deer Valley Airport. An escort will be waiting for you when you arrive in D.C."

"Thank you," Maria said. She hung up and headed to the parking lot. She didn't expect to get such a quick audience but was pleased that President Baldwin took this so seriously. She grabbed her go bag from a cabinet in her office and requested a driver.

When she had completed her report back in February, showing that the GIS was responsible for the Capitol bombing, President Baldwin insisted Maria continue to monitor the Global Islamic State's activities. That also meant formally joining the CIA and expanding her team.

Unfortunately, Watkins insisted they utilize one of the remote offices. Until Maria arrived in Phoenix and set up shop, she was unaware there were any CIA offices outside Langley. Perhaps it was part of the new order of things. Whatever the reason, the CIA was given space inside an FBI facility on the edge of Phoenix. Maria now owned a home about ten miles away.

Her ride to the Deer Valley Airport wasn't long. The driver took her to a private hangar where a government jet was being fueled. As Maria walked to the plane, another car arrived with two pilots and a steward.

Ten minutes later, the plane pulled onto the runway.

Maria spent the three-hour flight assembling the photos and preparing other materials which the President probably would never ask for. Still, she had to stay busy.

Three Secret Service Agents waited for her on the tarmac as she exited the plane. "Agent Croix, good to see you again," Agent Bellman said.

"Likewise," Maria said. Bellman had worked security for the last eight Presidents now, and Maria had been his direct supervisor half of that time.

Bellman and at least two other agents escorted Maria from the airport to the White House and directly into the Oval Office, bypassing all the security checkpoints.

The Secret Manhunt

April 15th – Washington, D.C.

Senator Ryan Morgan blocked the path of Maria Croix and the three Secret Service agents around her. "You have something to report about the Global Islamic State?"

Maria shook her head. "This information is so sensitive, I can only show it to the President. I've just flown over two thousand miles to deliver this report in person. You are not going to stand in my way."

Ryan shook his head. "Perhaps you don't understand. Whatever special relationship you think you have with the President, he is a very busy man. To see him, you must convince me it is worth his time."

Maria scowled back at him. "I doubt you have the clearance level for this information."

"You listen here, little lady," Ryan began.

Maria took a step toward him, waving a finger in his face. "I don't care what kind of bureaucratic nonsense you're trying to pull here. I'm a top CIA analyst and high-level Secret Service agent with a special commission from the President himself to research this topic. When I tell you this information is for his eyes only, I mean it! Now, are you going to get out of my way, or do I need to have you escorted from the White House?"

Ryan involuntarily took a step back. That hadn't happened in more than a decade. He forced his frown to become a smile. "Thank you. I think you've made your point. Right this way." He led Maria down the hall into the war room.

President Baldwin was deep in discussion with the newly appointed Secretary of State, Secretary of Defense, and the Secretary of Homeland Security. Edwin Torres was there too. It was rare now to see Baldwin without his dark shadow. Baldwin looked up briefly, and Ryan nodded.

Another two minutes of the conversation went by before President Baldwin interrupted. "Thank you for this report. I need fifteen minutes to deal with a developing situation."

The three Secretaries nodded, gathered up their materials, and left.

Once they were gone, President Baldwin looked up at Maria. "I understand you have something you need to show me?"

Maria nodded. "Are you sure you want the Senator and the media mogul to see this?"

"If it has to do with the new leadership of the Global Islamic State, yes," Baldwin replied.

Ryan smiled in triumph.

Maria nodded, then placed a photo on the table. "This was taken seven hours ago."

Baldwin scowled. "That's impossible."

Ryan looked at the photo but didn't see what was so disturbing. It was just an average-looking Arab man. "Who is that?"

Maria looked up at him. "Jamil Noury."

"The terrorist who blew up the Capitol Building?" Ryan asked.

Maria nodded. She turned back to the President and placed several more photos on the desk. "All of them are alive. Zakaria Nicator, Ahlam al-Alwani, Abu el-Abboubi, and half a dozen others listed as killed by the nuclear strike in Jordan."

"Now I understand why you insisted on such secrecy," Ryan said.

"Good," Maria said. "I was beginning to doubt your intelligence."

Ryan scowled down at her, an insult forming in his mind. Before he could utter it, President Baldwin said, "Thank you for bringing this to my attention so quickly. Prepare a report on where each of these men is and keep track of them. I'll let you know whom to send the report to as soon as I decide who I trust enough to capture them."

A New Teacher

April 17th - Kasur, Pakistan

Mohammad Al-Mahdi walked the streets of Kasur well after midnight. This was the only time he could go outside. His tall frame, fair skin, and prominent features would stand out too much in the light of day.

No one greeted him, recognized him, or even looked in his direction. The two bodyguards who could hardly be seen didn't count. They were already following him. Someday, he thought, everyone in this city will bow before me. But for now, they lived their lives as best they could, preparing for the day when he would reveal himself.[33]

Sadly, today was not that day. Today he was meeting a new teacher. He knew little about this teacher, except he was very strict. Ten tutors had taught Al-Mahdi. Each one taught a different specialty; primary schooling, religion, strategy. In short, every subject he needed to know when he could finally take his place in the world. He was thirty-two years old, and for the last two decades, all he had done with his life was learn and train. All his training, and the small attacks over the previous several years, finally paid off when his operatives assassinated the Pope.

Why he needed a new tutor now, he could not understand. But when The Council commands, he obeys. After all, they were paying the bills. Yet the question remained in his mind, what could this new tutor teach him that the others had not?

The three men entered the house without knocking, went directly to the dining room, and sat down. Al-Mahdi had been here before, but not for several years. After all, this was one of his parents' homes. This new tutor must have a family connection to be meeting here. After a few minutes, his father, Abdullah, and mother, Aamina, joined them at the table, followed by a man Al-Mahdi didn't recognize.[49] This man was about the same height as Al-Mahdi, and with a few wrinkles on his face, was probably ten years or more his senior.

"As-salam alaikum," Mohammad said.

"Wa Alaikum as-salaam," the man replied in the traditional greeting. "I think you kno-w why I am here." The man's stutter was slight but noticeable.

Al-Mahdi thought the man might be making fun of his own stutter, but there was no hint of levity on his light-colored face. "Yes. You are the n-new tutor with knowledge so precious we had to meet here in the city, r-rather than at the camp."

The man let out a long sigh. "We are mee-ting here because I do not want to cause your friends to dou-bt their faith."

Al-Mahdi's eyes showed a slight twinkle of confidence. "My f-friends are very devout. Nothing could shake them from their r-resolve to follow Allah."

"I do not mean their faith in Allah. I mean their faith in y-ou." The tutor gave a wry smile.

"I am but a hum-ble servant of Allah, striving to do his w-will."

"If only that were true." The tutor frowned.

"Then tell me what you might do to s-shake their faith so much." Mohammad was finding less and less patience for this man.

"My name, until a few precious yea-rs ago, was Mohammad Al-Mahdi."

Silence rang around the table. Mohammad tried to find the significance of the man's claim but could not see how it was relevant. "W-what do you mean 'was'? W-what is your name now?"

"My current name is not important. What you need to kn-ow is that I gave up my name on my forty-first birthday when it became clear the time was not ri-ght for the 12th Imam to reveal himself."

"I know the time isn't right. I w-won't turn forty until— " A different meaning slammed into Al-Mahdi's mind, and he paused to take it all in.

Like himself, this man was tall, fair-skinned, had a high bridge on his nose, spoke with a stutter, and carried himself with an air of importance.[49] A horrible thought occurred to him for the first time in his life. He knew others had laid claim upon the mantel of the returning Imam. There were over three thousand men currently imprisoned for making such a claim without the strength or right to come forward in such a way. But until today, he'd never met one who fit the prophecies at least as well as himself.

Were there a select few who looked the part and were prepared but not announced? What if he were not the first man to truly be prepared? How many people right now actually qualified the way he did to lead all of Islam into a Holy War?

Al-Mahdi eyed the man warily. "W-why are you here?"

"I am here because you need to kn-ow what I have learned in the last few years, Brother. I was t-trained as you have been. I was r-raised to believe I would one d-day unite all of Islam and end the sensel-less battles over minor p-points of doctrine. I have come to t-teach you what precious f-few can understand. I am here to tell you why y-ou might fail."

An Offer He Can't Refuse

April 18th – Notre Dame, Indiana

Gideon Shumway was so consumed by studying for finals that he didn't hear the doorbell when it rang the first time. Part of him acknowledged the second time it rang. Still, it was the persistent knocking that finally tore him away from the deep thoughts surrounding the finer points of the crusades.

The face which greeted him was familiar, but it took Gideon a moment to place it. "Hello. Can I help you?" The two security guards on either side helped jog Gideon's memory.

"I truly hope so. I'm Senator Ryan Morgan, and I have a job offer for you."

Gideon blinked twice before his manners kicked in. "Come on in and have a seat." He motioned toward the couch.

Ryan shook his head. "Actually, I'm famished. Why don't you join me for dinner?"

Gideon nodded. "Give me two minutes."

Ryan smiled and nodded back.

Gideon shut the door and rushed to the bathroom. He reset his hair, put on deodorant, and emptied his bladder. Then Gideon washed his hands, grabbed a dress shirt, and replaced his t-shirt. He put on his shoes and made it out the door in under three minutes, feeling much more presentable.

"Where are we headed?" Gideon asked.

"We have a table waiting for us at The Carriage House," Senator Morgan said.

During the twenty-minute drive, Senator Morgan peppered Gideon with questions. "How are your studies going?"

"Quite well," Gideon said. "I have a good shot at being the top in my class."

Senator Morgan smiled. "And your preparations for Law School?"

"I've been accepted at Brigham Young University." A thought occurred to Gideon, and he verbalized it before he really thought it through. "Which state do you represent?"

"Arizona," Morgan shot back. "As I recall, you've also been accepted to the Sandra Day O'Connor College of Law."

Gideon nodded. "Is that why you're here? To convince me to attend ASU instead?"

"No, no," Morgan said. "That would be a side note. As I said, I want to offer you a job."

"What kind of job?" Gideon asked.

The security guard sitting next to Gideon was so motionless, he was almost invisible.

"We'll get to that," Morgan said. "Why did you write that book?"

"My term paper predicted the death of President Towers," Gideon explained. "Five months after I handed it in, Towers was dead. My professor encouraged me to expand the paper to explain what happened next. I wanted to help people understand that all this chaos is according to God's will."

Morgan nodded to this, not saying another word to Gideon until they arrived at the restaurant and were shown their seats.

The conversation was delayed further by the need to select a meal. Morgan ordered the daily fish special and recommended Gideon get the lobster roll. Gideon agreed and handed the menu back to the waiter.

As soon as the waiter left, Morgan said, "Would you say everything that has happened since Towers's death has been according to God's will?"

Gideon shook his head. "No. The Thanksgiving poisoning and the bombing in January weren't directed by God. But God did foresee the goals of the deep state in our day."

"What about President Baldwin?" Morgan asked. "Is he President because it was prophesied?"

Once more, Gideon shook his head. "He may be fulfilling a prophecy, but that doesn't mean he is there because God chose him to do so."

"Then you do believe Baldwin is part of the Deep State?" Morgan asked.

"Even that isn't clear yet," Gideon said.

"How so?" Morgan pressed. "Your book was very clear. We've been through the four short feathers. Doesn't that mean President Baldwin is the first eagle head?"

The waiters arrived with their meals, giving Gideon a few minutes to carefully consider his answer. This man was here to offer him a job. Gideon's reply was clearly a determining factor.

When the lobster roll was half gone, Gideon cleared his throat and said, "I'm not sure yet whether President Baldwin actually is the first eagle head. We're talking about ancient prophecy here.

Sometimes events play out in such a way that they can only be understood in hindsight."

Senator Morgan studied Gideon, chewing on his words as much as the fish. "We're forming a new subcommittee. Your name is at the top of the list as an analyst to advise the committee."

"What kind of analysis?" Gideon asked. He placed the last bite of his lobster roll into his mouth.

"Religious analysis of foreign events." Morgan kept his tone so flat that Gideon knew the line was practiced.

"Only foreign events?" Gideon clarified.

Senator Morgan nodded before sipping his wine.

Gideon's mind raced, searching for the catch. The Spirit offered no warning, but logic told Gideon there was more to this than a simple job offer. "What's the catch?"

"The catch?"

Gideon cleared his throat. "You're the only surviving Senator. Surely a simple job offer is well below your pay scale. Why are you here to offer me this job?"

Morgan smiled. "So there really is more to your book than feedback from your professor. Yes, there is a catch. You won't be able to write a sequel to your book."

"Why not?"

"Because religious analysis will be your work product," Morgan said. "You'll have access to classified information. Any book on religious analysis you might write would have to be cleared by your superiors."

"Meaning you," Gideon said.

Morgan nodded. "Of course, I acknowledge that you've had great success with your book sales thus far. As such, we are prepared to compensate you with a sizeable salary. Well over six figures."

The Spirit continued to offer no warnings. If anything, it was urging him to accept. Unfortunately, there was a logical flaw in what Senator Morgan was asking Gideon to do. "No."

"No?" Morgan repeated.

"Thank you for the meal," Gideon said. "I have to decline your generous job offer."

"Why?"

"You're asking to purchase my religious opinions to provide them to the Baldwin Administration," Gideon said. "I'm already on record calling Baldwin corrupt. Don't think I haven't noticed the presence of Edwin Torres every time the President speaks. There must be more to this offer than preventing me from writing another book. If you aren't willing to put all the cards on the table, I'm not willing to take a risk on the ace up your sleeve."

Senator Morgan's nostrils flared briefly, though he showed no other signs of anger. "I'm not a man who takes 'no' lightly."

"All the more reason why I must decline," Gideon replied. He stood up. "Thank you again for the meal." He turned and started walking out of the restaurant.

"Hold on," Morgan said. "I have one more card to show before you leave."

Gideon turned around. "I doubt there is anything else you have to offer that would interest me."

Senator Morgan smiled, sending a shiver down Gideon's spine. "It's not what I have to offer, but what I can hold back."

Gideon frowned. "What are you talking about?"

"There's a certain young woman who gave birth last month," Morgan began.

"She has nothing to do with this," Gideon spat out.

"I think she does," Morgan shot back. "How would your readers feel if they knew you have a son with your teenage cousin?"

"Young Gid isn't my son," Gideon said.

Morgan shrugged. "She didn't name a father on the birth certificate, and it didn't take much digging to find out you paid her hospital bills. Add to that the baby's name, and no matter what you say, people will assume you're the father."

"Unless I work for you," Gideon clarified.

Morgan shook his head. "It wouldn't be me releasing this information to the media. No, I got the reporter who found all this to hold the story. If you work for me, it will be in my interest to continue protecting your reputation. But if you refuse—"

Gideon heaved a huge sigh. "Can you give me twenty-four hours to think it over?"

Morgan shook his head. "I have to give the reporter an answer within the hour. If you're working for me, I'll tell him your payments were merely a charitable reflection of your newfound wealth and that you haven't even seen your cousin in two years. That should effectively kill his story."

Gideon nodded his head. "It appears I have little choice. I'll work for you."

Senator Morgan's wide smile returned. "Welcome to the team! I'll be in touch after graduation. Oh, I'll also take the liberty of informing BYU that you've decided to attend ASU instead."

Gideon sighed again. He felt like he needed a long shower.

A New Pope

April 29th – The Vatican

Cardinal Guy Torchon fumed outside the Sistine Chapel, wishing beyond reason that he could be inside with the electors. But he was chosen as the Master of Ceremonies, making him ineligible for election.

The thirtieth vote was taking place inside, which meant there were only two candidates left. He glanced up at the smokestack, which would indicate the results of the vote.

"Fumata bianca!" someone called out.

Cardinal Torchon repeated the cry. "Fumata bianca!" Somehow they'd reached a two-thirds majority vote among the hundred or so Cardinals. He pulled out the key and unlocked the chapel.

People were congratulating Cardinal Romano.

The Great Scarlet Reset

Torchon involuntarily clenched one hand into a fist. It took him about ten seconds to get his temper under control and return a festive look. "Congratulations!"

"Thank you," Cardinal Romano replied.

"Have you thought about your regnal name?" Torchon asked.

Romano nodded. "I need a few hours to research the name, but I'm heavily favoring Pius."

Torchon smiled. "There have been twelve Pope Pius's. Are you sure you want to be number thirteen?"

Romano laughed. "That old superstition doesn't apply here."

"No, of course not," Torchon said.

The New G30

May 1st – Paris, France

President Frank Baldwin entered the large conference room, looking at the faces of the other world leaders who had already arrived. More than seventy seats were already filled. Three seats were reserved for Secretary of State Lake Paulsen, Secretary of the Treasury Harold Barnes, and himself. Agent Hadley stood behind them, the only Secret Service Agent allowed in the room. Edwin Torres hadn't come.

Su Xiannian had taken over as President of China less than a year ago, after the sudden and still mysterious death of President Xi Jinping. He brought only one aide with him, though most of the other leaders had two. Perhaps this was meant to portray his confidence.

Jacques Pompidou of France sat at the head of the table, given that his country was hosting this world summit. President Lothar Durchdenwald of Germany sat at the other end, flanked by

The Great Scarlet Reset

Katarina Nachtnebel, the German Chancellor, and someone Baldwin didn't recognize.

President Fabio Almeida of Portugal had a scowl on his face as if he weren't sure why he was here. President Hakeen Azikiwe of Nigeria wore a slight smile and gave Baldwin a small nod. His invitation had been a big boost for his popularity back home. President Art Lansky of Poland attempted to pull off a poker face, though his eyes betrayed the fear he felt. Baldwin and his two aides took their seats as the doors opened one last time to let in the Russian delegation.

Oleg Nevsky, the President of Russia, was fashionably late. However, the presence of Four at Nevsky's side caused Baldwin to raise an eyebrow. A high-ranking member of the Shadow Council at this meeting gave him hope of success, despite their dire predictions only a few weeks earlier.

"We all know why we are here," Pompidou declared once the Russians were seated. "President Baldwin claims another Islamic State has cropped up in Syria, only a few short years after we rounded up the last members of ISIS."

"There is no doubt that a Syrian national transported a bomb across the United States," Baldwin shot back. "A bomb which was used to wipe out most of our leadership."

"And you claim this same man is a high-ranking leader of the new Islamic State," Nevsky clarified. "How did such a man get his hands on one of our most prized weapons?"

"There are factions within your military who are still aligned with Hezbollah,"[50] Baldwin said. "At least, I hope they are only factions."

Nevsky scowled. "If I were working with Hezbollah, I would have given them a small nuke instead of a FOAB."

Baldwin nodded. "I made the same argument to my chief analyst. She assured me this plot could not have succeeded with a nuclear bomb. That being said, I have no interest in accusing you of sanctioning this attack. No, this was the work of Islamic extremists. I am asking permission to send my troops into Syria unimpeded to wipe out this small group of rebels."

Nevsky shook his head. "I cannot allow American troops into an area partially controlled by Russian soldiers. Besides, there are also Iranian troops and Hezbollah soldiers you claim gave this group such powerful weapons. I don't see Supreme Leader Legwan here. Perhaps you've already reached an agreement with him? Or are you planning to attack everyone else with interest in Syria?"

Baldwin shook his head. "I believe if this body condones this action, Iran will withdraw its troops from the region rather than risk war with the United States. I was hoping Russia would do the same. I'm more than happy to take on any Islamist extremists who get in my way, whether they claim allegiance to the Global Islamic State or Hezbollah."

"But you are indirectly accusing Iran of an act of war, are you not?" President Xiannian asked.

"What do you mean?" Baldwin asked. He already knew but didn't want to seem too prepared for this question.

"You say this small group is working with Hezbollah," Xiannian clarified. "Past American leaders have claimed Hezbollah is nothing more than an unofficial arm of the Iranian military.[51] Therefore, by extension, you are claiming Iran bombed the United States."

Baldwin did his best to look shocked. "Believe me, if I had proof of Iran's direct involvement in bombing my nation's Capital, I would return the favor ten-fold. As yet, Iran has remained silent on this subject. Any act on their part to prevent us from bringing this radical group to justice would be seen as collusion."

The Great Scarlet Reset

"And why should we condone this action?" Pompidou asked. "What reassurances would we receive that you won't use this as an excuse to change the balance of power in the region?"

"Further, why should we believe hunting down yet another Islamic group will make any difference?" Nevsky asked. "Another one will just pop up in a few years, and we'll be right back in the same position."

"They bombed Washington!" Baldwin shouted. He took a moment to compose himself. "I can't let that go unanswered. None of you would stand for such an insult."

"Israel supports this action," Prime Minister David Peres declared. "We intercepted a bomb nearly identical to the device detonated in D.C."

"When was this?" Nevsky asked.

"Six weeks ago," Peres said flatly.

"You've had one of our bombs in custody for six weeks, and this is the first I hear of it?" Nevsky shot back. "This is an outrage."

"The outrage is your country's mishandling of not one but two powerful bombs," Peres said calmly. "Bombs which, by your own words, are among your country's most prized weapons."

"You will return that bomb to us immediately!" Nevsky pounded his fist on the table.

The discussion devolved into shouting, and it took Pompidou two minutes of banging on the table to bring the room to order. "We will have decorum in the room," Pompidou declared when he could be heard. "This body does not have the authority to authorize an invasion of Syria by foreign troops." [52]

"That's true," Baldwin said. "I came to you first to gather support before presenting these facts before the United Nations. The real reason I've asked you all here is to propose a solution to the world's current financial woes."

"Are you in a position to cover our debts?" President Durchdenwald asked.

Baldwin shook his head. "No. I'm not proposing we try to resurrect the European Union. Its time has come and gone. America has its own financial problems at the moment. But suppose we band together to form a true world currency. In that case, we can jump past the inevitable economic collapse of every country represented in this room and any others able to meet the requirements we will set forth."

"This is the true reason you have gathered us together?" Pompidou asked. "France does not need American control over our currency."

"Nor does Poland," President Lansky affirmed.

"We should hear the details before we reject such a proposal," Prime Minister John McBride of the United Kingdom said.

A brief spat of affirmations and rejections made their way around the table before the world leaders calmed down to listen to Baldwin's plan.

"An economy thrives or starves based on the availability of money for profitable business transactions. Some argue for local banks printing their own money to establish a system of savings and lending. In today's global economy, such local banks become untenable.

"Today, there are more than two hundred currencies recognized by the UN. Fortunes are made and lost merely on the exchange rate between the 150 or so independent currencies. This has allowed such economic disparity that the average worker in Iceland has four times the average Mexican worker's buying power. And neighboring countries like the United States and Mexico have an exchange rate higher than twenty to one.

"By establishing a single world currency, we could mandate a truly global minimum wage and put an end to what many

Americans refer to as slave labor. We can also easily eliminate our national debts. We just need to preferentially set the exchange rate for our current currencies so that our debts in the new currency are easily paid off."

"And you will be the one to set such rates?" Nevsky scowled heavily. His objections to the whole plan were written all over his face.

"France does not need to be bailed out!" Pompidou spat out.

Several more objections echoed around the room. Baldwin sat there, allowing them to have their say. When the room quieted once more, he said softly, "Without this plan, or one equally ambitious, a global depression is at our doors. You may be able to survive another three or four years before your national currencies are so devalued that you will be begging for relief. Don't let yourselves become another Venezuela." [53]

Shouts and objections echoed around the room once more. Not everyone was objecting verbally. Some of them stood up and quietly left the room. Ten minutes later, the table was almost empty.

Baldwin watched them go. He didn't expect complete agreement or even enough countries to justify moving forward with this plan. But they would remember his proposal. And when they finally agreed to join him, he'd make them wish they'd signed up today.

"Sir, we've just received word," Agent Hadley said. "A new Pope has been selected."

"Has he announced a regnal name?" President Baldwin asked.

Hadley nodded. "Pope Pius XIII."

Friends in High Places

May 15th – New York City, New York

President Frank Baldwin gritted his teeth as he left the U.N. building. There was no support for his invasion of Syria. If one more missile was fired into Syria, it would mean war. Even if that missile only killed Jamil Noury, Syria, Russia, Jordan, and Iran would all consider it an act of war. They each threatened to retaliate for whatever force was used in the future and the two nuclear bombs already used.

Their nearly-empty threats weren't enough to stop Baldwin from violating any nation's borders to bring Jamil to justice. If he sent in a spy, there was the risk of capture and retaliation. But if he sent in a large force, they would come under attack. He needed a different path.

The worst part was that even the Shadow Council was protecting this man. So Baldwin's loyalties were divided. As the POTUS, he had to capture or kill this man. Privately, he had sworn not to do more than required to bring this man and his cohorts to justice.

The Global Islamic State was funded and protected by the Shadow Council, provided they continued to deliver instability in the region. Very little happened that the Shadow Council did not know about. Frank climbed into the stretch hummer and reached for the phone.

"Didn't get the outcome you wanted, Sir?" Major General Matthew Benson asked. His short-cropped red hair was starting to fade.

The vehicle rocked slightly as the convoy pulled out into traffic.

"Aren't you supposed to be in Iraq?" Frank asked back.

Matt shrugged. "I'm on leave this week. I leave in two days."

"And you sweet-talked your way past my Secret Service guards," Frank said. "All to avoid a phone call?"

Matt's broad smile made his wrinkles appear. "I knew if the U.N. denied your request, your next call would be to me. I wanted to meet in person back at the Oval Office, but your Chief of Staff suggested this instead."

"Sharon is like that sometimes," Frank replied. "Do you think you can capture Jamil without entering Syria?"

"That depends," Matt said slowly.

"On?"

"On whether or not I can send in a commando team." Matt kept his expression blank.

Frank shook his head. "The border is patrolled by Iranian forces. Russians control the city, not to mention the local Syrian troops. Now that the U.N. has officially denied my request, all three armies will be increasing security and manpower in that region. No, you're going to have to get more creative."

"So, the rules of engagement are no U.S. troops in Syria, and no U.S. equipment can cross the border. Correct?"

"That sums it up," Frank replied. "Can you do it?"

"Of course," Matt said, "but it will take time."

"I understand," Frank said with a frown. "Just don't come back without him. Dead or alive."

Matt saluted. "Yes, Sir. Now that business is out of the way, how are Betty and Hannah? I heard they took things pretty hard last year."

"Last year was tough for all of us," Frank said. "But Betty is as loving as ever now, and Hannah is struggling with being in the spotlight."

Matt nodded. "When was the last time there was a ten-year-old First Daughter?"

"Natasha Obama was only seven when her father took office," Frank replied. "And Brandon Towers was only ten on his father's inauguration day."

"Oh, yeah. I forgot about Sasha," Matt mused. "Technically, she was the Second Daughter. The media pretty much left her alone. They also all but ignored Brandon, despite how they felt about his father. Do you think they'll extend the same courtesy to Hannah?"

Frank shook his head. "Paparazzi follow her everywhere she goes, whether I'm with her or not. I thought she'd have at least two more years before she became First Daughter."

Matt nodded. "Life is changing fast right now."

"It sure is."

General Inspection

May 16th – New York City, New York

Bryan Benson was halfway through his Macroeconomics homework when there was a knock at the door. He ignored the first knock, trying to finish up the exercise he was on. He gave up and answered the door after the third knock.

Major General Matthew Benson saluted Bryan, and Bryan saluted him back. Dad wore his usual combat uniform

"Dad! What are you doing here?" Bryan asked as he let his father inside.

"I'm on leave, heading back to Iraq tomorrow," Matt replied. "I wanted to see how you're doing."

"You mean you want to inspect my barracks and verify my performance levels," Bryan said. "This really isn't a good time."

"Nonsense," Matt said. "There's always time for family."

Bryan shook his head. "I have homework to finish before my date." He bit his lower lip, regretting that he even mentioned dating. After all, this was a weeknight.

"Must be getting serious if you're dating during the week," Matt said.

This was the mildest reaction Bryan could have hoped for.

"If you let me tag along, I'll buy."

Bryan raised one eyebrow at this. "Did your promotion come with a pay raise?"

Matt nodded. "It did, but that's not the source of my generosity. My investments have been paying off quite well this year. Plus, you got a full scholarship, so I don't have to pay your college expenses."

Bryan was torn. This was a critical phase of his relationship with Claire. They'd been dating long enough that he'd bought an engagement ring a couple of days ago. However, Dad had a way of driving people away. Still, she would eventually have to learn to deal with General Dad, as Bryan called him.

"Can we go to Il Mulino?" Bryan asked.

Matt nodded. "Sure. Why not."

"Great," Bryan said. "We'll pick her up in an hour. Let me just text her, so she knows what to expect. In the meantime, I really need to finish my Macroeconomics homework. Feel free to conduct your inspection."

Two hours later, Bryan sat in front of a sixty-dollar salmon fillet after partaking in a thirty-dollar plate of octopus. Matt ordered the seventy-five-dollar steak, and Claire ordered a fifty dollar plate of seafood pasta. It was the most expensive meal Bryan had ever ordered.

The Great Scarlet Reset

What's more, Dad was on his fifteenth question for Claire about how Bryan was treating her. So far, all her answers had satisfied Dad.

"Are you planning to stay on campus when you get married?" Dad asked.

Bryan nearly choked on his salmon.

Claire just smiled and said, "I like what I've seen at Washington Square Village."

Matt raised one eyebrow at this. "So, you've looked into this."

Claire nodded. "I like to plan things out."

The ring in Bryan's pocket started to feel very heavy.

"Did I miss an announcement?" Matt turned to Bryan. "Did you already ask her?"

Bryan shook his head.

"What are you waiting for?" Matt asked. "A woman like this doesn't come along every day."

"I was looking for the right time," Bryan said.

Claire gasped.

Bryan looked over at her. He realized he'd just told her he was planning to propose.

"Is that why you wanted to come here tonight?" Matt asked.

Bryan just ignored him, realizing the situation was running away without him. Any delay now would only lessen the impact. So he got down on one knee, pulled the ring out of his pocket, and asked, "Claire Romano, will you marry me?"

Claire nodded as she stared at the ring.

Bryan took the ring and placed it carefully on her finger. Perfect fit.

"Yes!" Claire gasped, finally able to speak. "Yes, yes, yes."

A brief cheer from the restaurant brought Bryan back to his surroundings. Everyone was staring at him. They quickly went back to their meals, and Bryan got back in his seat.

Claire didn't seem to notice. She was too busy staring at her ring. "I'm thinking of a June wedding."

Bryan swallowed hard. "June of next year?"

Claire shook her head. "You know I'm a good Catholic girl."

Bryan blushed.

"You mean you two haven't— You're still a—" It was the first time Bryan had ever seen Dad struggle with words.

Claire and Bryan both nodded.

"We're both good Catholics," Bryan said, taking her hand.

"I'm planning to leave the country tomorrow, and I don't know when I'll be back," Matt said.

Claire frowned. "Is there any way you can delay?"

"Maybe a few weeks—" Matt began.

"That's all we'll need," Claire interrupted. "I'll call my mother, and she can get started on the preparations. She can handle arranging a small wedding. My last final is in two days, and then I can focus full-time on the wedding. How does June 3rd sound?"

"June 3rd sounds great!" Matt announced.

Bryan looked back and forth between the two of them. When his brain caught up to his ears, he smiled broadly. "I'm getting married in three weeks!"

New Beginnings

May 20th – Notre Dame, Indiana

Gideon Shumway made it through final exams without thinking about Senator Morgan and his slimy tactics. It wasn't until he accepted his diploma that he spotted Senator Morgan sitting in the audience. The Senator stood out by having four bodyguards around him.

The smile fell off Gideon's face as he walked back to his seat. He'd hoped to have a whole week after graduation to try and figure out how to get out of his deal with the devil.

When all the pomp and circumstance were done, Gideon made plans to meet up with his friends and told them he'd be there soon. As expected, Senator Morgan approached.

"Congratulations!" Morgan said. "I'll expect to see you in Phoenix on Monday."

Gideon shook his head. "I'm afraid that's impossible. I have to pack things up here, find a place to stay in Arizona, and visit my parents. I won't even start doing any of that until Monday."

"You said you'd start working for me after graduation," Morgan said, frowning.

Gideon nodded. "And I will. Two weeks from Monday."

Morgan's frown slowly turned to a smile. "You've got balls, kid. I'll see you on June 5th." He handed Gideon a card.

Gideon looked down at it.

Perry Chivas
21711 N. 7th Street
Phoenix, AZ 85024
(623) 555-1999

"That's your new supervisor and work address," Morgan said. "We've completed your background check. You passed with flying colors. Your law school classes don't start until August, so you'll have more than two months to get through the training and adjust to our procedures. Now go catch up with your friends and celebrate! After all, you're starting a new chapter of your life!"

Gideon nodded and ran to catch up with his friends. The phrase stuck in his mind. A new chapter. It reminded him that any new book he wanted to publish would be subject to editing by Senator Morgan. Gideon grabbed his phone and sent a quick text to his agent.

Putting all that out of his mind, he enjoyed dinner with his friends and their families. Jon and Mom joined him. The food was good, and the conversation was better.

As he was finishing dessert, Gideon's phone rang, showing Gregg Horvath. "Hey, Gregg. I've been expecting your call."

"I should hope so," Gregg said. "Now that you've graduated, we've got to start working on a sequel to Ezra's Eagle. I've just heard that—"

"I can't participate, Gregg," Gideon said somberly.

"What? Why not?"

"I've signed an NDA," Gideon explained. "Any book where I give input will have to go through my new boss."

"What new boss?" Gregg asked. "Who do I have to convince to let you write another book."

"Senator Ryan Morgan."

"Morgan! But he's the one running the new—"

"I can't confirm or deny anything," Gideon said. "So please don't ask me to. If you want to publish another book, you'll have to rely on our existing contract and the information you already have."

There was a long pause before Gregg said, "You're talking about the work-product clause. Are you saying you're permanently unavailable?"

"That's right," Gideon said. "Just follow the contract. That's all I can say."

"Understood. Contact me when you can."

Wedding Bells Are Ringing

June 3rd – New York City, New York

Bryan Benson stared at himself in the mirror. The tuxedo was fancier than anything he'd ever worn, and he never imagined he'd be wearing it so soon. A three-week engagement was fast by any standard.

General Matthew Benson appeared behind Bryan in full dress uniform. "Son, I need to speak with you."

Bryan turned to face him. "Is this the standard father-son talk for a wedding?"

Matt shook his head. "Nothing standard about this day." He took a deep breath, clearly struggling with what he wanted to say. "Look, the day I met Claire was the day you proposed. It's been a whirlwind of preparations these last two weeks. I just want to make sure you're not rushing into something you'll regret because of my inflexible schedule."

Bryan scowled, looking his father in the eyes. "Do you think I'm making a mistake?"

Matt shook his head. "That's not what I'm saying. I honestly don't know if this marriage is a mistake. It's not my place to say. I'm only asking whether you have any doubts."

Bryan shook his head. "I was days away from proposing. You just accelerated things a bit."

"A bit?" Matt repeated. "A three-week engagement seems very accelerated. You haven't known her through all four seasons yet. I just want you to know that if you need to wait, I'll understand."

Bryan shook his head. "It's too late for that. If I tell Claire I need more time, she'll take it wrong. If I'd told her two weeks ago, it might have worked. But today is a little too late for delays."

"It's also the last time to turn back," Matt said. "If you have any hesitations, now is the time to say so."

"No, Dad. It's not." Bryan insisted. He heaved a huge sigh before blurting out, "The day after finals ended, I went on a very long walk. I was gone for four hours, walking through Central Park with my phone turned off. I asked myself all these questions on that day, two weeks ago. I love Claire. She loves me. We've been dating for months, and we've asked each other lots of questions.

"In the last two weeks, I've been asking her the last few questions I had before saying 'I do.' We've discussed money, children, religion, and how to deal with extended family. We aren't two starry-eyed college kids rushing into something we don't understand. We're two people in love with our eyes wide open."

Matt nodded and clapped his hand on Bryan's shoulder. "Thank you, Son. That makes me feel a lot better." He pulled Bryan into a brief hug.

"Come on, Dad," Bryan said as they separated. "Our friends are waiting. Let's get this done."

Matt nodded and followed him into the chapel.

Bryan took his place next to Jake Ritchey, the Best Man. They'd been friends since 2nd grade. Lots of Bryan's high school friends were here and a few of his college classmates. Claire's side of the chapel was utterly packed with people Bryan had never met.

The organist started playing Here Comes the Bride, and Bryan swung around, looking for Claire.

In slow, measured steps, Claire entered the chapel, accompanied by her father. Claire's face was veiled, but Bryan knew it was her. The dress was gorgeous, the pure white symbolizing what Claire possessed, which so few brides actually kept these days.

The priest performed the ceremony flawlessly, though Bryan was entranced, going through the practiced motions. When the priest said, "You may now kiss the bride," Bryan lifted the veil and gave Claire a short but passionate kiss. Anything more, and he wouldn't make it through the reception.

Bryan escorted his new bride back down the aisle and out to the waiting limousine, taking them to the hotel Bryan had checked into the night before.

An hour later, with both of them once more looking presentable, the limousine took them to the reception hall. Here the decorations were as lavish as Claire's dress. Clearly, someone in her family had deep pockets.

Matthew was there to greet them. "Glad to see you made it on time. I was starting to get worried."

Claire smiled up at him. "We waited until today. Neither of us could wait any longer."

Matthew blushed then cleared his throat. "Well, the guests have started to arrive. Shall we go greet them?"

The Great Scarlet Reset

Bryan and Claire both nodded, following Matthew to the flowered arch. Claire's parents joined them, followed quickly by the bridesmaids and groomsmen.

They stood there for almost two hours as people poured in, introducing themselves to whichever side of the family didn't know them and catching up with those who did. One such introduction stood out from the others in Bryan's mind.

"Hi, I'm Nikki, Claire's Uncle," the man said as he shook Bryan's hand.

"Wonderful to meet you," Bryan said. Claire had warned him that Uncle Nikki was a slick operator and that no one in the family actually knew what he did. Some suspected ties to the New York mob, while Claire's mom insisted nothing Nikki did was illegal. He just liked that kind of image.

"Claire's told me all about you, of course," Nikki said. "Listen, I know you've got your whole career planned out and everything. If there's one thing I've learned in life, it's that nothing goes exactly according to plan. So, if you ever want to do something more, uh, interesting, give me a call. Okay?" He shoved a business card in Bryan's pocket and moved on.

"What did you tell him about me?" Bryan asked Claire.

"I only said you were preparing for a military career," Claire shot back. "Don't worry about it."

Bryan nodded, moving on to the next guest. Yet, the encounter stuck with him. Nothing ever goes exactly according to plan. He knew that, but his military career wasn't something that would be easily derailed. Not for the son of someone as connected as Major General Matthew Benson.

New Pope, Old Hope

June 4th – Nephi, Utah

Gideon Shumway attended Church with his parents with plans to leave for Phoenix in the morning. Nothing had changed since his last visit, but his mother deserved to see him. Despite their differences, Gideon enjoyed hearing his father's commentary on Alma 5 in Gospel Doctrine.

Four years ago, that same chapter was confusing and unclear. This year, Gideon finally understood the mighty change of heart. Now he knew he needed to work just as hard, ensuring that he retained the change in his nature given him by God.[54]

His phone buzzed. It was a text from Duane.

Pope Pius made an announcement. You need to hear it. Start at 15:13

Gideon leaped up the stairs two at a time to get to his room. He opened his laptop and found a recording of the Pope's speech. He skipped the first fifteen minutes, as Duane suggested.

The Great Scarlet Reset

"In this age of pursuing the new," Pope Pius said, *"people need a link to the past."* He was clearly partway into his speech. *"That is why I have ordered the completion of a project that started in 1882. The Basilica of the Holy Family in Barcelona, Spain, has met with one delay after another, making it the longest-running construction project in modern history.*[55]

"Even recent attempts to complete this Basilica have met delay after delay. However, I will complete what Pope Leo XIII started. I will complete what the last ten Popes have not. In only five years, I will complete this Basilica, giving the people of Spain one of the finest Churches in the world."

So the new Pope was going to make a name for himself by completing the Basilica. Five years would only put the completion six months ahead of the current schedule. Still, he made a good speech.

Visual Aid

June 8th – Qa'im, Iraq

Major General Matthew Benson stood alone in a farmer's field, staring through binoculars across the border at the small farming town of Abu Kamal. Hiding among its streets was the new headquarters of the Global Islamic State. Jamil Noury was spotted there five times in the last two weeks. Now that Benson had dealt with the distractions of family obligations, he had only one focus. Capturing Jamil Noury.

Colonel Perry walked up and stood next to him. He knew better than to salute this close to the border. "Sir, you've been out here for three hours. Are you hoping Jamil will walk up and have a chat?"

Matt laughed. "I hope he doesn't even know I'm here."

"Then what are you doing, Sir?"

"Pondering."

"Yes, Sir," Perry said. "What exactly are you pondering?"

The Great Scarlet Reset

Matt cleared his throat. "When was the last time Jamil crossed the border into Iraq?"

"I'm not sure he ever has, Sir."

"Of course he has," Matt said. "Why else would he make his camp so close to the border?"

"Well, it's not technically his camp, Sir."

"It's not? Then whose camp is it? Why is he there?"

"He's the head lieutenant of a man calling himself Al-Mahdi," Perry explained. "Abu Kamal is Al-Mahdi's home town."

"Mahdi—" Matt let the name roll off his tongue, triggering a memory from long ago. "I know that name from somewhere."

"It's not a very common name—" Perry began.

"No," Matt interrupted. "It's not a name at all. It's a title. From that weird book series on the sand planet."

"Dune?"

"Yes! That's the one. It was the title the desert people gave to their leader." [56] Matt mulled that over while he gazed once more through his binoculars.

Several minutes passed in silence before Matt said, "If Jamil isn't the leader, then who is this Al-Mahdi? How often does he come across the border?"

"I really can't say," Perry said. "We've been focused on Jamil."

"Then widen your focus," Matt said. "I want to know everything there is to know about this group, and especially what ties they have to people and towns in Iraq."

"Yes, Sir," Perry said. "Will you be riding back with me?"

Matt nodded and followed Perry out of the field. "I've seen what I came to see. Let's get this dirtbag."

New Duties

June 12th – Phoenix, Arizona

Gideon Shumway endured a week of training at the FBI building in Phoenix, Arizona. He signed all the non-disclosure documents put before him. Advising a Senatorial Committee required several levels of clearance, which Gideon quickly obtained. Now it was time for him to get to work.

"Ready to learn what we do here?" Perry Chivas asked.

Gideon nodded. He had an excellent view of the top of Perry's head.

"We analyze world events and explain them to the half-witted Senators," Gideon said.

Perry's smile was brief. "Let me rephrase. Are you ready to learn how we advise the Senators?"

Gideon nodded.

"The data comes into our servers from many sources," Perry said. "Then our algorithms direct the relevant information to your inbox and flag it with a priority level. Your job is to write a brief summary of each item and a more detailed explanation of higher priority events. If even more detail is needed, it will arrive as a top priority request. Any questions?"

Gideon nodded. "Who else in the FBI is working with me?"

"FBI?" Perry repeated. "No. You're working for the CIA. The FBI's name is on the building. For now."

Gideon swallowed hard. Working for Senator Morgan was terrible enough. But everything Gideon had researched showed the CIA was a stronghold of the grand conspiracy spoken of in Ezra's Eagle. Still, if he quit, the press would run that fake story. He'd have to play along.

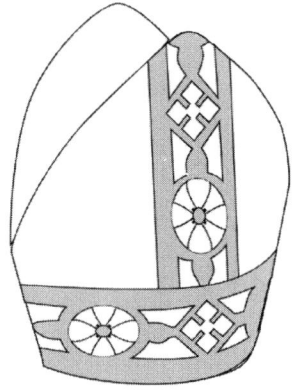

The Old Man and the See

June 14th –Vatican City

Pope Pius XIII looked up from the Basilica blueprints as an old friend came into the room.

"Supreme Pontiff, it is good to see you again," Bishop Grosvenor said.

"Gregori!" Pope Pius stood to greet his guest. "What brings you this far from Russia? I heard the Russian Orthodox Church made you an archbishop."

Grosvenor shook his head. "Not yet. It was proposed but not yet confirmed."

"Is that why you're here?" Pope Pius asked. "You've come to cash in on our friendship to become archbishop?"

Grosvenor shook his head. "Nothing like that. You know I supported your appointment as Pope, helped you get elected."

Pius nodded. "And I'm very grateful." He paused a moment, studying his old friend. "You've come to collect?"

Grosvenor nodded.

Pius took a seat and motioned for Grosvenor to do the same before asking, "Tell me then. What is the true cost of your support?"

"You must continue the work of Pope Ferdinand."

"Pope Ferdinand worked on many projects," Pius said carefully. "You'll have to be more specific."

"Unity," Grosvenor said. "You must continue the work to unify the Christian religions, or we will not be strong enough to survive what's coming."

"And what, exactly, is coming?"

"War."

Pius shook his head. "War is already upon this world. The destruction of Damascus and Wadi Mujib is enough to testify of that."

"I speak of a different form of war," Grosvenor said.

"What do you mean?"

"War between countries comes and goes more quickly than their leaders," Grosvenor explained. "I speak of a war between religions.[57] Such a war, once started, may never end. The Crusades officially lasted almost four hundred years and ended more than five hundred years ago. Yet, there are some Islamists who still fight that war."

"But as you say," Pius replied slowly, "war with the Muslims ended before the Great Protest began."

Grosvenor nodded. "War with the Muslims ended, but not war with the Islamists."[58]

"The difference between the two is razor-thin," Pius said. "I'm not sure how that difference applies here."

"That is why you must unite the Christian faiths," Grosvenor persisted. "If you cannot understand the difference between a faith and a political ideal, perhaps you aren't the leader we need."

Pope Pius shook his head. "Pope Ferdinand was misguided in trying to undo the Great Protest by uniting our faiths under some minimalist agreement. We should let the missionaries bring individuals back to the true faith rather than try negotiating with their leaders."

Grosvenor sighed. "My associates will not be pleased with your attitude."

"Yet I am the one who speaks the will of God, am I not?"

Grosvenor stood and headed toward the door.

Pius frowned, confused by his old friend's words. "If the Patriarch of Moscow wishes to discuss reuniting with the Catholic Church, I would be happy to receive him."

"I'm not speaking of the Patriarch," Grosvenor corrected as he turned back to face Pius.

"Then of whom do you speak?" Pope Pius insisted.

"My friends prefer to remain in the Shadows." Grosvenor's emphasis on the last word told Pope Pius precisely who he meant.

Pius scowled. "I had no idea you had friends in such low places."

"They can be your friends as well," Grosvenor offered. "Or they can see you as a threat."

Pope Pius stood. "A leader of the light cannot remain friends with those who prefer the darkness. It is time for you to go."

Grosvenor nodded, frowning deeply. "Goodbye, old friend."

"May the light of the gospel shine on you once more," Pope Pius offered.

Bishop Grosvenor left without saying another word.

Pope Pius studied the door for a long time after his old friend was gone. How could he be friends with a man for fifty years, watch him progress through the Priesthood, and remain woefully ignorant of the darkness within him?

What's worse, he feared he'd just made an enemy of the most dangerous people on the planet. Still, if such dark men desired unity of the Body of Christ, they must have some nefarious purpose for it. Pope Pius would never do the will of such men. Yet Grosvenor suggested Pius's selection as Pope was partly due to the support of those men of darkness.

This presented a real quandary. A kabbala of darkness wanted Pope Pius to continue Pope Ferdinand's work, suggesting they supported the last Pope's efforts. Did a disagreement with this dark council lead to Pope Ferdinand's death? And if so, had Pope Pius just signed his own death warrant by refusing them?

Pope Pius shook that thought off. He could not abandon his nature, even to save his own life. He would not work with agents of darkness. It bothered him that such men thought he could be reasoned with or even controlled.

New Foundations

June 16th – Washington, D.C.

Maria Croix took part of her day off to visit the massive hole where the Capitol Building once stood. She approached the edge of the pit, gazing down several stories. Workers measured the foundations of the building using lasers on tripods. Everything previously resting on that foundation was gone.

"I need you to take a few steps back, ma'am," someone said.

Maria took a step back, then turned to see who spoke. The man wore a grey hard hat and a suit. "Are you the construction foreman?"

The man nodded, removing his sunglasses. "Can I ask what you're doing here?"

"I have a professional interest in what happened here," Maria said. "I'm just here to satisfy my curiosity regarding the rebuilding process."

The foreman nodded. "Can I see some I.D.?"

Maria flashed her badge.

"Thank you. I'm John Cavanaugh. Only three kinds of people have a professional interest in this hole in the ground. I just wanted to make sure you were one of the first two."

"Law enforcement?" Maria asked.

"Investigators and construction workers are the first two," Cavanaugh replied. "The third category are those who made this hole."

Maria nodded at that. Would anyone who participated in this horror actually come back to stare at the hole they'd made? "So, how is the project going?"

"We've dug down to the original foundation," Cavanaugh said. "It isn't cracked, but I'm not sure if we can save it."

"Why not?"

"The foundation is strong, no question there. But the plans for the new Capitol Building require a larger footprint. Right now, we're measuring the old foundation to see if we can build upon it or whether we need to dig it out and start fresh."

Maria smirked. "Kind of like the Constitution."

"What do you mean?"

"Right now, President Baldwin is rebuilding the government," Maria said. "Is he going to look at the Constitution and decide it's too old, too small, or simply outdated?"

Cavanaugh laughed. "You're not seriously comparing the greatest document ever written to an old slab of concrete, are you?"

Maria shook her head. "I may not be, but I'm concerned our President is."

Selection Day

June 27th – Phoenix, Arizona

Ryan Morgan waved to the cameras as he approached the polling place. The video clip may or may not make national news, but it would certainly play on the local news, if only for all of two minutes. Ryan waited all of ten minutes before casting his vote. The cameras recorded him returning to his limousine. Yes, he'd cast his vote. However, much like this election, it was all a publicity stunt.

"No troubles in there?" Bastion Flick asked.

"Of course not," Ryan said. "Any troubles on your end?"

Bastion shook his head. "Payment to Lectus went through without a hitch. Honestly, even without Lectus, our numbers suggest you'll get more than sixty percent of the vote."

Ryan smiled. "You've run an effective campaign once more."

Bastion nodded. "Thank you. There is some pushback, claiming you're part of some grand conspiracy based solely on the fact that you did not attend the State of the Union address."

Ryan chuckled briefly. "Well, they're right."

"Of course," Bastion replied without humor. "Google, Facebook, Twitter, and Instagram are actively demonetizing and suppressing the channels of anyone who puts forth such theories."

"Good. Do we have a report yet on how effective the Lectus machines are?"

Bastion shook his head. "These machines aren't connected to the internet. We won't see results until polls close and the votes are reported."

"How can they possibly control those machines without a network feed?" Ryan asked.

"More than twenty states placed wi-fi blockers in the polling places to prevent it," Bastion explained. "The Muta machines don't need an internet connection to do their jobs."

"How is that possible? The algorithms might need adjustment."

"It's all handled within the machine."

"This has been tested?" Ryan asked.

Bastion nodded. "These machines were used in dozens of states during the midterm election."

"What about states that don't use voting machines?"

"All gone," Bastion said. "President Baldwin got the machines in every voting district in every state."

Ryan nodded. "Good. We can't have any more mistakes like Towers."

Bastion shook his head once more. "It will never happen again."

"So this demand for the results being posted on the blockchain is just smoke?"

"No, that's actually going to happen," Bastion explained.

"But that gives too much transparency," Ryan shot back.

"The Muta machines will report the results to the blockchain, allowing everyone to view it and preventing it from being modified."

"How is that blockchain supported?" Ryan asked.

"The Muta machines themselves are running that blockchain."

Ryan laughed. "So if we want to change the blockchain, we just have to send an update to the Muta machines."

"You can't change the blockchain," Bastion said. "That's what makes it secure."

Ryan continued to chuckle. "Yeah. That's what the average person believes. They don't know about a 51% attack."[59]

"I'm sorry. What is that?"

"If someone controls more than half of the computing power behind a blockchain," Ryan explained, "they can edit a blockchain. For any blockchain to be secure, all you need is at least three genuinely independent parties. The blockchain is secure as long as no single party has more than half of the computing power. But if the Muta machines themselves are supporting the blockchain, then only one entity, Lectus Voting Systems, controls that blockchain and can edit that chain at will."

The Middle Game

July 2nd – Washington, D.C.

President Frank Baldwin watched with eleven other members of the Shadow Council as One entered the room.

"It's so nice to see you all here," One said as he took his seat. "Centuries of planning have led us to this moment. We have control of the major countries of the world. We have enough sway over the major religions of the world to ensure our plans come to fruition. All that remains is total domination over the economic forces of the world. Two, you will crash all the stock exchanges at once."

Two nodded. "I am ready."

"Good," One said. "Thirteen, once that is done, you will address the United States. The new Senate and Congress will do exactly what we tell them to do."

Baldwin nodded. "Of course, Great One."

One frowned. "Don't call me that. One will do."

"Sorry, One," Baldwin said.

One nodded. "You are still new to this council. It is a mistake everyone is allowed to make once. Six, what is the status of the new Pope? Will he follow our commands?"

Six shook his head. "No. With only two serious candidates available, the Council of the Cardinals chose poorly. I attempted to persuade my old friend, but he sees himself as a man of ideals. He believes God gave him the power he now wields."

"No matter," One said. "Have the new Pope eliminated. Then there will be only one possible choice."

"What is the time frame required?" Six asked.

One smiled. "Smart of you to ask. Switching the world to a digital currency will take about a decade. That is how long you have."

Six nodded. "It will be done."

DCEP Forever

July 13th – Beijing, China

Su Xiannian approached the podium with a big smile on his face. Today was the day he'd worked toward since he'd replaced Xi as President of China. This announcement would ensure China's place as the premiere Superpower within five years.

"Yesterday, the Bank of China began divesting our holdings in U.S. Bonds," Su declared. "This divesting will continue until we have sold off all foreign bonds."

The crowd cheered on cue.

"These foreign bonds' proceeds will bolster the Digital Currency Electronic Payment,[60] which is now the only official currency of China."

More cheers.

"Chinese citizens have two weeks to finish converting their Yuan holdings into the DCEP. The DCEP will spread from our borders across the world as the new world currency!" Su shouted.

The crowd cheered again.

"This will improve your lives in every way, making it easier to pay for all your goods and services and receive your payments."

The cheers were getting weaker now.

"As we embrace the future of digital currency, we will let go of the evils caused by physical currency. Namely, poverty, greed, and financial oppression."

Their cheers continued long after the mandated ten seconds. They really were excited about this new future.

Black Thursday

July 20th – Phoenix, Arizona

Gideon Shumway quickly settled into his new life in Phoenix, Arizona. He only worked twenty-five hours per week, giving him plenty of time to study and prepare for his classes starting in August.

Book sales continued at a slightly subdued rate since he'd left the talk show and seminar circuit. Still, the millions he'd already collected in profits were distributed in a wide array of investments. As he opened his stock portfolio, something was wrong. Last week he had a quarter-million dollars worth of stocks. Today, they were only worth $187,000. Gideon checked YouTube for answers. It didn't take long to find them.

"Today marked the largest single-day drop in the history of the stock market," James Jones reported. *"The Dow Jones Industrial Average dropped from an all-time high of $42,500 to $32,800. The Level 1 safeguard was tripped only minutes after the stock market*

opened in New York this morning.[61] Trading closed after four hours. While the S&P 500 fell only twenty percent, the Dow Jones fell twenty-five percent. Indicators are already showing trading will resume tomorrow, with many stocks down another five percent after the closing bell.

"What makes this day truly unique is that the New York Stock Exchange was not the only one hit. Euronext, London Stock Exchange, Frankfurt Stock Exchange, all six Swiss Exchanges, and many other European countries saw similar declines. Some of these European exchanges were down significantly before the New York Stock Exchange opened. Still, all of them saw a marked decline shortly after the S&P 500 took a nosedive."

Gideon switched to his real estate portfolio and saw it was down one percent from a week ago. But his cryptocurrency holdings were up five percent in the same period. Overall, his investments lost about eighty thousand out of two and a half million.

Gideon sighed. Tomorrow morning there would probably be a request in his inbox to analyze this crash from a religious perspective. His mind was already working on a response.

Shadow Request

July 25th – Kasur, Pakistan

Mohammed Ali Malik listened to one proposal after another, waiting to hear something worthy of his attention. "None of th-these targets are l-large enough," he concluded. "We n-need something to s-strike f-fear into the hearts of our en-nemies.

"I'm sorry, Mahdi," Izad said. "These are the types of operations we've been running for years."

"Exactly," Ali said. "We n-need to ch-change our m-methods. We must in-ncrease the s-spectacle of our attacks."

"There is one plan we haven't discussed," Karim said.

"Do tell," Ali said.

"We could send in a suicide bomber as Christmas Mass is letting out," Karim said. "There will be plenty of casualties. Many headlines. Much chaos."

"N-now there is a p-plan worth discussing," Ali said. "But there are t-two p-problems."

"Perhaps we can solve them," Karim offered.

"First, o-one bombing is n-not enough," Ali explained.

"Then we will plan multiple attacks," Karim said. "All set for the same Christmas morning."

Ali said. "Y-yes. That's w-what I'm asking f-for."

"What is the second problem, Mahdi?" Izad asked.

"S-suicide b-bombings decrease our numbers too q-quickly," Ali explained. "W-we've discussed this b-before."

Karim nodded. "We can send three men to America who will recruit others to die for our cause. Given enough time, we can easily recruit seven to ten teams that will each independently launch attacks at the same time."

"You c-can accomplish this w-with only three m-men?" Ali asked.

Karim nodded. "It will take several years of planning, but it can be done."

"G-good," Ali said. "T-that is the kind of i-ideas I'm l-looking for."

"It would take at least five years of preparations to pull off an attack of such a scale," Izad said. "And each person recruited would add to the risk of all being caught."

"No single recruit needs to know about more than two other people," Karim explained. "If we plan for ten teams and three are caught, the authorities will think they have thwarted our efforts entirely."

"You would intentionally hand over recruits to allay suspicion?" Izad asked. "Allah forbid."

"No," Karim shot back. "I'm only saying that if the Americans are smart enough to stop two or three of the teams, they will think they have them all and stop looking. If we plan for a level of failure, it assures our overall success."

Ali smiled. "Very g-good, Karim. "Izad says it w-will take f-five years. I g-give you six."

"You wish me to personally go to America?" Karim asked.

Ali shook his head. "N-no. You are t-too well known to the CIA."

Karim chuckled. "I did work for them for a time."

"S-so I've heard," Ali said, smiling back. "T-that's why I know y-you'll pick the r-right three men."

"Mahdi," Eshiram said as he entered the room. "You have a visitor."

"Did he give the correct signs?" Karim asked.

Eshiram nodded.

"Then show him in," Karim confirmed.

Eshiram shook his head. "He insists on meeting with the Mahdi alone."

"What!" Izad protested. "No visitor is afforded that honor."

"One with the right signs may have what he requests," Eshiram shot back.

"But the only people who can make such a request—" Izad began.

"T-tell him I w-will be r-right there," Ali interrupted. If Twelve had returned so soon, it must mean he was doing something right. Or that something had gone horribly wrong.

"As you wish, Mahdi," Eshiram said.

"Karim, please p-proceed," Ali said. He bowed his head slightly to each member of his council who bowed back. Then Ali went to his private study. It was Twelve. Still, Ali offered the signs and got the countersigns in return.

"I am Twelve," Twelve said.

Ali nodded. "Then our s-success did not y-yet earn you an adv-vancement."

Twelve shook his head. "No. Sadly, Pope Pius is not the man we wanted for the job."

"Then you w-wish me t-to take action again?" Ali asked.

Twelve nodded. "You are very insightful."

Ali smiled. "My new m-mentor has been t-teaching me well."

"Your new mentor?" Twelve asked. "Who are you talking about?"

"He d-didn't g-give his n-name." Ali suddenly became very concerned that he shouldn't have brought The Teacher into his confidence. "I t-thought you s-sent him."

"Tell me more about him," Twelve said.

"T-teacher!" Ali called. "C-come and answer f-for y-yourself!"

The Teacher strolled into the room. "He kn-knows who I am."

"You call yourself Teacher now?" Twelve asked.

The Teacher nodded. "The m-man you knew b-before is gone, j-just as you r-requested."

"Yet here you are," Twelve said.

The Teacher shook his head. "N-no man kn-knows who I w-was, save those w-who are now l-loyal to Al-Mahdi."

Twelve nodded. "Very well. Then you can guide the future Mahdi on this assignment."

The Teacher nodded. "You w-wish us to eliminate P-pius?"

Twelve shook his head. "I don't care who or how. I just need the conclave to convene again and select a new Pope."

"H-how q-quickly?" Ali asked.

Twelve shook his head. "Five to ten years would be soon enough."

"It s-shall be d-done," Ali and The Teacher said in unison. They even stuttered at the same time.

The First Order

July 31st – Sacramento, California

Michael Ward logged in to his Zoom account, still trying to figure out why he got an invitation from the White House to join a meeting. To his surprise, President Baldwin's face appeared on his screen.

"Hello, old friend," Baldwin said.

"Frank! The invitation was from you?"

Baldwin nodded. "The first digital meeting of the new Senate starts in fifteen minutes, and I need to discuss the first order of business with you before that happens."

"With me?" Michael asked. "In case you haven't heard, I'm not a federal Senator. I'm still a California state representative."

"I'm well aware of your office," Baldwin said. "The first order of business is to approve my selection for Vice President."

"I see." Michael was still confused. "How can I help?"

"You can agree to be my Vice President."

Michael's answer caught in his throat. He couldn't get the words out.

"I'm sorry," Baldwin said. "I didn't catch that. I think the video must have frozen."

Michael swallowed hard before spitting out, "I'd be honored."

Baldwin smiled. "Wonderful. I'll be putting your name forward in about half an hour. Please join us for that Zoom call."

Michael nodded. "Of course, Sir." As soon as the call ended, he let out the breath he didn't realize he'd been holding in. Then he leaped out of his seat and shouted for joy.

"What's wrong?" Joanna came running into the room. "I heard screaming."

"I'm the new Vice President!"

"Of what?"

"Of the United States!"

"What! When did that happen?"

Michael gave his wife a huge hug and kiss. "The Senate is about to meet, and the first order of business is confirming me as Vice President."

"Really? Does that mean we get to live in the White House?"

Michael shook his head. "The Vice President lives a couple miles away at the Naval Observatory."

Joanna shrugged. "But we'll still be at the White House a lot, right?"

Michael nodded. "That we will."

"Did he say why he chose you?" Joanna asked.

"Not today," Michael said. "But when Frank put me on the list six weeks ago, he said he valued my insights and my connections."

"Your connections?"

The computer beeped.

"It's time to join the meeting!"

"The Senate is meeting on Zoom?" Joanna asked.

Michael nodded. "Until the new Capitol Building is complete, all Senate and House meetings will be via Zoom."

Legal Beginnings

August 16th – Phoenix, Arizona

Gideon Shumway showed up to his first class with thirty seconds to spare. He nearly panicked when he saw his $2.5 million portfolios were now worth only $1.7 million. The stock market was in a nosedive. Real estate was barely holding its value, and cryptocurrencies were in a slight decline.

As Gideon took his seat, the teacher cleared his throat. "For those of you who are serious about a career in law," he took a long pause to stare at Gideon. "Legal Writing is the basis of everything you will do, no matter what area of law you practice. If you get an A in my course, your entire career will be easier. If you only put in enough effort to get a passing grade, you'll struggle in your career for the rest of your life."

Gideon thought the professor was laying it on a little thick. Still, he had a point.

"I'd like to get a thorough understanding of your current writing styles," Professor Stewart said. "With the recent passing of our school's namesake, I feel it is appropriate that each of you write a tribute to Sandra Day O'Connor. It will not affect your final grade, but I will score it as if it were your final paper. This will show you how much improvement you need to make. Papers are due on Monday."

"Monday?" Gideon said in unison with twenty others.

"Yes, Monday," Professor Stewart confirmed. "There's plenty of information floating around the web right now but beware of plagiarism. Your papers will be submitted electronically. This is only partially so they can easily endure my app designed to detect phrases plucked from the news or other sources. Is that clear?"

Gideon joined a small handful of others in saying, "Yes, Professor."

"I'm sorry," Professor Stewart said. "I couldn't hear you. Let's try that again. Is that clear?"

"Yes, Professor!" the whole class roared.

Swimming Buddies

August 25th – Phoenix, Arizona

"That will be all for today," Professor Stewart said. "Though I would like to see Gideon Shumway in my office."

The rest of the class cleared out as Gideon slowly collected his things. He followed the professor to his office, wondering what was going on.

Once the door was closed behind them, Professor Stewart turned and smiled at him. "I did a lot of checking up on you after reading your paper on Justice O'Connor."

"Was there something wrong with my work?" Gideon asked.

Professor Stewart shook his head. "No, absolutely not. That's why I wanted to talk to you."

"I don't understand."

"Most of the kids I get in my class can barely write at an eighth-grade level," Professor Stewart explained.

"But this is a graduate-level course," Gideon replied. "You make it sound like your students are straight out of high school."

Professor Stewart laughed. "It often feels like they are. I'm basically teaching an undergraduate-level English writing course with an emphasis on law. Your paper shows your undergrad included classes in persuasive writing."

Gideon nodded. "Comparing religions required me to persuasively write to people with very different backgrounds."

"But it's more than that," Professor Stewart said. "I thumbed through your book." He lifted a copy of Gideon's book off his desk. "You must have learned how to reference sources to write this book to this level."

Gideon shrugged. "Professor Jenkins was quite clear in how he wanted sources cited."

Stewart nodded. "I know. I spoke with him."

"Why?" Both of Gideon's eyebrows rose.

"I had to be sure you actually wrote this paper on Sandra Day O'Connor. It's the best such paper I've gotten in ten years."

Gideon wasn't sure how to react. So he just softly said, "Thank you."

"Right now, you're probably wondering why I called you in here," Stewart said.

Gideon nodded.

"By most measures, you don't need my course. I could give you a final exam right now, and you'd get a passing grade." He paused. "But not an A. I know you could put my course on cruise control and get a B. But if you don't work hard and get an A in my course, you're doing yourself a disservice."

"I fully agree," Gideon said.

"Then why in God's name are you a part-time law student?"

This meeting finally made sense. "I have a part-time job."

"Why?" Jenkins insisted. "You're already a millionaire."

Gideon cleared his throat. "It wasn't exactly my idea."

Jenkins blinked several times, trying to understand that. "Do you need a lawyer?"

"I've been thrown in dangerous waters," Gideon said slowly. "I'm not sure whether you want to be my swimming buddy right now."

Jenkins nodded. "Senator Morgan."

Gideon nodded very slightly.

Stewart sighed. "If you want my help with this matter, I'm willing to act as your lead attorney."

Gideon paused, weighing this unexpected turn of events. "I'll have to think about it."

Stewart nodded. "Please do."

Crash and Boom

October 2nd – Amalfi, Italy

Scott Knox pulled up his cryptocurrency portfolio to see if the stock market crash was affecting him. He knew diversification was a key to protecting wealth. Still, so far, all he'd done was spread his millions across three dozen cryptocurrencies recommended by an expert.

"Scott, what are you doing?" Tonya called from the next room.

"Checking my portfolio," Scott shouted back. Over the last ten weeks, the Dow Jones dove from an all-time high at $42,500 down to $17,000, erasing over eight years of growth. It was a more significant dive than the Halo virus crash of 2020, only this time, no one could blame it on a virus or a government shutdown.

"Okay," Tonya said. "We're heading to the beach."

Scott opened his portfolio monitor and set it to display the last three months. "I'll be down in twenty minutes." Something didn't look right. His portfolio performance was nearly the exact opposite of the Stock Market. Except, the scale of the increase was different.

In March 2020, when the stock market hit its low, with a thirty percent drop in the DJIA, Bitcoin, and nearly every other cryptocurrency was cut in half.

Now, with the stock market down 60%, Scott's portfolio had risen from $30 million to $75 million, a 150% rise. He'd paid only $10,000 for the advice, which had just earned him $45 million.

Over the last three years, he'd turned the $10 million bounty into a $75 million fortune. It was more money than he'd ever imagined having. Yet it was his, without the IRS knowing he had it. Scott smiled wide as he closed the laptop.

Analyzing God's Hands

October 3rd – Phoenix, Arizona

Gideon Shumway got a text alert on his way to work. He waited until he was parked, then checked it.

Large Deposit: $1000 U.S. Treasury

So the new stimulus check had been approved and deposited into his account. Gideon was a little surprised to get a check at all, considering how much income he'd reported on his taxes last year. All his friends received various amounts based on reportable income and how many children they had. It started with two checks to everyone. Then they sent out advances on the Child Tax Credit.

More and more groups of people starting to receive a monthly check from the IRS for various reasons. If they were sending a check to people like Gideon, it meant everyone was getting a check now.

Gideon left his phone in the car and proceeded to his office. There were no new requests, so he continued with the unfinished low priority items from last week. Less than ten minutes passed before he got the email he'd been expecting for more than a month.

Analyze the recent drop in the stock market. Priority: Low

Low priority meant no more than a one-page summary. Gideon was tempted to simply leave it at: 'No religious aspect' as he'd done half a dozen times. However, before giving up so quickly, he did a quick search for 'Stock Market Crash God.'

The top result was an article written right after the 2020 crash. This was followed by philosophical arguments about whether stock investments were truly part of Christian life or merely socially acceptable gambling.

None of that really helped. So Gideon tried another search. 'market crash is god's punishment.'

This search yielded much better results. There were statements by Pat Robertson and debates about various stock market corrections being God's punishment for various reasons. He reviewed several of them before writing up his report.

There will always be those who blame God for every setback in life. However, there is no biblical justification for assigning this market drop to God's punishment. Nor can it be appropriately associated with any specific sins committed by the nation's people.

There is no specific prophecy relating to a worldwide stock market decline. Only time will tell whether this is part of some more extensive series of events fulfilling prophecy.

He included a few quotes with references and submitted the report.

Universal Basic Income

January 3rd – Phoenix, Arizona

Gideon Shumway groaned as he opened the door to Professor Stewart's office.

"That's not a good way to start our meeting," Professor Stewart said.

Gideon smiled as he looked up and put away his phone. "Sorry. I just got a text that the government has made another deposit into my account."

Stewart laughed. "Most people are pleased when that happens."

"That's because most people are getting two thousand dollars each month," Gideon said. "Enough money to change their lifestyle. But every time they write another of these checks, it devalues the dollar, forcing me to keep as little as possible in cash. I hope this is the last stimulus check."

"Nope," Stewart said. "They've just made those checks semi-permanent."

"What?"

Stewart nodded. "Every month this year with a vote every six months to extend the checks by six months."

"For how long?"

Stewart shrugged. "Until politicians no longer need votes?"

Gideon sighed more deeply. "This isn't what I came to talk to you about."

"No. You came because I promised answers."

"Exactly," Gideon said. "What have you found?"

"Before we get to that," Stewart said, "I need to know why you wrote that book."

"What do you mean?"

"You put a lot of time and effort into explaining Ezra's Eagle," Stewart said. "What were you hoping to accomplish?"

"I wanted to inform people about an ancient prophecy coming true right now."

"Sure," Stewart said. "You could have done that with a website or an eBook you gave away. But you published a book and sold hundreds of thousands of copies, making a fortune along the way."

Gideon nodded. "I had something of value and found a way to get paid for it."

"So you got paid for your analysis and opinions," Stewart concluded.

"That's one way to put it."

"Now, let me ask another question. When you've graduated from law school, what kind of career do you want?"

Gideon thought about that. It wasn't the first time this question came up. But each time he considered it, the answer changed. Then he remembered the promises made by the angel. "I want to make a difference in the world. I want to have a front-row seat for the major changes I outlined in that book."

Stewart nodded. "You seem well-positioned to do that."

Gideon involuntarily took a step back. Then he sat down. He'd repeated the words of the angel, then been told his job with the CIA was the perfect way to accomplish that. "I never thought of it that way."

"Perhaps you should," Stewart said. "I can certainly get you out of your contract with the CIA. I can advise you on managing the possibility of a smear campaign, accusing you of being the father of your cousin's child. But, given your life goals, I'd much rather advise you on increasing your influence within the CIA so that you gain the ear of the President."

"You can do that?"

Stewart nodded. "It would be my honor to act as legal counsel to someone who advises the President. Right now, you have a back-row seat. Everything you write passes through several layers of bureaucracy before it reaches the desk of the President. With a little work, you can make yourself so valuable that the President himself will ask to speak with you in person. I can help you make that happen."

The Spirit burned in Gideon's heart. This was the right thing to do. Despite being in the belly of the beast, as he saw it, this job with the CIA was the right place to be.

At least for now.

Third Time's the Charm?

January 6th – Houston, Texas

"Blue forty-two!" Benjamin Shumway Jr. called out to his team. "Blue forty-two! Hut, hut, hike!"

Isieli snapped the ball back to Ben, then became part of the blue wall protecting him.

Ben faked a hand-off to Laione, then looked for Kaelo.

He wasn't there.

It took Ben half a second to realize Kaelo was down, and three orange-clad Clemson players were charging.

Ten yards away, Fokisi was struggling to get through the orange line. The play was falling apart fast.

Ben tucked the ball into his elbow and took off, running away from the three large orange blobs coming toward him. "Dozer!" Ben shouted to his fellow BYU players.

Laione and Isieli grunted and gave an extra push, creating a hole for Ben to slip through.

The Great Scarlet Reset

Ben took advantage of that hole in the orange line and shot through. He crossed the line of scrimmage before the Clemson defense realized what was happening. But now they were too late.

Laione and Isieli closed the hole behind him, blocking the three players who had been on Ben's tail. The resulting collision caused enormous confusion. It was another two seconds before any orange players realized it wasn't a tackle pile.

Ben crossed the forty-yard line, leaving all the Clemson players behind him. Hitting the fifty-yard line, he felt like he was flying. Pumping his legs for all they were worth, he crossed the forty, the thirty, the twenty, the ten, and into the endzone.

Cheers erupted from the stands.

Ben held the ball in the air like a trophy, the thrill of the chase coursing through his body. He glanced up at the scoreboard.

BYU 41, Clemson 40.

It was a very narrow lead, but it was a lead, and it was the fourth quarter. Elated, Ben headed to the sidelines to watch the field goal kick.

"Good job, Son," Ben Sr. said as Ben Jr. jogged past him.

"Thanks, Dad." Ben Jr. felt his leg muscles starting to cramp. Rather than sitting, he walked up and down the sidelines, helping his muscles calm down after the enormous strain.

The field goal was good, bringing the score to 42, 40.

Ben Jr. took a seat, hydrating in anticipation of getting back on the field. There were three minutes left in the game, and if BYU could get the ball back, it would be up to Ben to run that clock out without losing the ball.

He watched with amusement as Clemson got a first down, bringing them to their own thirty-yard line. Seventy yards was a long way to go in two minutes and thirty seconds.

Their next play gained them eight yards and cost them thirty seconds. Then BYU pushed Clemson back by two yards, shaving another thirty seconds off the clock.

Then Clemson made a big play, almost a copy of what Ben had just done, except the Clemson quarterback was tackled on the BYU twenty-yard line.

A gasp circled the stadium as the QB didn't get up.

Medics ran onto the field, stood around him for twenty seconds, then carried him off.

Ben waited for the announcement of penalties, but it never came. There were no flags on the play. The tackle was utterly legit, but the Clemson first-string quarterback was out.

Three seconds remained on the clock.

The Clemson team gave a shout and took the field. Including the kicker.

Ben watched as a field goal ended the championship game. BYU, 42. Clemson, 43. Despite all his hard work, it all came down to three seconds. For the third year in a row, he lost the championship.

The entire Clemson team took the field, cheering and rejoicing. The BYU team slowly started heading to the locker room.

Painful Award

January 9th - Provo, Utah

Benjamin Shumway Sr. was in the locker room with the team when he heard his name mentioned on ESPN. "Silence!"

The locker room went quiet as Ben turned up the volume. They'd spent the afternoon nursing their bruised egos by lifting weights to bulk up for next season.

"The biggest surprise of the College Playoffs this year isn't who won," Harold Barton said.

"We gave Clemson a thirty-five percent chance of winning before the season began," Nathan Jurek agreed. *"No, the big surprise is the Heisman Trophy going to someone other than Vance Jackson."*

"That's right, Nathan," Harold jumped in. *"Vance had an amazing season, taking Clemson all the way to the Championship Game once more, only to be injured with three seconds left in the game."*

"And what an injury it was!" Nathan blurted out. *"A broken leg and a torn ACL. His dreams of the NFL may be history."*

"We're all rooting for your full recovery," Harold said somberly. *"However, the Heisman Trophy this year goes to Ben Shumway."*

The locker room erupted in a brief cheer.

"That's right," Nathan said. *"For the third year in a row, Ben Shumway has taken the BYU team to the Championship game, and for the third year in a row, the BYU defense was unable to hold on to the win."*

"Some credit has to go to Shumway's father, Ben Sr.," Harold said. *"A man involved in BYU football at one level or another since he played for the team in the early '90s."*

"I don't know how you can say that," Nathan shot back. *"After all, he's the defensive line coach for BYU, and it's the defensive line that lost the championship for BYU three years running."*

"I'm fully aware of that," Harold said. *"But this man raised not just one, but two college quarterbacks who took their teams to the championships."*

"He did?" Nathan asked. *"Who are you talking about?"*

"Is your memory really so short?" Harold asked. *"I'm talking about Gideon Shumway, former quarterback for Notre Dame."*

"But where is he now?" Nathan asked. *"If my memory serves, Gideon quit football after losing to the combined might of his brother and father."*

Harold nodded. *"Yes. We were all surprised to find Patrick O'Hare leading the Fighting Irish last year. If memory serves, Gideon wrote a book that's still selling well."*

"I don't remember seeing that," Nathan said. *"Believe me, if someone had written a first-hand account of battling in the Holy War of college football, I would have read that book."*

"No, no," Harold clarified. *"The book was about some ancient prophecy. It's actually—"*

"Anyway," Nathan interrupted. *"Congratulations to Benjamin Shumway Jr. on winning the Heisman trophy. I'm sure NFL recruiters will be watching next season very closely."*

"Three cheers for the Shumways!" someone called out. "Hip, Hip, Hooray! Hip Hip, Hooray! Hip Hip, Hooray!" Each cheer grew louder until the last was a deafening roar.

Ben Sr. was crying as his son came into the room and gave him a hug. Those around Ben assumed they were tears of joy. In truth, it was a bittersweet joy. Junior had won the Heisman, even earned himself a spot in the NFL draft next year. But at the same time, it was a reminder of Gideon's choices, abandoning football, and leaving a stain on the Shumway name. Not even the Heisman had wiped that stain away.

Godfather Gideon

March 10th – Phoenix, Arizona

Gideon Shumway got a face time request from his brother Jon two hours after Church. Jon rarely called, so something significant must have happened. "Hello, Jon," Gideon said as he opened the chat.

Jon looked tired, but there was a big goofy grin on his face. "Hey, Gideon. He's here."

"He who?"

Jon laughed. "My son, of course. Your new nephew, Zachary Benjamin Shumway, was born about four hours ago."

"Congratulations!" Gideon said. "How is Liz?"

"She's doing well," Jon said. "They are both sleeping right now. Just wanted to call you in person before I take a nap myself."

Gideon smiled. "You look like you could use one. Been up all night?"

Jon nodded. "Eighteen hours of labor, and all I had to do was stay awake through the whole thing."

Gideon chuckled at that. "Have you told the rest of the family yet?"

Jon shrugged. "I called Mom and Dad. Ben is next on my list. Everyone else will have to wait for the email I'm going to send tomorrow."

"Got it. Thanks for calling. Give Ben a call, then get some rest."

Jon nodded again. "Will do, little brother. One more thing before I go."

"What's up?"

"We're naming you as the godfather."

Gideon frowned. "That's a Catholic tradition."

"I know," Jon said. "But if something should happen to us, we want you to take care of our children."

"Oh. Of course. Is this because I make more money than you?"

"Ha-ha. Only a little," Jon admitted. "Liz and I have plenty of money. The fact that you do too is only one of the reasons we're choosing you."

Gideon nodded. "That makes sense. What about Mom and Dad?"

Jon shook his head. "They're busy caring for Grandma. So busy they can't even make it to the baby blessing. By the way, can you make it out here at the start of May?"

Gideon nodded. "I can do that."

"Great! Well, I gotta go. Talk to you soon!"

Gideon waved goodbye. The silence that followed made him realize just how empty his life was now. He didn't have any roommates, and Sunday was the only day he had to take a break from school and work duties.

He tried dating, but none of the women in his Ward deserved a second date so far. Some of them were intimidated by his wealth, while others found it his most endearing quality. Neither was a good trait in an eternal companion.

Gideon sighed. "Maybe I should get a dog," he told the empty house.

Dogs require a lot of your time, he thought. He was often gone ten to twelve hours a day and needed his time at home for studying. Still, he needed some kind of companionship. Perhaps if he got a housekeeper, they would be able to walk and feed the dog as well. He certainly could afford that.

Those Who Wait

June 15th – Camp Snake Pit, Iraq

Major General Matthew Benson stood at the gates of Camp Snake Pit, clapping along with every other soldier on base as the convoy drove in with the prisoners.

Six months of analysis, followed by six months of waiting, had finally paid off. Jamil and his GIS friends had crossed into Iraq twenty hours earlier to join their extended families for their annual pilgrimage into Syria. Perry and his men were waiting for them.

When the gates were closed behind the last vehicle, Colonel Perry got out of the lead vehicle and saluted General Benson. "All HVT's present and accounted for, Sir!"

The cheering doubled.

"Escort the prisoners to the guardhouse," General Benson declared.

Perry stood and called out, "Disembark the prisoners!"

Two dozen soldiers exited the vehicles along with seven men in local garb. The soldiers marched the prisoners toward the guardhouse.

Once the prisoners were all inside and the door slammed shut behind them, Colonel Perry declared, "Mission accomplished, Sir!"

"Mission accomplished," General Benson repeated. "Time to go home."

Puppy Love

June 15th – Phoenix, Arizona

Tamara Bushman was halfway through her shift at Lookout Mountain Veterinary Clinic. She was handling intakes because both receptionists had called in ill. Apparently, the new variant of the Halo Virus was making another resurgence. "Next!"

A tall redhead brought a beautiful chocolate Labrador puppy to the counter. "Chip is here for his booster shots."

"Great!" Tamara said. "How old is he?"

"4 months," the redhead said. "He was born on Valentine's Day. How old are you?"

"Twenty-three," Tamara replied before she even thought about the question. Realizing her mistake, she tried to recover. "And how old are you?"

"Twenty-eight." The man smiled. "I haven't seen you here before."

Tamara shook her head as she entered Chip's information into the computer. "I usually work in the back."

"So you're a veterinarian?"

Tamara shook her head. "I'm a Vet Tech. I'm sorry, I can't find a dog named Chip in our database. Have you brought him here before?"

The man nodded. "His full name is Chocolate Chip Shumway."

Tamara tapped a few more buttons before the information appeared on the screen. "That would make you Gid Shumway?"

Gid nodded.

"Good. I have your file up now," Tamara said. "Looks like you're a few minutes early for your appointment. Have a seat, and we'll call you when we're ready."

"What would it take to get a private appointment with you?" Gid asked. "Maybe, dinner and a movie?"

Tamara blushed. "More than you can imagine," she spat out. "Next!"

Gid chuckled before walking away.

"Was he flirting with you?" Sharon asked.

Tamara nodded.

"Did you say yes?" Sharon persisted.

Tamara shook her head. "I don't date people outside my faith."

"How do you know he wasn't Mormon?" Sharon asked.

"Oh, come on," Tamara said. "The chances of meeting another Latter-day Saint here are less than one in twenty."

"Meaning it is possible."

Tamara nodded. "Possible, yes. But not likely."

"You Mormons and your rules," Sharon said.

"Right," Tamara said under her breath. "Take over. I need a break."

Sharon gave her a huge smile as the next customer came forward. "I think he got to you."

Tamara shook her head, trying to clear it. "I hope not."

The Third Star

June 28th – New York City, New York

Bryan Benson answered the door and scowled at his father. "Hello, General. I heard you got your man." He waved his father inside.

"I got a lot more than one man," Matt replied as he walked in. He was once more dressed in his combat uniform. "I honestly expected you to be more pleased."

"Pleased?" Bryan repeated more loudly. "I would have been pleased if you'd splashed that dirtbag's blood all over the news instead of showing him in handcuffs!" He slammed the door.

"I suppose you'd rather have our soldiers kill every enemy we encounter on the battlefield." Matt scowled back.

"That would prevent them from escaping and returning to the battlefield," Bryan said.

"It would also anger the survivors and the families of the dead," Matt explained. "All life has value, even your enemies."

"Anyone who has sworn to—" Bryan began.

"Dad!" Claire interrupted. "What a surprise! Dinner isn't for another hour."

"Any chance we can move that dinner to a restaurant?" Matt asked. "I came to celebrate."

They held a brief discussion, followed by an even shorter cab ride before arriving at Eleven Madison Park. Any mention of the GIS or captured enemy combatants in general ceased.

Instead, Matt steered the conversation to Bryan and Claire's recent anniversary, how school was going, and how Bryan treated Claire. That got them through the appetizers, salad, and halfway through the main course before Matt brought up the possibility of grandchildren.

"Actually," Claire began slowly, "we had a miscarriage in December." The pain Bryan had seen last Christmas was evident on her face once more.

"I'm so sorry," Matt said, patting Claire's hand. "What did the doctor say?"

"She said our insurance doesn't cover the kinds of tests we need to learn more." Bryan failed to keep the bitterness out of his voice. Not only had the miscarriage put Claire into a brief depression, but it also felt like an attack on Bryan's manhood and his ability to provide for his family.

Matt frowned. "That doesn't sound right. Are you with USAA?"

Claire shook her head. "We can't afford the premiums. Bryan got coverage as part of his scholarship with the ROTC, but we couldn't afford to add me to the policy."

"What insurance do you have now?" Matt asked.

"The basic policy through NYU Student Health Insurance," Claire said. "Infertility treatments aren't covered."

"They often aren't," Matt mused. "Would you object if I covered your premiums next year so that you can upgrade to the USAA policy?"

"You would do that?" Claire asked.

Matt nodded.

Bryan sat quietly, trying to sort through his emotions on that offer. He knew how much Claire wanted to have children. He also knew his dad's investments had been far more successful since his old college roommate became President. "So, what are we celebrating?" Bryan asked, desperate to change the subject.

"I'm sorry," Matt said. "I thought you knew. I got a promotion!"

Claire gasped. "You got your third star."

Matt nodded. "I'm only in town for a week before I head back to Iraq."

"They need a Lieutenant General to interrogate the prisoners?" Bryan asked. His tone and his scowl showed how little he thought of that.

"Far more than that," Matt said. "In a few weeks, I'll be overseeing all military operations in Iraq instead of just the western front."

"So the promotion isn't just ceremonial," Claire said. "You're getting more responsibility as well."

Matt nodded.

"Great," Bryan said through gritted teeth. "Soon, every enemy combatant in Iraq will have a cozy cell."

"Something like that." Matt frowned. "I hoped you'd be happy for me."

Bryan nodded. "I am. I really am. I just think that religious fanatics don't make good prisoners."

"So it's only the religious fanatics we should shoot on sight," Matt said. "I suppose next you're going to tell me all Muslims should be arrested."

Bryan began to answer but then paused. Years of history classes buzzed through his head. Everything from David Koresh and the Branch Davidians to the Spanish Inquisition was suddenly painted in a new light. "No," he said weakly. "No, Dad. You're right. That's taking things too far."

Matt paused with a bite of steak on his fork, forgotten halfway to his mouth. He set the fork down. "I'm glad to hear that, Son."

Bryan heaved a huge sigh and hung his head. "I'm sorry, Father. I shouldn't have yelled at you about your capture of the GIS leaders. You're right. We can't kill every enemy soldier, even if the uniform they wear bears the insignia of their God instead of their country."

"That's quite a change of heart." Claire took Bryan's hand. "I'm proud of you for admitting it so quickly."

Bryan looked up at her loving gaze and couldn't help but mirror her smile. "Thanks, honey."

Nationality Override

July 10th – Camp Snake Pit, Iraq

Lieutenant General Matthew Benson scowled at the transfer order. "This isn't right. These prisoners have a VIP suite waiting for them in Guantanamo. Why are they being taken to a Syrian prison?"

"They are Syrian nationals," Brigadier General Perry explained. His promotion came on the same day as Matt's. "Our treaties in this region demand they be held in their country of origin unless there is a compelling reason for them to remain in American custody."

"There *is* a compelling reason," Matt shot back. "They killed the President of the United States! Not to mention most of Congress and the Supreme Court. Need I go on?"

Perry shook his head. "I agree with you completely, Sir. But orders are orders."

"Ugh." Matt wanted to tear up the order and take the prisoners to Cuba. "Fine. Get them out of here. Just make sure the Syrian prison is strong enough to hold them."

"These devils are headed to the same prison that's been holding the former members of ISIS," Perry replied. "I'm sure it can hold a few more radicals."

"I'm not," Matt said. "Maybe Bryan was right. We should have killed them instead of capturing them."

"Again, orders are orders," Perry said.

Matt nodded. "President Baldwin himself asked me to bring in those men alive. I just hope, for his sake, they don't get loose."

Pioneer Day

July 24th – Phoenix, Arizona

Gideon Shumway showed up for the Pioneer Day[62] Party put on by the Singles Stake. It was the first such activity he'd been to in months. But Pioneer Day was one celebration he'd enjoyed as a kid. No one in Illinois celebrated it the way his parents did.

"Gideon!" Paul called. "You decided to come!"

Gideon nodded, placing his stack of pizza boxes on the table. Few people brought anything satisfying to a potluck party.

"Five large pizzas," Paul said. "These parties are always better when you attend."

Gideon laughed. "So you only enjoy the food I bring?"

"No," Paul said as he grabbed a slice. "But I always enjoy the food you bring. Besides, there's someone I think you should meet."

"You have a new girlfriend?" Gideon asked. Paul had gone through five relationships in the last year. Who knows how many the year before.

"No," Paul said. "Well, actually, I do, but that's not who you need to meet."

Gideon groaned. "You want to set me up with your new girlfriend's friend?"

"Sister, actually," Paul admitted.

"No," Gideon said flatly. "I don't need your help finding a date."

"You're twenty-seven years old," Paul said. "Brigham Young would say you've been a menace to society for years."

Gideon laughed. "I'm twenty-eight, actually. And what about you? Aren't you twenty-five? You'll be a menace in less than a year."

Paul shook his head. "I'm working hard to get married before my next birthday. Susan understands. She feels the same way I do. We—"

"Are you engaged?" Gideon asked.

Paul shook his head. "Not yet. Two more dates and I'll plan the proposal."

"Practically engaged again?" Gideon asked. "That's the third time this year."

Paul nodded. "I know. But I have a plan. Susan and I have some serious topics to discuss, and the last two women didn't like my answers."

"And you think that Susan's older sister would make a good match for me?"

Paul shook his head. "Younger sister, actually. She recently finished her training as a Vet Tech."

The words shot through Gideon as he remembered his last experience at the vet's office. "That's not going to work."

"What? Why?"

"Let's just say I was recently rejected by a vet tech, and it's left a sour taste in my mouth."

"But I told them both to find us," Paul said. "They should be here soon."

Gideon sighed. "Time to make myself scarce."

"You're leaving?" Paul said. "I thought you loved Pioneer Day."

"I do," Gideon agreed. "I'm not leaving. I'm going to check on the fireworks." He grabbed two slices of pizza and headed outside.

Tamara Bushman followed her sister through the crowd. "What makes you think this guy is right for me?"

"Paul speaks very highly of him," Susan said. "He's a law student. There's Paul."

Tamara caught sight of a tall redhead walking away. Something about him looked familiar. "What's this law student's name?"

"Shumway. Gideon Shumway."

Tamara swallowed. "Does he go by Gid?"

Susan nodded. "Sometimes."

"And he has a chocolate Labrador puppy named Chocolate Chip?"

Susan turned to look at her. "You know him?"

Tamara nodded. "We met."

"Then it isn't really a blind date," Susan said.

"It would have to be." Tamara stared at the floor. "I shut him down pretty hard when he asked me out."

"Why?"

Tamara sighed. "I didn't know he was a Church member. Most of the people I meet at work aren't members."

Susan nodded. "I'll see what I can do."

The Wrong Place at the Right Time

July 29th – Provo, Utah

Benjamin Shumway Jr. got dressed after the first day of practice with a sense of disconnection. He'd gone through the drills, but his mind kept wandering. He'd lived the last six months knowing he was a shoo-in for the NFL draft as long as he could repeat his performance from last season.

For the first week, he was elated. He'd fulfilled his promise to Gideon, to keep his father's hope of a son in the NFL alive and well. Yet as time went on, the idea of playing in the NFL became less and less appealing. He felt drawn toward something else, though he couldn't figure out exactly what.

"Great job out there, General." Kaelo slapped him on the back. "Some of the new troops were watching you pretty closely."

"Troops?" Ben repeated. Something about the word struck a chord in his heart.

"Well, yeah," Kaelo said. "Football was created as training for the Army.[63] You're our General, and we're your infantry on the field of battle. The freshmen look rather green. They're going to need a lot of training if we're going to take the championship this year."

"Yeah," Ben said. "Thanks." The title General Shumway bounced around in his mind. Officially, he was the captain of the team. It would take a lot of rising in the ranks to reach the level of General, yet that would be a worthwhile life.

As he walked back to his apartment, his mind weighed two paths in his life. If he stayed on his present course, the best he could hope for was playing football for the next ten or twelve years, perhaps leading his team to a few Superbowl victories.

But if he changed course now, he could prepare for a military career and help protect his country from terrorists and other threats. It might never lead to public fame or a massive fortune, but neither of those would survive into the next life. A life of service to his country, of saving lives, sounded like a cause he could live for.

He would have to play out this season, no doubts there. It was far too late to find another quarterback. No, he would stay with the team, play out his final season. But instead of preparing for the NFL, he'd be preparing for military command.

This was going to break his father's heart.

Group Date

August 9th – Phoenix, Arizona

Gideon Shumway pulled up to Let It Roll with Bryan and Mark in tow. He'd been talked into another group date. "When will Paul get here?"

Bryan pointed to a red Honda Accord. "He's already here."

Gideon got out and followed Bryan's finger. "That's not Paul's car."

"No," Bryan explained as he got out. "It's Susan's."

"He's still dating Susan?" Gideon asked. "I thought this group date was his typical post-breakup ritual."

"He didn't tell you?" Mark asked as he shut the door.

"Tell me what?" Gideon asked.

"Paul's engaged," Bryan said.

Gideon scowled. There could only be one reason why Paul failed to mention that detail. He was trying to set Gideon up with Susan's sister. Unfortunately, Gideon was their ride tonight. He couldn't just abandon Mark and Bryan. "Fine. Let's get this over with."

"What are you talking about?" Mark asked.

"Paul is trying to set me up with his fiancée's sister," Gideon explained. "Some young vet tech."

"What's wrong with that?" Mark shot back.

"Gideon got shot down hard by a vet tech a couple months ago," Bryan told Mark. "He's still a little bitter."

"Oh, please," Mark said. "Like there's any chance it was the same person. Besides, I heard Tamara was really looking forward to meeting you."

That thought brought Gideon up short. He paused with one hand on the door. "She is?"

Mark nodded. "Susan's been talking you up to her sister for two weeks."

"Up is right," Bryan said. "You're one of only a dozen guys in the Stake taller than Tamara."

Gideon opened the door and let the other two go in first. At 6' 4", Gideon often felt like he was towering over most women. The thought of meeting a tall girl made him smile. As he went inside, he spotted a tall redhead at the counter. Something about her was familiar.

"Gideon!" Paul called. "Glad you could make it. Have you met Susan?"

"We've met," Susan said as she came around the counter.

Gideon nodded. "Good to see you again, Susan. You didn't tell him?"

Susan chuckled. "I thought he knew."

"Knew what?" Paul asked. "What am I missing?"

"Gideon and I dated," Susan said.

"You two had a relationship?" Paul asked.

"We went on two dates," Gideon said. "I'd hardly call that a relationship."

Susan nodded.

"But now you think I'd hit it off with your sister?" Gideon asked.

"Why not ask her yourself?" Susan asked. She stepped aside.

The redhead Gideon saw earlier stood up, holding a bowling ball. "Good to see you again, Gid. How's Chip?" She gave him a smile.

Yet all Gideon saw was the same face that shut him down in June. "Chip is fine, thanks." Gideon turned to Bryan. "I thought you said she was eager to meet me."

"I am," Tamara said.

Gideon turned back to her. "That's not how it appeared after our last encounter."

Tamara blushed. "Sorry about that. Can we just start over?"

Gideon smiled. "I'd love to. I'm Gideon Shumway." He offered his hand.

"Tamara Bushman. A pleasure to meet you. Are you any good at bowling?"

Gideon chuckled. "Good enough."

Tamara nodded. "Then you can be on my team."

"That's not fair!" Susan whined. "I was counting on having you on my team."

Tamara smiled at her. "Sorry, sis. You're playing on team Black now."

"But Paul's never scored over 120," Susan shot back.

"Look, we both know I've been carrying your low score for years," Tamara said. She turned to Gideon. "What's your average score?"

"185," Gideon replied instantly. "What's yours?"

"165," Tamara said with a smile. "This is going to be fun!"

Islamic State Reborn

November 5th – Tell Tamir, Syria

Jamil Noury looked over at Mohammad Al-Mahdi, waiting for the signal. Four months of confinement hadn't gone to waste. The little satan arrested seven leaders of the Global Islamic State back in June. Since July, those leaders had visited a dozen prisons like this one, all in preparation for today.

"Allahu Akbar!" Al-Mahdi shouted.

Two thousand prisoners echoed the cry as their cell doors opened. They rushed the guards, only half of whom stood in their way. In less than two minutes, fifty of the prisoners were armed.

The prisoners swarmed into the yard.

Two of the tower guards fired into the crowd.

Dozens of bullets converged on each of the tower guards.

Jamil pushed through the crowd to the large gate where the busses waited. Thankfully, someone left the padlock open. One less obstacle to overcome. He recruited two others to help him open the gate.

"To the busses!" Al-Mahdi shouted.

The crowd cheered as they swarmed into the busses.

Jamil hopped into the driver's seat of the bus Al-Mahdi boarded. He didn't wait for people to board. He just grabbed the key above the sunshield and started it up. He slammed on the gas and lurched forward, forcing the crowd to dive out of his way.

A glance in the mirror showed about seventy people had boarded, leaving almost half of them standing up. Jamil didn't care. He just kept accelerating toward the main gates.

The bus slammed into the inner metal fence, slowing briefly as the chain gave way. The second fence offered a little more resistance, but the bus pushed through.

Cheers rose from passengers.

Jamil kept going, continuing to accelerate. The side-view mirror showed the other nine busses were pulling out now, along with hundreds of people running behind.

As they crossed the Nahr al Khabur River, Al-Mahdi stood and shouted, "Freedom!"

"Freedom!" the others echoed.

"No prison can hold Al-Mahdi!" Al-Mahdi continued. "I chose to be captured. I chose to endure those walls so I could bring all of you into the true light of Allah!"

"Allahu Akbar!" several people shouted.

"Onward, to Ar Raqqah!" Al-Mahdi shouted.

Failed Inspection

November 13th – New York City, New York

Bryan Benson answered the door and scowled at his father. "What do you want?"

"I want to see you and Claire," Matt said. "I heard about the baby."

The hairs on the back of Bryan's neck bristled. Less than two years of marriage, and Claire already had two miscarriages. The second one was only three days ago. "You've come to berate me for my shortcomings?"

Matt scowled. "Of course not! I've come to mourn with you. Can I come in?"

Bryan stepped out of the way. Claire wouldn't want General Dad turned away. "Come on in, General," Bryan said through gritted teeth. "Barracks are ready for inspection."

"It isn't like that," Matt said as he entered.

Claire came out of the bedroom. "Bryan? Is someone here?"

"Hello, Claire." Matt took her hand. "How are you?"

Claire's expression fell. "This one is harder. Six months of treatment just to get pregnant again, and I still lost her."

"Her? It was a girl?" Matt asked.

Claire shrugged. "Just a feeling."

Bryan slammed the door shut. "Can't you see she's hurting? Why can't you just leave us alone?"

"She's not the only one," Matt said softly.

"What did you say?" Bryan stomped over to look his father in the eye.

"I said, she's not the only one who's hurting," Matt said firmly. "Any soldier in your situation would be within their rights to request a brief leave of absence."

Bryan's fingers clenched into fists. "I don't need a leave of absence. I'm still fit for duty!"

"That's not what I'm saying," Matt said. "I just—"

"You just meant showing weakness is okay," Bryan shot back. "Like you did in Iraq!"

"Now, just a minute there, cadet!" Matt roared back. "That's going too far."

"Bryan—" Claire took Bryan's hand, trying to calm him down.

Bryan shook Claire off. "I don't think so! You tried twice to kill those terrorists who bombed D.C. Then, you sat on your hands for a whole year, waiting for them to fall into your trap. But when you finally had them in your sights, you let them live. And then the bureaucrats took over and shipped them into a poorly guarded jail in Syria.

"It was only a matter of time before they escaped. Now the terrorists got thousands of new recruits, thanks to the fall of ISIS. I'm telling you, there's only one way to deal with these rag heads. Shoot them on sight!"

Claire and Matt just stood there, staring at Bryan as he stomped out of the room. He hung his head and walked into the bedroom, unsure where else to go. He could still hear their voices from the front room. One of the joys of apartment living.

"He didn't mean it," Claire said.

Matt shook his head. "The man has spoken. He's definitely not fit for duty."

Claire gasped. "You can't mean that."

"I'd better report back," Matt said. The door opened and shut.

Bryan sat on the edge of the bed, trying to calm down and clear his head. His emotions were everywhere, but anger colored everything else.

Claire slowly walked back and joined Bryan, sitting next to him, resting her head on his shoulder.

"Why did he even come?" Bryan asked. "Was he trying to make me feel worse for my failure?"

"No," Claire said, rubbing his arm. "He's just not very good with words."

Bryan shook his head. "How did he even find out? Did you tell him?"

"No," Claire said. "Dad gets reports directly from the doctors."

"He does? Why?"

"Because he's paying the bills, remember?" Claire reached up and gently guided Bryan's face to hers before kissing him.

Bryan's anger slowly faded. Claire was the only one who could calm him down when he flew off like that. And for whatever reason, Dad was one of those people who was really good at rubbing Bryan the wrong way.

"I'm sorry, Claire. I just—"

"You're just mourning," Claire interrupted. "It's okay. So am I. Your father will understand."

Collateral Damage

November 28th – New York City, New York

Bryan Benson finished off Claire's homemade pumpkin pie and took a seat on the couch. A stack of mail waited for him. The Discover bill sat on top. He pushed that aside and found a letter from the NYU Scholarship Department. He ripped the letter open, curious about how much his stipend would increase to offset increased living expenses next year.

> Mr. Bryan Benson,
>
> *We are sorry to inform you that the funds for your ROTC Scholarship have been withdrawn. For details as to the cause, please contact Sergeant Connors, ROTC Scholarship Team Leader.*
>
> *Please make other arrangements to pay your tuition before registering for Winter Semester.*

Bryan dropped the letter, too stunned to do anything.

That's how Claire found him half an hour later. "What is it, honey? What's wrong?"

Bryan just pointed to the letter on the floor.

Claire picked it up and read it. "What? This can't be right."

"It's got their official seal and everything," Bryan managed to say. "I don't think it's a joke."

"Then it has to be a mistake," Claire said. "Don't worry. We'll give Sergeant Connors a call tomorrow. He's always been friendly in the past. I'm sure he can clear this up."

"What if he can't?" Bryan asked. "We can't afford to pay for my college."

Claire shook her head. "Put it out of your mind for now. We'll get it straightened out."

The Last Touchdown

January 4th – Phoenix, Arizona

Benjamin Shumway Jr. threw the football from the BYU thirty-yard line. It sailed twenty yards through the air before Kaelo reached up and grabbed it.

Kaelo dodged the red-clad Ohio State warriors who tried to tackle him. He crossed the forty-yard line only three steps ahead of the nearest foe.

By the time Kaelo crossed the twenty-yard line, his lead had grown to five steps.

The game clock hit zero.

Kaelo stepped into the end zone seven steps ahead of anyone else, slowing to celebrate his victory. He had to dive out of the way as the red-clad 12 tried to tackle him.

Late tackles were illegal but sometimes hard to stop. Still, Kaelo managed to get out of the way in time.

Ben breathed a sigh of relief as he gazed up at the scoreboard. Ohio State, 33. BYU, 37. They'd finally won the College Football National Championship!

The team and support staff swarmed onto the field, lifting Ben and others upon their shoulders as they did the victory dance. Even Gideon came down from the stands to help carry Ben off the field.

The next hour was a blur of joy and elation from a victory hard-fought and finally won. It was followed by a victory dinner with Gideon, Mom, Dad, and the entire team.

When all was said and done, the four Shumway's relaxed in Gideon's living room.

"It took four tries," Gideon said, "but you finally did it. You won the College Football National Playoffs. For the first time in almost two decades, BYU is the national champion once more."

"Yes," Dad agreed. "Well done, Son. You're sure to be a first-round draft pick this year."

Ben Jr. felt like he'd been slapped in the face. He wanted to let this day go by without tainting the victory for his father. He held in what he wanted to say. Instead, he just nodded and said, "That could easily happen."

Gideon studied Ben for a moment before blurting out, "I also have some happy news."

"You do?" Mom asked. "What?"

"I got engaged," Gideon said.

Ben smiled and nodded at him. Only life-changing news could change the subject. If Dad started probing, the truth would come out. This wasn't the right day for that fight.

"You are?" Dad asked. "Who is she?"

"Is it that Bushman girl you told me about?" Mom asked.

"What Bushman girl?" Dad asked Mom.

"I've been dating Tamara Bushman for the last five months," Gideon explained. "She's a veterinary technician, sometimes called an animal nurse."

"When did you propose?" Ben Jr. asked.

"New Year's Eve," Gideon replied. "At midnight."

"How romantic," Mom said. "Why didn't you tell us sooner?"

Gideon shrugged. "I didn't want to overshadow Ben's big day. And if he lost, I wanted some good news to lighten the mood."

"If you're engaged, where is she?" Ben asked. "Why didn't she come with you to the game?"

Gideon sighed. "She had to work."

"If you didn't want to step on my big day," Ben asked, "why are you telling us now?"

The doorbell rang.

"Because she's here," Gideon said as he stood up. He walked to the door and let Tamara in. He gave her a kiss before saying, "Come on in and meet my family. This is my father, Benjamin, my mother, Ruth, and my little brother, the hero of the day, Ben Jr. Everyone, this is Tamara."

Tamara approached Ben Jr. first, shaking his hand. "So, you won! That's wonderful."

"Thanks," Ben Jr. said. "Nice to meet you. I never thought Gid would find someone to marry him, let alone someone as tall as me."

Tamara chuckled. "I wasn't sure I'd ever find a man I could look up to." She walked over to Ben Sr. "I've been looking forward to meeting you."

Ben Sr. just grunted as he shook her hand. "Nice to meet you."

Ruth gave Tamara a great big hug. "Welcome to the family. When is the wedding?"

"We're still discussing that," Tamara said. "Right now, we're looking at late July. Gideon is advocating for Pioneer Day. I'm pushing for a weekend wedding."

Ben Sr. smiled. "Pioneer Day has always been my favorite holiday."

"That's what Gideon keeps saying," Tamara replied. She sighed. "I guess July twenty-fourth it is."

From Land to Sea

January 5th – New York City, New York

"What did Sergeant Connors say?" Claire Benson asked as she came back into the room.

"After a thorough review," Bryan said slowly, barely able to believe what he'd just heard, "the ROTC Scholarship will not be renewed. I am no longer a good candidate for military leadership."

"Why?" Claire asked. "What happened?"

Bryan clenched his fists. "I failed the psych eval."

"You what?" Claire stammered. "But how? Why?"

"Connors was very tight-lipped about the details, but he said my interview marks me as a danger on the battlefield."

"You don't mean—"

Bryan nodded slowly. "The Army doesn't want me anymore. Today was the deadline. Without that scholarship, I'll have to take a semester off."

Claire paced in front of the couch. "Okay. So you'll take a semester off. That will give you time to apply for another scholarship."

"The Army isn't going to give me another scholarship, no matter how long I have."

"Then apply to the Navy."

Bryan blinked, a little stunned. "The Navy?"

Claire nodded. "You've got plenty of skills. I'm sure the Navy would be happy to have you."

Bryan slammed his fist on the couch. "My dad hates the Navy. He says they're just ... just perfect!" A smile broke over Bryan's face. "Yes! That'll show him, if I become an officer in the Navy, he'll see I was right!"

Claire nodded and matched his smile, handing him the laptop.

Forging A New Path

January 16th - Provo, Utah

Benjamin Shumway Jr. walked into the Marines recruiting office after he'd finished his classes. One Marine stood in field camos by the door, a gun displayed on his hip. Another Marine sat behind a desk in dress uniform.

The man behind the desk stood and smiled as he shook Ben's hand. "Benjamin Shumway! What can I do for you?"

Ben smiled. "You recognize me?"

"Two-time Heisman winner and captain of the BYU football team. Of course I recognize you! I'm Staff Sergeant Mills. What brings you in today?"

Ben took in a deep breath before blurting out, "I'm here to explore joining the Marines after I graduate."

Mills took a step back. "You want to join the Marines instead of the NFL?"

Ben nodded.

"Why?"

"I need a life with meaning," Ben explained. "Carrying a football over the line five hundred times just isn't what I want."

Mills nodded. "I see. Well, if you're certain—"

Ben nodded.

Mills pulled out a clipboard and handed it to Ben. "Here's the enlistment form. Make sure you fill out every box properly."

Ben shook his head. "I'm not signing anything today. I'm here to make sure when I do sign up that I'm fully prepared and have no regrets."

Mills's smile grew wider. "Brains as well as guts. Why don't we discuss your strengths and interests." He motioned for Ben to sit.

Ben took a seat. "Well, to start, I'm a Linguistics Major, with a focus on middle east dialects."

"Pashto?"

Ben nodded.

"Urdu? Saraki? Punjabi? Sindhi?"

"My Saraki needs work, but I can read it and understand most of it. The others, I've passed a fluency exam."

Mills nearly choked. "How did you learn so many languages?"

Ben shrugged. "I served my mission in India. I spent an hour every day for two years studying five of the major languages of India. Hindi, Punjabi, Marathi, Telugu, and Odia. When I got home, I kept studying. For the last four years, I increased it to three hours per day."

Mills studied Ben, measuring more than his physical fitness. "Have you ever considered Special Forces?"

Ben shrugged. "As far as I know, they have to pick you. You don't pick them."

Mills nodded. "That's mostly true. But there are ways to get their attention."

"How?"

Mills smiled. "Let me make some calls first. Come back next week, and I'll be able to give you more specifics."

Ben stood and shook Mills's hand. "Alright. See you next week."

"I'm looking forward to it," Mills said.

Aggressive Recruiting

January 17th – Provo, Utah

Benjamin Shumway Jr. left his last class of the day feeling very confident. His Saraki had improved a lot over the Fall semester, and now he could focus on his language skills without worrying about football.

"Ben Shumway!" someone called out. A man in a pin-striped suit was staring at Ben.

Ben pulled a Sharpie out of his backpack. "Do you have a football for me to sign?"

The man laughed. "I'm definitely a fan, but I want you to sign something a little more valuable than a football.

"A helmet or a jersey?" Ben asked. "I heard my rookie jersey recently sold for $12,000."

"Yeah, I saw that," the man said. "No, I didn't win it."

"Then what do you have for me to sign?"

"I want to be your agent."

Ben shook his head and started to walk away. "I don't need an agent."

The man took a few quick steps to walk beside Ben. "That's only because you don't know what an agent can do for you. I'm talking everything from merchandising to book sales."

Ben glanced over at him. "My brother is the author, not me."

"Oh, you wouldn't have to write any of it yourself. We can hire a ghostwriter. But that's not the point. You're going to need an agent."

"What's your name?"

"Max Cash."

"Seriously?" Ben raised an eyebrow at that.

"Absolutely. My birth name is Maxwell Cash. Very convenient in my line of work."

"How did you know where I was?"

Max cleared his throat. "You posted publicly on Facebook that you were heading into your Sarachi class. Now that you're done with college football, it's time to plan out your future."

"Well, I won't need your services, Mr. Cash," Ben said. "I'm not joining the NFL."

"How is that even possible?" Max asked. "You're going to pass up forty million dollars for a single year's work?"

Ben stopped dead in his tracks. He swallowed hard. "Forty million?"

Max nodded. "You're the number one draft pick this year. The funding pool assigns a $13.4 million salary for your first year and a $26.5 million signing bonus. And, as if that's not enough, I can make sure your autobiography outsells your brother's book."

Ben's heart was pounding. Forty million dollars was too large an offer to pass up.

"I see I've finally got your attention," Max said. "Why don't we discuss the details over dinner?"

"Because I'm having dinner with my family."

"They can come along," Max said.

"In Nephi."

"Nephi? What is Nephi?"

"My hometown," Ben explained. "Where my parents live."

"I can meet you there if you'd like," Max said. "Or I can arrange a meeting tomorrow. Whichever you'd prefer."

Ben started walking again. "From what my brother tells me, the standard agent fee is ten percent."

Max kept pace with him, almost running to keep up with Ben's longer legs. "That's right."

"I appreciate that you're the first one offering their services," Ben said. "But if I'm going to pay someone four million dollars, I need to know a lot more about them."

"Absolutely," Max said. "I know there will be others reaching out to you, but I'm confident when all is asked and answered, you'll see I'm the best agent for you."

"And why is that?"

"Because I can guarantee you won't be doing any beer commercials."

Ben laughed. "You've done your research on my religious beliefs but don't know my hometown?"

"I currently represent several BYU alumni in a variety of matters. What matters to my clients matters to me."

"I'll think about it," Ben said.

Max whipped out a business card and handed it over. "All I ask is that you don't sign anything without talking to me first."

Ben nodded as he took the card. "I can do that."

The Final Rejection

April 25th - New York City, New York

Bryan Benson set the letter down. He'd been rejected from the Army, the Navy, and now the CIA. He crumpled the paper and tossed it in the trash. One bad interview with a psychologist, and he was banned from working in or around the military.

"What letter was that?" Claire asked. Her six-inch heels gave her a slight height advantage over Bryan, which he guessed was why she always wore them. Her dark hair clashed with Bryan's dirty blond.

"Another rejection letter."

"Already? From the CIA?"

Bryan nodded.

"Did they give a reason?"

Bryan let out a long sigh. "Same reason as always. The psychiatric evaluation."

"What? That was months ago."

"I know. Something isn't right."

"Do you think your father has anything to do with this?"

"Dad? He's been supportive of me going into the military."

"Yes, but you did have quite the fight a couple weeks before the Army pulled your scholarship."

"I doubt he would sabotage my military career by blackballing me," Bryan replied.

"Yes, he would. He's conceited enough, and you wounded his pride. It's the only thing that explains these rejections," Claire said.

"I don't see how."

Claire smiled at him with that look. The one that said this was so obvious you should see it for yourself.

"Wait, you think he sent a letter to the Army, which was forwarded to the Navy when I applied there, and then to the CIA when I applied? You really think the CIA would go that far into my past, digging up records of a failed application?"

Claire laughed. "Intelligence is their middle name. Of course they did. I wouldn't be surprised if they found your kindergarten report card to see if you were the kind of kid who couldn't keep his hands to himself."

"I knew I should never have shown that to you." Bryan knew she was right but didn't want to admit it. If she was right, his hopes of joining the military or any other government agency were over. And if so, what was left for him? He was working nights as a security guard, but the pay was awful. If anything happened and he actually got into a firefight, he would most likely also be fired the next day. If he wanted to use all the skills he had, and the legitimate agencies wouldn't have him, perhaps it was time to call Claire's Uncle Nikki. The one who told Bryan at the wedding, 'If you ever want to do something more uh, interesting, give me a call.'

Decision Time

April 27th – Nephi, Utah

Benjamin Shumway Jr. sat at his parents' kitchen table with a big decision to make. His parents sat at either end, with Staff Sergeant Mills and Max Cash sitting across from him. They'd both brought forms for him to sign.

"The NFL draft starts in a few days," Max said. "You can't delay this decision any longer."

"I know," Ben Jr. said. "I'm not even sure why I'm hesitating."

"I am," Mills said.

"You are?" Dad asked.

Mills nodded.

"How could you possibly know more about my son's decision than he does?" Dad pressed.

"Because before Mr. Cash approached him with an insane amount of money, your son came into my office and told me what he really wants," Mills explained.

"That was months ago," Ben Jr. said. "I don't really remember what I said that day."

"You told me that a life of making touchdowns isn't enough for you," Mills reminded him. "I know the Marines can't offer you anywhere near the amount of pay the NFL is offering. The only thing I can promise is that you'll find more meaning with the Marines than you ever will in the NFL."

"I'm only asking for one year," Max countered. "One year of work, and you're guaranteed forty million dollars."

Mills nodded. "Yes, and at the end of that year, you'll either be offered even more money, or you'll be injured so badly you can't play for the NFL or train for the special forces. The choice is yours, Ben. Chase the money or make a difference in this world."

Ben Jr. sighed. It wasn't just about the money. Signing an NFL contract would fulfill his father's life ambition to have a son in the NFL. Gideon had given up on that dream, even though he probably would have made it by now.

"The San Francisco 49'ers are ready to trade three sophomore linemen to the St. Louis Rams to get you," Max said. "The way you transformed the BYU football team into a force with a fighting chance got multiple teams bargaining for you. In the end, the 49'ers offer was superior."

"You've been quiet for a while now," Mills said. "What's going through your mind?"

Ben Jr. sighed deeply. "Both of you make valid points. I have two wonderful futures ahead of me, and I have to pick between them."

"Fame and fortune," Max began.

"Or duty and purpose," Mills finished.

"That's one way to put it," Ben Jr. said.

Dad cleared his throat. "Listen, Son. I know I've been pretty hard on Gideon for giving up on football. And just knowing that the NFL offered you a contract is enough for me. Don't let an old man's dreams change your decision. Either way, I'll be proud of you."

Ben Jr. closed his eyes and took a deep breath. He said a quick prayer in his heart. As his mind calmed down, the choice became clear. He opened his eyes and said, "I've known for months what the right choice is. The truth is, I made this choice almost a year ago." He sighed again, then smiled. "I'm going to fight terrorists. I'm joining the Marines."

Dad smiled.

Mom ran over and gave Ben Jr. a hug.

Max scowled.

Staff Sergeant Mills just nodded.

Guard Duty

July 1st - Carmel, New York

Bryan Benson stood watch outside a private residence in upstate New York. It was 3 a.m., and all Bryan really knew about this particular job was someone important was inside the house. He was one of six security guards stationed here to ensure no one disturbed the big guy, whoever that was. Bryan had been working for Uncle Nikki for almost a year now, mainly getting night shifts. He never complained, though. The pay was far higher than his old job.

A noise came from the bushes to his left.

"Frank, please tell me that's you in the bushes." He spoke softly into his earpiece. "Frank, are you there?" No response. "All guards, check-in." Bryan walked toward the disturbance. Someone was there, but Bryan couldn't tell who.

"Haskins checking in. All clear."

"Jenkins checking in. All clear."

Three guards were missing. Bryan fired into the shadow. "Come out, whoever you are." He pulled out his flashlight and held it over his head as he was trained to do.

Someone sprang from the shadows far closer than Bryan had suspected. There was no time to aim before the gun was knocked out of Bryan's hand. Bryan grabbed his secondary weapon and brought his flashlight down hard on the intruder's head. It was a Maglite 6-cell D flashlight. The intruder crumpled at Bryan's feet. That's when he saw the knife the intruder had been holding. It was covered in blood.

Quickly Bryan patted himself, checking for injuries. The blood wasn't his. "Code Purple," Bryan said into his earpiece. "Repeat, Code Purple." The code told the others there was a wounded guard somewhere. Bryan called the local police, per regulation. The first cop showed up five minutes later. Two minutes after that, the first ambulance arrived.

Within fifteen minutes, three police cruisers appeared on the scene, helping them search for the missing guards. By the time half an hour had passed, two more ambulances had arrived. The first ambulance hauled away the wounded intruder under police escort. Two of the guards were dead, the third critically injured. The paramedics spent three minutes patching up the injured guard before hauling him on a stretcher into the second ambulance.

The other two ambulances left without passengers. The county coroner showed up to collect the bodies.

Tomorrow Starts Today

Pioneer Day – Phoenix, Arizona

Gideon got a text from his agent as he was getting dressed. Gregg wrote: *Book 2 launches today.* Gideon sighed, wishing once more that he could have written that book with Gregg. As it was, per the contract, Gideon hadn't even read the book. That wouldn't stop Senator Morgan from popping a vein over what might be in it.

Setting his phone down, Gideon grabbed his tuxedo and put it on. Today wasn't the right day to worry about books or Senators. This was Pioneer Day and Gideon's wedding day. Today was all about Tamara and the covenants Gideon would enter into today with her.

As Gideon came out of the bedroom, Ben Jr. handed him a protein smoothie. "I was starting to worry about you. You've got five minutes to down that."

Gideon downed half the smoothie in the first gulp. "I hope you planned more for my breakfast than this."

"What do you mean? That's got plenty of protein to get you through the morning."

Gideon nodded. "I know it does, but it's all liquid. I need something solid in my stomach as well."

Ben sighed and handed over his toaster strudel before heading to the freezer to grab another one.

"Thanks, Ben. I knew I picked the right brother to be my best man."

"Of course you did," Ben said. "Jon's not even awake."

"Yes, I am," Jon said as he came into the kitchen. "And I'm right on time."

"Well, I have to get Gideon there half an hour earlier," Ben said. "You, eat," he commanded.

Gideon saluted and downed the rest of the smoothie before attacking the toaster strudel.

A few minutes later, Ben herded Gideon into the car and drove him to the Phoenix Temple. When they got out of the vehicle, Gideon handed Ben his phone. "Do me a favor. Hold on to this until after the reception."

"Expecting a phone call?"

"I really hope not."

The wedding ceremony was simple and profound, with a couple dozen family members from each side. They spent an hour taking family photos before taking a break for lunch.

As they arrived at the reception hall, Ben whispered in Gideon's ear, "Your phone has been going nuts. Someone named Ryan has been calling every five minutes."

"Text him that I'm unavailable for a few more hours," Gideon replied. "No matter what he replies, I don't want to hear it until the reception is over."

"Got it."

The Great Scarlet Reset

Gideon knew that was an explosion waiting to happen, but it would have to wait. He focused on meeting the members of Tamara's extended family, many of whom were locals.

After four hours of shaking hands, dancing, and cutting the cake, Gideon escorted Tamara to his car, which had been appropriately decorated by the groomsmen.

The cheers all died as four men in suits surrounded the car. "Senator Morgan needs to speak with you."

"As you can see, I'm rather busy," Gideon said. "Whatever he wants, I'm sure it can wait."

The agent who spoke shook his head. "That's not how this works, Mr. Shumway. You're coming with me."

"Where are you taking him?" Tamara asked.

"Washington, D.C."

"Then I'm going too."

"That's not possible."

Gideon shook his head. "If I'm not under arrest, she comes with me."

The agent sighed. "Fine. Let's go."

Ben grabbed Gideon's suitcase out of the car and handed it to him along with his phone. "At least you're already packed."

Gideon smiled at him. "Thanks." Then he turned to Tamara. "I promise, this will only be a short delay before we get to our honeymoon."

The agents led the couple to a waiting limousine and climbed in with them, putting the luggage in the trunk.

As they approached the Deer Valley Airport, the lead agent said, "I don't know what you did, but Senator Morgan is furious."

"I know," Gideon said. "And it has nothing to do with what I've done."

"We will see."

Endnotes

1. Ezra's Eagle Explanation
   Thanksgiving Day – Notre Dame, Indiana

   Ezra's Eagle refers to the apocryphal prophecy of the Old Testament Prophet Ezra found in the 11th and 12th chapters of the book 4th Ezra (also called 2nd Esdras). The best book on the subject can be found at ezraseagle.com

2. Contrary Feathers Three and Four
   November 27th – Atlanta, Georgia
   January 24th – Washington, D.C.

   The Second Book of Esdras, Chapter 11
   28 And I beheld, and, lo, the two that remained thought also in themselves to reign:
   29 And when they so thought, behold, there awaked one of the heads that were at rest, namely, it that was in the midst; for that was greater than the two other heads.
   30 And then I saw that the two other heads were joined with it.
   31 And, behold, the head was turned with them that were with it, and did eat up the two feathers under the wing that would have reigned.

3. The World Loves Only Its Own
   November 27th – Nephi, Utah

   John 15:19
   If ye were of the world, the world would love his own: but because ye are not of the world, but I have chosen you out of the world, therefore the world hateth you.

4. The First Contrary Feather
   November 29th – Washington, D.C.

   The Second Book of Esdras, Chapter 11
   25 And I beheld, and, lo, the feathers that were under the wing thought to set up themselves and to have the rule.
   26 And I beheld, and, lo, there was one set up, but shortly it appeared no more.

5. The Second Contrary Feather
   November 29th – Washington, D.C.

   The Second Book of Esdras, Chapter 11
   27 And the second was sooner away than the first.

6. Wikileaks Arrest
   December 1st – San Francisco, California

   The WikiLeaks founder Julian Assange was arrested on Thursday in London to face a charge in the United States of conspiring to hack into a Pentagon computer network in 2010, bringing to an abrupt end a seven-year saga in which he had holed up in Ecuador's embassy in Britain to avoid capture.
   https://www.nytimes.com/2019/04/11/world/europe/julian-assange-wikileaks-ecuador-embassy.html

7. The Adam and Eve Story
   December 1st – San Francisco, California

   "Cuvier, in his 'Theory of the Earth,' first published in 1812, based his conclusions on his unparalleled correlative research in stratigraphy, comparative anatomy, and palaeontology. At that time he wrote: 'Every part of the earth, every hemisphere, every continent, exhibits the same phenomenon. [...] There has, therefore, been a succession of variations in the economy of organic nature [...] the various catastrophes which have disturbed the strata [...] have given rise to numerous shiftings of this (continental) basin. [...] It is of much importance to mark, that these repeated irruptions and retreats of the sea have neither been slow nor gradual; on the contrary, most of the catastrophes which occasioned them have been sudden; and this is specially easy to be proved, with regard to the last of these catastrophes. [...] I agree, therefore, [...] in thinking, that if anything in geology be established, it is, that the surface of our globe has undergone a great and sudden revolution, the date of which [...] cannot be [...] much earlier than five or six thousand years ago [...] (also), one preceding revolution at least had put (the continents) under water [...] perhaps two or three irruptions of the sea."

— Chan Thomas, The Adam and Eve Story: The History of Cataclysms

https://www.cia.gov/library/readingroom/docs/CIA-RDP79B00752A000300070001-8.pdf

8. Silver Alert
   December 2nd – McLean, Virginia

   A Silver Alert is a public notification system in the United States to broadcast information about missing persons – especially senior citizens with Alzheimer's disease, dementia, or other mental disabilities – in order to aid in locating them.
   https://en.wikipedia.org/wiki/Silver_Alert

9. Deepfakes
   December 2nd – McLean, Virginia

   Deepfake (a portmanteau of "deep learning" and "fake") is a technique for human image synthesis based on artificial intelligence. It is used to combine and superimpose existing images and videos onto source images or videos using a machine learning technique known as generative adversarial network. The phrase "deepfake" was coined in 2017.
   https://en.wikipedia.org/wiki/Deepfake

10. The Ever-Present Secret Combinations
    December 2nd – McLean, Virginia

    The Second Book of Nephi, Chapter 26
    22 And there are also secret combinations, even as in times of old, according to the combinations of the devil, for he is the founder of all these things; yea, the founder of murder, and works of darkness; yea, and he leadeth them by the neck with a flaxen cord, until he bindeth them with his strong cords forever.

11. Paris on Fire
    December 14th – Paris, France

    In Paris, people initially gathered peacefully around the main courthouse holding signs that reflected those thousands of miles away in the United States, including "Black Lives Matter" and "without justice there is no peace."
    Later, however, after around two hours of calm, video circulated of at least two fires breaking out and reports of tear gas being fired. Paris police said a total of 18 arrests were made during the protest for vandalism.

https://www.nbcnews.com/news/world/fires-break-out-thousands-join-anti-police-violence-protest-paris-n1223201

12. The Rift in the Republican Party
    December 26th – Washington, D.C.

    So describing Republicans as divided between pro-Trump and anti-Trump forces no longer makes much sense … the GOP is overwhelmingly a pro-Trump party. That said, just like Democrats, the broader Republican Party does have some distinct blocs and factions worth understanding. The parties don't have the same kinds of differences. Democrats have deep divides over policy. In contrast, Republicans, at both the state and federal levels, are largely unified around an agenda of cutting spending for programs such as Medicaid that are targeted at low-income people, defending Americans' ability to own and purchase guns, limiting abortion, and reducing regulations and taxes on businesses.

    Instead, the most important dividing line in the Republican Party right now is probably this: How much should the GOP adhere to Trumpism?
    https://fivethirtyeight.com/features/the-five-wings-of-the-republican-party/

13. World-Wide Secret Combination
    January 2nd – New York City

    Concerning the United States, the Lord revealed to his prophets that its greatest threat would be a vast, world-wide secret combination which would not only threaten the United States but seek to overthrow the freedom of all lands, nations and countries. In connection with the

attack on the United States, the Lord told his prophet there would be an attempt to overthrow the country by destroying the Constitution.
Ezra Taft Benson, Oct. 1961 General Conference, Page 69

14. The Assassination Marketplace
January 2nd – New York City

The Rise Of An "Assassination Marketplace" Shows The Dark Side of Decentralized Networks

Augur was intended to allow people to predict things without interference of a central authority. But, of course, the internet ruined it.

Right now, there's an online bidding war over whether or not Donald Trump will die before the year is out. All a would-be assassin has to do is stake a whole bunch of money on "yes" and they'd make a fortune.

These not-quite death threats reportedly lodged against the president and other public figures, including Jeff Bezos, John McCain, and Betty White, can be found on Augur, a decentralized app recently launched by the nonprofit Forecast Foundation. Augur is a protocol through which people can create prediction markets, which are crowdsourced platforms where people stake cryptocurrency (in this case Ethereum and the Augur-specific token Reputation) on a prediction's most likely outcome.

Winners get a payoff while losers part ways with their crypto. Ideally, it would be like betting on roulette but instead of colors and numbers, you're trying to predict the future to create an accurate record of important events in the process.

https://futurism.com/augur-assassination-marketplace-decentralized-blockchain

15. Pizzagate
    January 2nd – New York City

    What is Pizzagate?
    It all started in early November 2016, when Clinton campaign manager John Podesta's email was hacked and the messages were published by Wikileaks. One of the emails, according to The New York Times, was between Podesta and James Alefantis, the owner of D.C. pizzeria Comet Ping Pong. The message discussed Alefantis hosting a possible fundraiser for Clinton.
    Users of the website 4Chan began speculating about the links between Comet Ping Pong and the Democratic Party, according to the BBC, with one particularly vile connection burbling to the surface: the pizzeria is the headquarters of a child trafficking ring led by Clinton and Podesta.
    https://www.esquire.com/news-politics/news/a51268/what-is-pizzagate/

16. Sandy Hook Elementary Conspiracy Theory
    January 2nd – New York City

    The Sandy Hook Elementary School shooting occurred on December 14, 2012, in Newtown, Connecticut. The perpetrator, Adam Lanza, fatally shot his mother before murdering 20 students and six staff members at Sandy Hook Elementary School, and later committed suicide. A number of fringe figures have promoted conspiracy theories that doubt or dispute what occurred at Sandy Hook. Various conspiracy theorists have claimed, for

example, that the massacre was actually orchestrated by the U.S. government as part of an elaborate plot to promote stricter gun control laws. The more common conspiracy theory, initially disseminated by Alex Jones on InfoWars, denied that the massacre actually occurred, asserting that it was "completely fake." (After being sued by some parents of the victims, Jones reversed his stance and admitted that the massacre was real.)
https://en.wikipedia.org/wiki/Sandy_Hook_Elementary_School_shooting_conspiracy_theories

17. Earth's Failing Magnetic Field
    January 2nd – New York City

Over the last 200 years, the magnetic field has lost around 9% of its strength on a global average. A large region of reduced magnetic intensity has developed between Africa and South America and is known as the South Atlantic Anomaly.

It has been speculated whether the current weakening of the field is a sign that Earth is heading for an eminent pole reversal – in which the north and south magnetic poles switch places. Such events have occurred many times throughout the planet's history and even though we are long overdue by the average rate at which these reversals take place (roughly every 250 000 years), the intensity dip in the South Atlantic occurring now is well within what is considered normal levels of fluctuations.

https://www.esa.int/Applications/Observing_the_Earth/Swarm/Swarm_probes_weakening_of_Earth_s_magnetic_field

18. All In the Family
    January 22nd – Springfield, Missouri

    "Homosexuals have a right to be a part of the family. They're children of God and have a right to a family. Nobody should be thrown out, or be made miserable because of it." – Pope Francis
    https://www.catholicnewsagency.com/news/pope-francis-calls-for-civil-union-law-for-same-sex-couples-in-shift-from-vatican-stance-12462
    https://apnews.com/article/pope-endorse-same-sex-civil-unions-eb3509b30ebac35e91aa7cbda2013de2

19. Brazil's New Holy War
    January 22nd – Springfield, Missouri

    Evangelical gangs in Rio de Janeiro wage 'holy war' on Afro-Brazilian faiths.
    The expression "evangelical drug trafficker" may sound incongruous, but in the Brazilian city of Rio de Janeiro, it's widespread.
    Many Brazilian Protestants attend mainstream services, and are horrified by rising discrimination against those who practice other faiths.
    But the fastest-growing denominations in Brazil are the harder-line Pentecostals and Neopentecostal churches – including the wildly successful Assembly of God and the Universal Church of the Kingdom of God.
    https://theconversation.com/evangelical-gangs-in-rio-de-janeiro-wage-holy-war-on-afro-brazilian-faiths-128679

20. Catholic Child Abuse Network
    January 22nd – Springfield, Missouri

    In a lawsuit, they charged other priests serving as "procurers" to bring victims to McCarrick at his beach house on the Jersey Shore, where he "assigned sleeping arrangements, choosing his victims from the boys, seminarians and clerics present at the beach house," and that they were paired with adult clerics.
    https://www.nj.com/crime/2020/07/former-cardinal-mccarrick-accused-of-participating-in-beach-house-sex-ring-lawyers-allege.html

21. Designated Survivor
    January 24th – Washington, D.C.
    January 24th – Hauvers, Maryland

    In the United States, a designated survivor (or designated successor) is a named individual in the presidential line of succession, chosen to stay (at a secure and undisclosed location) away from events such as State of the Union addresses and presidential inaugurations. The practice of designating a successor is intended to safeguard continuity in the office of the president in the event the president along with the vice president and multiple other officials in the presidential line of succession died in a mass-casualty incident. The procedure originated in the 1950s during the Cold War with its risk of nuclear attack.
    https://en.wikipedia.org/wiki/Designated_survivor

22. Presidential Line of Succession
    January 24th – Hauvers, Maryland

No.	Office
1	Vice President
2	Speaker of the House of Representatives
3	President pro tempore of the Senate
4	Secretary of State
5	Secretary of the Treasury
6	Secretary of Defense
7	Attorney General
8	Secretary of the Interior
9	Secretary of Agriculture
10	Secretary of Commerce
11	Secretary of Labor
12	Secretary of Health and Human Services
13	Secretary of Housing and Urban Development
14	Secretary of Transportation
15	Secretary of Energy
16	Secretary of Education
17	Secretary of Veterans Affairs
18	Secretary of Homeland Security

https://en.wikipedia.org/wiki/United_States_presidential_line_of_succession

23. Hanging by a Thread
    January 24th – Hauvers, Maryland

Brigham Young, July 4, 1854
Journal of Discourses Volume 7, Discourse 2, Pages 9-15
Celebration of the Fourth of July, A Discourse by President Brigham Young, Delivered in the Tabernacle, Great Salt Lake City, July 4, 1854.
He operated upon that pusillanimous king to excite the colonists to rebellion; and he is still operating with this

nation, and taking away their wisdom, until by-and-by they will get mad and rush to certain destruction.

Will the Constitution be destroyed? No: it will be held inviolate by this people; and, as Joseph Smith said, "The time will come when the destiny of the nation will hang upon a single thread. At that critical juncture, this people will step forth and save it from the threatened destruction." It will be so.

24. Suitcase Nuclear Device
    January 24th – Washington, D.C.

    A suitcase nuclear device (also suitcase nuke, suitcase bomb, backpack nuke, mini-nuke, and pocket nuke) is a tactical nuclear weapon that is portable enough that it could use a suitcase as its delivery method.

    Nuclear weapons designer Ted Taylor has alleged that a 105 mm (4.1 inch) diameter shell with a mass of 19 kg is theoretically possible.
    https://en.wikipedia.org/wiki/Suitcase_nuclear_device

25. The Last Two Feathers
    January 25th – Bethesda, Maryland

    2 Esdras 11:24 (KJV)
    24 Then saw I also that two little feathers divided themselves from the six, and remained under the head that was upon the right side: for the four continued in their place.

The Great Scarlet Reset

26. Ancient Betrayal
    January 25th – Bethesda, Maryland

    Moses 5:53-54
    53 And among the daughters of men these things were not spoken, because that Lamech had spoken the secret unto his wives, and they rebelled against him, and declared these things abroad, and had not compassion;
    54 Wherefore Lamech was despised, and cast out, and came not among the sons of men, lest he should die.

27. The First Eagle Head
    January 25th – Bern, Switzerland
    January 25th – Irving, Texas

    2 Esdras 11:29-30 (KJV)
    29 And when they so thought, behold, there awaked one of the heads that were at rest, namely, it that was in the midst; for that was greater than the two other heads.
    30 And then I saw that the two other heads were joined with it.
    31 And, behold, the head was turned with them that were with it, and did eat up the two feathers under the wing that would have reigned.

28. The Eagle Heads's Goals
    January 25th – Irving, Texas

    2nd Esdras 11
    32 Moreover this head gained control of the whole earth, and with much oppression dominated its inhabitants; and it had greater power over the world than all the wings that had gone before.

29. The Third Beast Kingdom
January 25th – Irving, Texas

Daniel 7

> 6 After this I beheld, and lo another, like a leopard, which had upon the back of it four wings of a fowl; the beast had also four heads; and dominion was given to it.

See Chapter 2 of The Last Days Timeline Volume 1 by James T. Prout for more information on the third beast kingdom.

30. The Fourth Beast Kingdom
January 25th – Irving, Texas

Revelation 13

> 1 And I stood upon the sand of the sea, and saw a beast rise up out of the sea, having seven heads and ten horns, and upon his horns ten crowns, and upon his heads the name of blasphemy.
> 2 And the beast which I saw was like unto a leopard, and his feet were as the feet of a bear, and his mouth as the mouth of a lion: and the dragon gave him his power, and his seat, and great authority.

Daniel 7

> 7 After this I saw in the night visions, and behold a fourth beast, dreadful and terrible, and strong exceedingly; and it had great iron teeth: it devoured and brake in pieces, and stamped the residue with the feet of it: and it was diverse from all the beasts that were before it; and it had ten horns.

See Chapter 3 of The Last Days Timeline Volume 1 by James T. Prout for more information on the fourth beast kingdom.

The Great Scarlet Reset

31. Babylon the Great
    January 25th – Irving, Texas

    Revelation 17
    > 3 So he carried me away in the spirit into the wilderness: and I saw a woman sit upon a scarlet coloured beast, full of names of blasphemy, having seven heads and ten horns.
    > 4 And the woman was arrayed in purple and scarlet colour, and decked with gold and precious stones and pearls, having a golden cup in her hand full of abominations and filthiness of her fornication:
    > 5 And upon her forehead was a name written, MYSTERY, BABYLON THE GREAT, THE MOTHER OF HARLOTS AND ABOMINATIONS OF THE EARTH.

32. Father Of All Bombs (FOAB)
    January 30th – New York City
    February 2nd – Washington, D.C.
    February 3rd – Langley, Virginia

    Aviation Thermobaric Bomb of Increased Power (ATBIP; Russian: Авиационная вакуумная бомба повышенной мощности, АВБПМ), nicknamed "Father of All Bombs" (FOAB; Russian: "Папа всех бомб", "ПвБ"), is a Russian-designed, bomber-delivered thermobaric weapon.

    The thermobaric device yields the equivalent of 44 tons of TNT using about seven tons of a new type of high explosive. Because of this, the bomb's blast and pressure wave have a similar effect to a small tactical nuclear weapon.

    https://en.wikipedia.org/wiki/Father_of_All_Bombs

33. The Muslim Messiah
   January 31st – Kasur, Pakistan
   April 17th - Kasur, Pakistan

   Twelve Shi'as cite various references from the Qur'an and reports, or Hadith, from Imam Mahdi and the Twelve Imams with regard to the reappearance of al-Mahdi who would, in accordance with Allah's command, bring justice and peace to the world by establishing Islam throughout the world.
   The Hadith is a collection of writings by those who knew the Prophet Mohammad while he was alive. A quick search of Wikipedia will give you more information on this subject.

34. Confusion Before the Imam Mahdi Returns
   February 13th – Langley, Virginia

   There are many signs that will precede him, a general and very important sign is that he will come at a time when there is great confutation, intense disputes and violent deaths. When people are afflicted by disturbance and experiencing great fear. Calamities will fall upon the people, so much so that a man shall not find a shelter to shelter himself from oppression. There will be battles and fitnaas before his appearance. Every time a fitnaa has come to end, another will start, spread and intensify. The people will be troubled to such an extent that they will long for death. It is then that Imam Mahdi will be sent.
   For clarification, a confutation is an act of refuting someone's point forcefully. Accused criminals must offer confutation if they hope to be found innocent.

The Hadith is a collection of writings by those who knew the Prophet Mohammad while he was alive. A quick search of Wikipedia will give you more information on this subject.

35. Restorationism Explained
February 19th – Salt Lake City, Utah

Restorationism (or Christian primitivism) is the belief that Christianity has been or should be restored along the lines of what is known about the apostolic early church, which restorationists see as the search for a purer and more ancient form of the religion. Fundamentally, "this vision seeks to correct faults or deficiencies (in the church) by appealing to the primitive church as a normative model."
https://en.wikipedia.org/wiki/Restorationism

36. The Name of Christ's Church
February 19th – Salt Lake City, Utah

D&C 115
4 For thus shall my church be called in the last days, even The Church of Jesus Christ of Latter-day Saints.

37. Restoration of the Priesthood
February 19th – Salt Lake City, Utah

Joseph Smith - History
68 [...] While we were thus employed, praying and calling upon the Lord, a messenger from heaven descended in a cloud of light, and having laid his hands upon us, he ordained us, saying:
69 Upon you my fellow servants, in the name of Messiah, I confer the Priesthood of Aaron, which holds the keys of the ministering of angels, and of the gospel of repentance,

and of baptism by immersion for the remission of sins; and this shall never be taken again from the earth until the sons of Levi do offer again an offering unto the Lord in righteousness.

D&C 27

12 And also with Peter, and James, and John, whom I have sent unto you, by whom I have ordained you and confirmed you to be apostles, and especial witnesses of my name, and bear the keys of your ministry and of the same things which I revealed unto them;

13 Unto whom I have committed the keys of my kingdom, and a dispensation of the gospel for the last times; and for the fulness of times, in the which I will gather together in one all things, both which are in heaven, and which are on earth;

38. The Articles of Faith of the Church of Jesus Christ of Latter-day Saints
February 19th – Salt Lake City, Utah

11 We claim the privilege of worshiping Almighty God according to the dictates of our own conscience, and allow all men the same privilege, let them worship how, where, or what they may.

39. Chinese Government Bribes Catholic Church
February 19th – Salt Lake City, Utah

"The Chinese Communist Party allocates 2 billion U.S. dollars each year" to gain influence over the Vatican's internal policy making and to pay for its silence on the CCP's repression of religious freedom, said the controversial billionaire whistleblower.

https://www.breitbart.com/national-security/2020/06/23/whistleblower-claims-chinese-communists-pay-vatican-2-billion-in-bribes/

40. The One-World Church
    February 19th – Salt Lake City, Utah

    The plans for the United Religions Organization, a one-world church, is about to become institutionalized. Collaborating are Episcopalian Bishop William Swing, the Gorbachev Foundation and certain leaders of the Catholic Church.
    https://www.catholicculture.org/culture/library/view.cfm?recnum=166

41. The Business of Catholicism
    February 19th – Salt Lake City, Utah

    MORE than 12,000 Catholic churches applied for PPP loans meant to hold small businesses together in the U.S.
    Three in four had them granted as small businesses are forced to make life-changing and devastating decisions over their futures after being denied the money that was specifically meant for them.
    https://www.the-sun.com/news/804987/catholic-churches-us-given-small-business-loans-coronavirus-emergency/

42. Global Warming and the Pope
    February 19th – Salt Lake City, Utah

    VATICAN CITY, April 22 (Reuters) - Pope Francis made an impassioned plea for protection of the environment on Wednesday's 50th anniversary of the first Earth Day, saying the coronavirus pandemic had shown that some challenges had to be met with a global response.

Francis praised the environmental movement, saying it was necessary for young people to "take to the streets to teach us what is obvious, that is, that there will be no future for us if we destroy the environment that sustains us".
https://news.trust.org/item/20200422104126-w4mdr

43. The Burden of Damascus
    February 20th – Damascus, Syria

    Isaiah 17
    1 The burden of Damascus. Behold, Damascus is taken away from being a city, and it shall be a ruinous heap.

44. Voting Fraud by Algorithm
    February 20th – Washington, D.C.

    After we went to bed, in the early morning hours of Wednesday November 4th, the "deep state" went to work in their attempt to steal the election. Around 3:30 am, "magically" out of nowhere, Joe Biden's Wisconsin tally jumped up almost 200,000 votes without a single vote for President Donald Trump. You don't have to be a math genius to realize that this is mathematically impossible!
    https://thetruthaboutcancer.com/america-banana-republic-voter-fraud-alert/

45. Surviving at Ground Zero
    February 28th – Wadi Mujib, Jordan

    Can you survive a nuclear blast underground?
    It's even possible to survive a nuclear blast near ground zero if you happen to be inside a robust building, such as a fortified structure or an underground facility, says Brooke Buddemeier, a certified health physicist at

Lawrence Livermore National Laboratory in Livermore, California.
https://www.atlassurvivalshelters.com/faq/

46. The Cities of Aroer
    February 28th – Wadi Mujib, Jordan

    Isaiah 17
    2 The cities of Aroer are forsaken: they shall be for flocks, which shall lie down, and none shall make them afraid.

47. The Virtue of Poverty
    March 1st – Notre Dame, Indiana

    'The poor will have the Gospel preached to them' (Matt 11:6), we read in Scripture, precisely as one of the signs which mark the arrival of the Kingdom of God. Those who do not love and practice the virtue of poverty do not have Christ's spirit. This holds true for everyone. For the hermit who retires to the desert; and for the ordinary Christian who lives among his fellow men, whether he enjoys the use of this world's resources or is short of many of them. – St. Josemaria Escriva
    https://stjosemaria.org/the-virtue-of-poverty/

48. The Great Reset
    April 2nd – Washington, D.C.

    There is an urgent need for global stakeholders to cooperate in simultaneously managing the direct consequences of the COVID-19 crisis. To improve the state of the world, the World Economic Forum is starting The Great Reset initiative.

As we enter a unique window of opportunity to shape the recovery, this initiative will offer insights to help inform all those determining the future state of global relations, the direction of national economies, the priorities of societies, the nature of business models and the management of a global commons. Drawing from the vision and vast expertise of the leaders engaged across the Forum's communities, the Great Reset initiative has a set of dimensions to build a new social contract that honours the dignity of every human being.
https://www.weforum.org/great-reset/

49. Description of the 12th Imam
    April 17th - Kasur, Pakistan

He will be tall;
He will be fair complexioned;
His facial features will be similar to those of Rasulullah (Sallallahu Alayhi Wasallam);
His character will be exactly like that of Rasulullah (Sallallahu Alayhi Wasallam);
His father's name will be Abdullah;
His mother's name will be Aamina;
He will speak with a slight stutter and occasionally this stutter will frustrate him causing him to hit his hand upon his thigh.;
His age at the time of his emergence will be forty years;
He will receive Knowledge from Allah.
    - Mufti A.H. Elias and Mohammad Ali ibn Zubair Ali.
    www.islam.tc/prophecies/imam.html

50. Russia's Ties to Hezbollah
    May 1st – Paris, France

Hezbollah has been a useful non-state partner to Russian forces in Syria. The Lebanese Shia militia and Iranian proxy currently fields between 6,000 and 8,000 fighters in that country's civil war, with some estimates as high as 10,000. Having suffered roughly 2,000 deaths and over 5,000 injured since their involvement in the conflict, Hezbollah has continued to be a stalwart ally of the Assad regime, fighting as far away as Deir ez-Zor. Since September 2015 this has included working closely with the Russian military, which intervened in an apparently effective attempt to save the Assad regime. Hezbollah's success on the ground in Syria has been noted by Moscow, which views it as a capable ally that has strongly contributed to the survival of the Syrian government.
https://carnegieendowment.org/sada/67651

51. Hezbollah and Iran
    May 1st – Paris, France

    Hezbollah does not reveal its manpower and estimates vary widely. In 2017, Jane's Information Group assessed that Hezbollah had more than 25,000 full-time fighters and perhaps 20,000–30,000 reservists. They are financed in part by Iran and trained by Iran's Islamic Revolutionary Guard Corps.
    https://en.wikipedia.org/wiki/Hezbollah_armed_strength

52. The G20 vs. the U.N.
    May 1st – Paris, France

    The UN and the G20's intended aims are different: the UN is "committed to maintaining international peace and security", whereas the G20 is the so-called "premier forum for international economic development". ... The

G20 was never intended to be a global organization resembling the UN.
https://www.cigionline.org/articles/un-and-g20-efficiency-vs-legitimacy

53. Hyperinflation in Venezuela
    May 1st – Paris, France

Hyperinflation in Venezuela is the currency instability in Venezuela that began in 2016 during the country's ongoing socioeconomic and political crisis.[1] Venezuela began experiencing continuous and uninterrupted inflation in 1983, with double-digit annual inflation rates. From 2006 to 2012, the government of Hugo Chávez reported decreasing inflation rates during the entire period. Inflation rates increased again in 2013 under Nicolás Maduro, and continued to increase in the following years, with inflation exceeding 1,000,000% by 2018. In comparison to previous hyperinflationary episodes, the ongoing hyperinflation crisis is more severe than those of Argentina, Bolivia, Brazil, Nicaragua, and Peru in the 1980s and 1990s, and that of Zimbabwe in the late-2000s.

In 2014, the annual inflation rate reached 69%, the highest in the world. In 2015, the inflation rate was 181%, again the highest in the world and the highest in the country's history at the time. The rate reached 800% in 2016, over 4,000% in 2017, and about 1,700,000% in 2018, with Venezuela spiraling into hyperinflation. While the Venezuelan government "had essentially stopped" producing official inflation estimates as of early 2018, inflation economist Steve Hanke estimated the rate at that time to be 5,220%. In April 2019, the International

Monetary Fund estimated that inflation would reach 10,000,000% by the end of 2019. The Central Bank of Venezuela (BCV) officially estimates that the inflation rate increased to 53,798,500% between 2016 and April 2019.
https://en.wikipedia.org/wiki/Hyperinflation_in_Venezuela

54. The Mighty Change of Heart
    June 4th – Nephi, Utah

    Alma Chapter 5
    26 And now behold, I say unto you, my brethren, if ye have experienced a change of heart, and if ye have felt to sing the song of redeeming love, I would ask, can ye feel so now?

55. The Basilica of the Holy Family
    June 4th – Nephi, Utah

    The Basílica de la Sagrada Família (Spanish: Basílica de la Sagrada Familia; 'Basilica of the Holy Family'), also known as the Sagrada Família, is a large unfinished Roman Catholic minor basilica in the Eixample district of Barcelona, Catalonia, Spain. Designed by Spanish/Catalan architect Antoni Gaudí (1852–1926), his work on the building is part of a UNESCO World Heritage Site. On 7 November 2010, Pope Benedict XVI consecrated the church and proclaimed it a minor basilica.
    On 19 March 1882, construction of the Sagrada Família began under architect Francisco de Paula del Villar. In 1883, when Villar resigned, Gaudí took over as chief architect, transforming the project with his architectural and engineering style, combining Gothic and curvilinear Art Nouveau forms. Gaudí devoted the remainder of his

life to the project, and he is buried in the crypt. At the time of his death in 1926, less than a quarter of the project was complete.
https://en.wikipedia.org/wiki/Sagrada_Fam%C3%ADlia

56. Mahdi of Dune
    June 8th – Qa'im, Iraq

    Mahdi, Arabic "المهدي" (al-Mahdi, lit. "the Guided One") or "المنقذ" (al-Munaqadh, lit. "the Savior"), was the name used by the Fremen to describe their savior in their messianic legend. The term equated roughly to "The one who will lead us to paradise."
https://dune.fandom.com/wiki/Mahdi

57. The Holy War
    June 14th –Vatican City

    I saw next international war break out with its center upon the Pacific Ocean, but sweeping and encircling the whole globe. I saw that the opposing forces were roughly divided by so-called Christianity on one side, and by the so-called followers of Mohammed and Buddha upon the other. I saw the great driving power within these so-called Christian Nations was the Great Apostasy in all its political, social, and religious aspects.
Vision of Sols Guardisto in 1923
    As printed in Prophecy; Key to the Future, Pages 199-201

58. Islam vs. Islamist
    June 14th –Vatican City

    While Islam is the faith of 1.4 billion people, Islamism is not a form of the Muslim faith or an expression of Muslim piety. Rather, it is a political ideology that strives to derive legitimacy from Islam. Islam and Islamism are not synonymous, and there is even a tension between the two, exemplified by the case of this Nigerian Muslim father turning in his Islamist son to the authorities.

So if Islam is a faith, then what is Islamism? It can be best described as an "anti-" ideology, in the sense that it defines itself only in opposition to things. That is, Islamism stands not for but against.

Soner Cagaptay

https://www.washingtoninstitute.org/policy-analysis/muslims-vs-islamists

59. 51% Attack

June 27th – Phoenix, Arizona

A 51% attack is a potential attack on a blockchain network, where a single entity or organization is able to control the majority of the hash rate, potentially causing a network disruption. In such a scenario, the attacker would have enough mining power to intentionally exclude or modify the ordering of transactions.

https://academy.binance.com/en/articles/what-is-a-51-percent-attack

60. China's Digital Currency

July 13th – Beijing, China

From the Bank of England to the European Union, to the United States Federal Reserve, central banks are leaning towards utilizing a central bank digital currencies (CBDCs) model in managing their nations' financial affairs. However, amid the growing list of countries developing a state-backed digital currency, China leads the global race with its DCEP.

Although the Chinese digital currency is yet to be fully rolled out, the country's central bank, the People's Bank of China (PBoC), had conducted a soft airdrop on the digital Renminbi to kick start the DCEP adoption process.

https://www.asiacryptotoday.com/dcep-adoption-how-to-use-the-digital-yuan/

61. Stock Market Safeguards
    July 20th – Phoenix, Arizona

Circuit Breakers

Since the crashes of 1929 and 1987, safeguards have been put in place to prevent crashes due to panicked stockholders selling their assets. Such safeguards include trading curbs, or circuit breakers, which prevent any trade activity whatsoever for a certain period of time following a sharp decline in stock prices, in hopes of stabilizing the market and preventing it from falling further.

For example, the New York Stock Exchange (NYSE) has a set of thresholds in place to guard against crashes. They provide for trading halts in all equities and options markets during a severe market decline as measured by a single-day decline in the S&P 500 Index. According to the NYSE:

A market-wide trading halt can be triggered if the S&P 500 Index declines in price as compared to the prior day's closing price of that index.

The triggers have been set by the markets at three circuit breaker thresholds—7% (Level 1), 13% (Level 2), and 20% (Level 3).

A market decline that triggers a Level 1 or Level 2 circuit breaker after 9:30 a.m. ET and before 3:25 p.m. ET will halt market-wide trading for 15 minutes, while a similar market decline at or after 3:25 p.m. ET will not halt market-wide trading.

A market decline that triggers a Level 3 circuit breaker, at any time during the trading day, will halt market-wide trading for the remainder of the trading day.

https://www.investopedia.com/terms/s/stock-market-crash.asp#:~:text=Such%20safeguards%20include%20trading%20curbs,preventing%20it%20from%20falling%20further.

62. Pioneer Day

July 24th – Phoenix, Arizona

Pioneer Day is an official holiday celebrated on July 24 in the American state of Utah, with some celebrations taking place in regions of surrounding states originally settled by Mormon pioneers. It commemorates the entry of Brigham Young and the first group of Mormon pioneers into the Salt Lake Valley on July 24, 1847, where the Latter-day Saints settled after being forced from Nauvoo, Illinois, and other locations in the eastern United States. Parades, fireworks, rodeos, and other festivities help commemorate the event. Similar to July 4, many local and all state-run government offices and many businesses are closed on Pioneer Day.

https://en.wikipedia.org/wiki/Pioneer_Day

63. History of American Football
   July 24th – Phoenix, Arizona

   The military both popularized football and developed rules to make it safer.

   During World War II, West Point's football team recruited athletes with the understanding that they could escape the draft.

   War-speak pervades football, and military institutions use high school and college games as recruiting opportunities.

   You might want to pause during this year's Super Bowl halftime show to give a nod to the military, which is closer to your Sunday night viewing experience than you probably realize.

   The armed forces, according to recent research, played a major role in turning football from an elitist college sport into an American pastime.

   https://www.seeker.com/football-shaped-by-military-discovery-news-1765639631.html

Appendix A

Selections from The Last Days Timeline

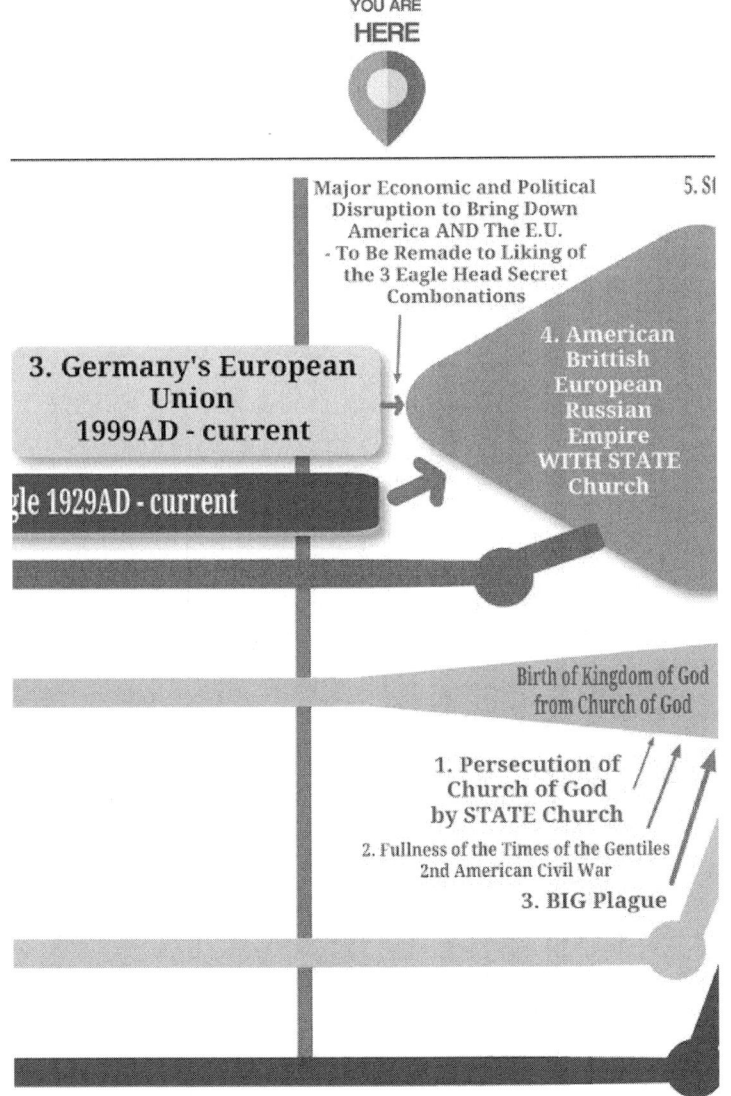

Simon Driscoll and James T. Prout

6: Daniel's 4ᵗʰ Beast rises as the 3ʳᵈ Beast Goes Down

On to the main event: Daniel's 4ᵗʰ Beast = Ezra's Eagle under the 3 Eagle Heads = The transformed United States of America into a conglomerate 10 nation global government entity Beast Kingdom of the Gentiles.

> (Daniel 7:7-8)
> "7 After this I saw in the night visions, and behold a **fourth beast, dreadful and terrible, and strong exceedingly**; and it had **great iron teeth**: it **devoured and brake in pieces**, and **stamped the residue** with the feet of it: and it *was* diverse from all the beasts that *were* **before** it; and it had **ten horns**.
> 8 I considered **the horns**, and, behold, there came up among them **another little horn**, before whom there **were three of the first horns plucked up by the roots**: and, behold, in this horn *were* **eyes like the eyes of man**, and a **mouth speaking great things**."

Learning Points:
A. This fourth beast is a kingdom that is very strong and hard to get along with.
B. It has large iron teeth for eating and with those teeth it eats and breaks nations up.
C. It crushes the remainder of nations that it doesn't swallow, with its heavy feet.
D. This beast is very different than the last 3 beasts that were **before** it: the plucked dancing lion, the laying down rib eating bear, and the flying leopard with 4 heads.
   a. (Author's Analysis): These 4 latter-day kingdoms do come in a series. Britain's Empire comes first. Second is Russia's Communist USSR. Third is Germany and France's European Union. And Fourth is this ferocious creature being described now. Notice that all 3 animals before it, came and went….Which means the EU **goes down too**…while the next 4ᵗʰ Beast Kingdom comes onto the stage.
E. It has 10 *horns*.
   a. (**Author's Analysis**): Wait a minute. Eagles don't have 10 horns….well, this Eagle will morph into a kingdom with 10 horns. Now this sounds like John the Revelator's Scarlet Beast with 7 Heads and 10 Horns that are kings. We will get there in just a bit.
F. A "little horn" came up *after* the first 10 horns were established. The "little horn" plucks up 3 of the first horns and supplants them. Kicks them out.
G. The "little horn" had eyes of a man, and a mouth that spoke large things. Many interpretations of these 2 special features of the 'little horn' could be made. I will not yet venture.

Author's Analysis:
This 4ᵗʰ beast, looking this way and doing these things, looks like America, but not quite. Some of these things make sense for the current *time*. But, I believe this 4ᵗʰ beast is *yet future* to 2017…because of what is contained in the 2ⁿᵈ half of Ezra's Eagle vision (demonstrated below).

This **last** Beast of Daniel Chap 7 is special. It doesn't have a strong animal descriptive

The Great Scarlet Reset

quality that the first 3 had. (ie. Lion, Bear, Leopard), However the Lord says that this 4th Beast starts out as an Eagle in 2nd Esdras Chapter 11, as seen below.

In Ezra's Eagle vision 2nd Esdras Chapter 12, Ezra receives the interpretation of the dream itself….and God gives **the link** to Daniel's 4th Beast.

> (2nd Esdras 12:11-12)
> "11 The eagle, whom thou sawest come up from the sea, is the kingdom **which was seen in the vision of thy brother Daniel**.
> 12 But it was **not expounded unto him, therefore now I declare it unto thee**."

> (also 2nd Esdras chapter 11:38-40)
> "38 Hear thou, I will talk with thee, and the highest shall say unto thee,
> 39 Art not thou it **that remainest of the four beasts**, whom I made to reign in my world, that the **end of their times might come through them**?
> 40 And **the fourth came and overcame all the beasts that were past**, and had power over the world with great fearfulness, and over the whole compass of the earth with much wicked oppression, and so long time dwelt he upon the earth with deceit."

Learning Points:
A. (v11-12) The Eagle shown to Ezra was the same **beast/animal** as the 4th Beast in Daniel Chapter 7….and **Ezra** received and recorded the interpretation, not Daniel.
B. (v38-40) God is saying that Daniel's 4th beast is the last beast of the 4 that is on earth *in the last days* during the end of their times. That 4th Beast was bigger and overcame the other 3 Beasts/animals that were also from Daniel's dream. Those other 3 beasts **came before the 4th**. The empires do not present their strength at the same time. They are sequential. (keep this in mind as we read Daniel 7 and Ezra's Eagle)

God said that this 10 horned ferocious animal, the 4th Beast Kingdom of Daniel's dream was the same animal as Ezra's Eagle. However, this 4th animal doesn't look anything like the Eagle described by Ezra. Not in the feathered/Presidential era, anyway.

The "3 Eagle Head" era that comes after the "18 feathers/Presidents" era; looks very much like this ferocious global government creature with 10 horns. Daniel's 4th Beast with 10 horns also lines up very nicely with John the Revelator's Scarlet Beast with 7 heads and 10 horns.

Follow along in the scriptures yourself here:
https://www.lds.org/scriptures/ot/dan/7?lang=eng

> (Daniel 7:11)
> "11 I beheld then because of **the voice of the great words which the horn spake**: I **beheld** *even* till the **beast was slain**, and his **body destroyed**, and given to the **burning flame**."

Learning Points:
A. IMPORTANT: - I skipped a few verses of Daniel Chapter 7 speaking of "The Ancient of Days" casting down the thrones of the 7+1 remaining horns of this 4th Beast.
B. Daniel watched as the Little Horn spoke his bad words.
C. Daniel watched until the 4th beast/animal was burned by fire. Important note: the end of this 4th Beast is to **be burned**. Ezra's Eagle vision says the same thing. There are many "hard links" between these 2 prophesies. Read them together as one.

>(Daniel 7:12)
>"12 As concerning the **rest of the beasts**, they had **their dominion taken away**: yet **their lives were prolonged** for a season and time."

Learning Points:
A. The other 3 earlier beast/animals/gentile nations **lived** for a time…yet their power was taken away from them….by what? The answer is in King Nebuchadnezzar's dream that Daniel interpreted (See Appendix 1) **and** in the 2nd half of Ezra's Eagle….which is yet in our future of 2017.

NOTE: God's interpretation of Daniel's 4 Beast Vision is Verse 17 through the end of the chapter 7. Remember, most of this material is yet future to 2017.

>(Daniel 7:17-18)
>"17 **These great beasts**, which are four, are **four kings**, which shall arise out of the earth.
>18 But the **saints of the most High shall take the kingdom**, and possess the kingdom for ever, even for ever and ever."

Learning Points:
A. "Four kings" ie. "Four kingdoms".
B. After the 4th Beast is slain, and judgment comes from "The Ancient of Days," then the Saints shall have their kingdom. Meaning the Zion society in Jackson County, Missouri can then begin… *after* this 4th Beast goes down in America and is no longer oppressive to the Saints of God, and is cleared out.

Daniel is Told the Truth of this 4th Beast Kingdom of the Gentiles

>(Daniel 7:19-20)
>"19 Then I would know the truth of the fourth beast, which was diverse from all the others, exceeding dreadful, whose teeth were of iron, and his **nails of brass**; which devoured, brake in pieces, and stamped the residue with his feet;
>20 And of **the ten horns that were in his head**, and of **the other [stout horn]** which came up, and before whom three fell; even of that horn that had eyes, and a mouth that spake very great things, whose look was more stout than his fellows."

The Great Scarlet Reset

Learning Points:
A. Daniel is rehashing what he saw. We now know that his nails were made of brass. This part was missing from the initial recording of the dream.

> (Daniel 7:21-22)
> "21 I beheld, and **the same horn made war with the saints**, and **prevailed** against them;
> 22 **Until the Ancient of days came**, and judgment was given to the **saints** of the most High; and the time came that the saints possessed the kingdom."

Learning Points:
A. Daniel saw that the "little horn" made warfare against the saints and **won** for a time….until the "Ancient of Days" comes and takes away the little horn's kingdom and gives it to the Saints.

Author's Analysis:
I have read many theories from prophecy book authors concerning the man called The Ancient of Days. They have stated at least 3 different meanings:
1. **Jesus Christ** – I don't think so, because we see in a later verse, the Son and The Ancient of Days are mentioned together. (See Dan 7:13-14)
2. **Adam** – Joseph Smith said this is the traditional LDS understanding of the Ancient of Days. Adam will collect all the Keys of the Priesthood at Adam-ondi-Ahman from the previous Prophets and return all keys back to Jesus Christ. So, this verse in Daniel may be referring to this event. I agree with this view.
3. **John the Beloved/Revelator** – This theory is newer. It does hold a little merit. Yet this idea does go against scripture. I do not subscribe to it.

The Ancient of Days judges the oppression of the evil Stout Horn ruler and gives the Saints the kingdom.

I think the Ancient of Days is Adam as Joseph Smith Jr. and Joseph F. Smith stated.

> (D&C 27:11)
> "11 And also with **Michael, or Adam, the father of all**, the prince of all, the **ancient of days**;"

> (D&C 116:1)
> "1 Spring Hill is named by the Lord Adam-ondi-Ahman, because, said he, it is the place where **Adam** shall come to visit his people, or the **Ancient of Days** shall sit, as **spoken of by Daniel the prophet**."

> (D&C 138:38)
> "38 Among the great and mighty ones who were assembled in this vast congregation of the righteous were **Father Adam**, the **Ancient of Days** and father of all,"

The translated John the Beloved/Revelator also plays a big part in freeing the Saints of God from the 4th Beast Kingdom. Then, the grand council at Adam-ondi-ahman

> with Adam receiving the keys and giving them to Christ takes place. Most likely, in that order.

The Beast Kingdom Lead By the Little Stout Horn Persecute the Saints of God

(Daniel 7:23-25)
"23 Thus he said, The fourth beast shall be the fourth kingdom upon earth, which shall be diverse from all kingdoms, and shall devour the whole earth, and shall tread it down, and break it in pieces.
24 And the ten horns out of this kingdom *are* **ten kings** *that* shall arise: and another [stout horn] shall rise **after** them; and he **shall be diverse from the first** [10 horns], and he shall **subdue three kings**.
25 And he shall speak *great* **words against the most High**, and shall **wear out the saints** of the most High, and think to **change times and laws: and they shall be given into his hand** until a **time and times and the dividing of time**."

Learning Points:
A. The first 10 kings of the 10 kingdoms will arise and collude to combine their power and will be doing a good job of that. *Then* a "little horn" rises up and takes out 3 of the previous kings and kingdoms of the 10 kingdom conglomerate.
B. This "little horn" is *the* bad guy. He speaks against the most High God. He makes war and wins over the Saints of God. He changes times and changes laws (as seen later). And the saints are put in bondage for a time. What type of bondage?
C. The "time and times and dividing of time" is typically understood by most scholars to be 3.5 years. This is a guestimate by the scholars and I happen to believe it.

(Daniel 7:26-28)
"26 But **the judgment** shall sit, and they shall **take away his dominion**, to **consume** and to destroy *it* **unto the end.**
27 And the kingdom and dominion, and the greatness of the kingdom under the whole heaven, **shall be given to the people of the saints** of the most High, whose kingdom *Is* an everlasting kingdom, and all dominions shall serve and obey him.
28 Hitherto *is* **the end of the matter**. As for me Daniel, my cogitations much troubled me, and my countenance changed in me: but I kept the matter in my heart."

Learning Points:
A. When "the Judgment shall sit"...the man who is to come and rescue the Saints of God from the oppression of the 10 nation 4th Beast......that beast will be destroyed **by fire and consumed**. That will be the *end* of the 10 nation conglomerate 4th Beast.
   a. Note: all 3 accounts of Daniel, Ezra, and John say this 4th Beast will be finally consumed by fire.
B. The Saints of God shall be given the kingdom after this Beast Kingdom is removed.

The Great Scarlet Reset

So if the 4th Beast of Daniel's vision is still in our future, we must also have a look at Nebuchadnezzar's Dream (Daniel Chapter 2) of the Kingdoms of the Earth from ancient to modern. The dream by Nebuchadnezzar King of Babylon relates directly with the latter-days and **the end** of this big ferocious kingdom in Daniel chapter 7. (See Appendix 1)

This full vision of Daniel's 4th Beast was left intact, however the part where the Ancient of Days comes and Judges the Beast and gives the Kingdom to the Saints of God is a bit further in our Timeline. However, this Author wanted to leave it in this section, of "the Rising Beast" so that you, the reader, will know that there is a very good happy ending for the Saints of God in America. Now, let's look at the *rise* of the Gentile Beast Kingdom in America from a few more perspectives.

7: Rev Chap 13, John's Scarlet Beast Becomes a Reality, Not Just in the Stars

As with Daniel, John the Beloved/Revelator saw the rise of the Gentile Beast Kingdom. It was not limited to the vision of the stars that John received in Chapter 12. Because in the very next Chapter 13, John sees the earthly creation of the figurative Beast he saw in the star constellation.

Remember: **important timeline point**..in Chapter 12, we saw the Kingdom of God being born *before* the full creation of the Scarlet Beast Kingdom's sign in the constellations.

There is a lessor known dragon constellation in the heavens named *Draco*. *Draco* does indeed fit the description of the Revelation 12 Dragon Constellation. It hugs and surrounds Polaris, the North Star. It's tail swings out over 1/3 of the stars in the sky as the world turns upon it's axis.

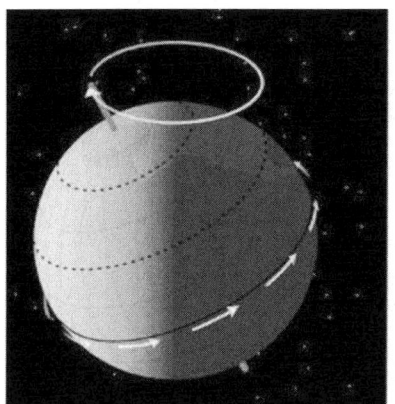 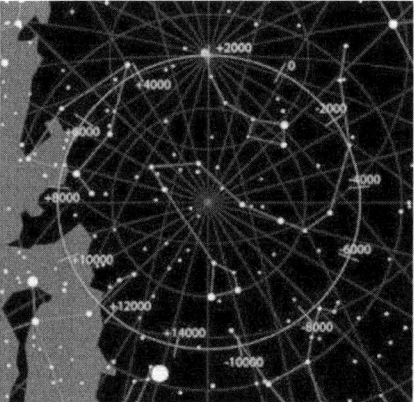

(Both images with permission from Seven Heavenly Witnesses of Jesus Christ)

I do not have any specific timely events happening with Draco after the September 23, 2017 date. I'll be researching this topic for a future edition of this work. If there is anything happening with Draco that you, the reader are aware of, please contact me at www.LastDaysTimeline.com.

And now the Scarlet Beast with 7 Heads with Crowns and 10 Horns is born into physical reality…in John's Revelation Chapter 13.

> (Revelation 13:1-2)
> "1 And I stood upon the sand of the sea, and saw **a beast rise up out of the sea**, having **seven heads and ten horns**, and upon his **horns ten crowns**, and **upon his heads the name of blasphemy.**
> 2 And the beast which I saw was **like unto a leopard**, and his feet were as the **feet of a bear**, and his mouth as the **mouth of a lion**: and **the dragon gave him his power**, and **his seat**, and **great authority.**"

The Great Scarlet Reset

Learning Points:
A. This 7 crowned Head and 10 Horned Beast rose up from the sea. Sea or "water" is usually people. This is very similar to how Ezra's Eagle rose up from the sea. However, most of these visionary beasts rise up from the sea. Only a few rise up from land.
B. On the heads was the "name of blasphemy". I do not venture to estimate what that name is.
C. This Beast looks to have the **body of a leopard, the feet of a bear, the mouth of a lion**. These are the same 3 animals as in Daniel's 3 Beasts that came before the 4th Beast. However, it appears from the evidence that we are describing the 4th Beast. Thus, the 4th Beast is an amalgam of Daniel's **first three beasts**. This is a direct link from Daniel's Vision to John's Vision. Make a note of it.
D. The Dragon Satan loves this Beast. He gives it *power*, his *seat*, and great authority in the Earth. This is Satan's mission. This Beast Kingdom is what he wants.

This Scarlet "red" Beast with 7 crowned Heads and 10 Horns looks like an *amalgam* of the 3 last-day Gentile kingdoms of England, Russia's USSR, and Germany's European Union. However, this time, there are even more clues.

The **body** of the beast is the leopard. Thus, the bulk of the body is the old European Union.

The **feet** of the beast is the bear. Thus, the moving force of this beast is Russia's USSR.

The **mouth** of the beast is the lion. Thus, the rhetoric and oratory of this beast is England and it's speaking English.

The Deadly Wound Comes to ONE of the Heads of the Beast Kingdom

> (Revelation 13:3-4)
> "3 And I saw **one of his heads** as it were **wounded** to death; and his **deadly wound was healed**: and all **the world wondered after the beast**.
> 4 And they **worshipped the dragon** which gave **power unto the beast**: and they **worshipped the beast**, saying, Who is like unto the beast? Who is able to make war with him?"

Learning Points:
A. One of the 7 crowned heads of this beast was almost taken down. Remember, this beast is a multi-state kingdom of multiple nations and kings. So, **after** the Beast is formed....one of the Heads goes down. But, then comes alive again after being healed.
   a. This piece of scripture has been interpreted to mean at least 20 different things by the prophecy writers. **However**, only *after* the Beast Kingdom is formed can this come to pass.
B. The world in general, goes toward the Beast.
C. The world in general, worships the dragon/serpent/Satan. This may be a reference to a **state** religion under the 10 Beast nations.

a. We have seen in Daniel chapter 7, that great persecutions come under this Beast upon the Saints of God. History tells us that the absolute worst persecutions upon religion comes directly from the **state**, which has power over life and death. (See *Foxes Book of the Martyrs* – by John Fox. Also *History of the Christian Church* – by Cheetham. Free audiobook downloads on www.LastDaysTimeline.com)
D. The world also worships this great 10 Nation Beast…mostly because of its great power of war in the world.

Author's Analysis:
We have not seen the "deadly wound" happen yet in 2017 because the Beast hasn't been formed, and the signs in the star constellations haven't come to pass yet. Remember, this Beast is Daniel's 4th big "empire" type kingdom that is initially formed by the 3 Eagle Heads in Ezra's Eagle.

Therefore, this whole "Beast" saga in John's Revelation takes place *after* the star constellation *signs* in the heavens of the birth of the Kingdom of God….and the Sign of the Dragon Beast in Heaven….*and* after Germany and France's European Union (Daniel's 3rd Beast) goes down.

(Revelation 13:5-8)
"5 And there was **given** unto him **a mouth** speaking **great things and blasphemies**; and power was given unto him to continue **forty and two months**.
6 And he opened his mouth **in blasphemy against God**, to blaspheme his **name**, and his **tabernacle**, and them that **dwell in heaven**.
7 And it was given unto him to **make war with the saints**, and **to overcome them**: and power was given him **over all kindreds, and tongues, and nations**.
8 And **all** that dwell upon the earth **shall worship him**, whose names are **not written** in the book of life of the Lamb slain from the foundation of the world."

Learning Points:
A. This 7 crowned Head 10 Horned Beast was "given" a mouth. Remember, the mouth of this Beast was as a Lion's mouth. The plucked dancing lion in Daniel 7 most likely is latter-day Gentile England. Remember, this beast has the "mouth of the lion". So, at this point the Lion shows up to speak.
B. "The Mouth" speaks of very bad things against God, his name, his temple, and his angels. So, this Beast Kingdom who now has an English mouth speaks against all Christian religions. *Yet*, as shown in the previous verses, will have a **state** religion of its' own. Remember, the Whore, Babylon-The Great will mount and ride this Beast Kingdom
C. This Beast Kingdom made war with the Saints of God and **won**….for a time.
D. This Beast has great power over **all** of Earth's peoples. Remember this Beast is a 10 Nation Government, *but* it is only 10 nations. All the nations of the world aren't on the team. However, all nations are within the influence of this Beast…
E. 42 months = 3.5 years – That is all the time that this Beast will be around… *in America*, before the Roaring Lion comes to take down the Beast. (Ezra's Eagle).

The Great Scarlet Reset

For the yet future Battle of Armageddon, the remnant of this Beast remains intact, because "the Anti-Christ" (Stout Horn leader of the Beast) is killed by Jesus in that final battle. But, America is freed *early* to restore the Constitution, and build the New Jerusalem (as shown in a few more chapters).

Author's Analysis:
Talk about "going backwards" in the world. American God-given liberties and civil liberties have been an institution in the world for 100s of years now. However, a return to a **state** religion under this 4th Beast would be really problematic for the Saints of God and all Christians that would rather die than worship something or someone who is false, to their understanding. Remember, freedom of religion was the very reason and basis the Pilgrims chose to leave their mother lands. To worship God according to the dictates of their own conscience....as recorded in the Holy Scriptures.

It would make sense that the new **state** religion of this Beast would cut-down the other Christian religions. As this new **state** religion would need to be promoted and made "the standard"... by official legal decree, then all the other Christian religions or otherwise would have to be degraded and demagogued. *And*, as we shall see, this new leader of The 4th Beast Kingdom will be an "Anti-Christ" that will have great super-natural power to show the world the dark-arts of Satan *openly*. Combine that material, with false religion and they will have what they need to make the masses bow down to their new **state** religion of The Beast.

The main influence which America has on the world is through money, debt/finance, and commerce. There are plenty of other influencing factors, but these are the top 3. It most likely will be much the same with other nations that are not in the 10 nations within this new 4th Beast....We can estimate this, because of *who* is going to start it up and run it. It is the same people (3 evil Eagle Heads) that are running America's systems from behind-the-curtain right now.

The next set of verses in Revelations Chap 13: 9-10, deal with *principles* of the patience for the Saints of God living through this time period. The wicked will kill the wicked. Let it happen.

Rev 13: 11-18 deals with *another* beast that looks like a goat with 2 horns. This *new* Beast raises an image to the *old* Beast and starts an economic system based upon the Mark of the Beast. (See Appendix 2)

Now that John and Daniel's Beast with 7 Heads and 10 Horns has been raised up. ...and it has gotten rich and powerful. It took some *time* to do that. Let us see what this 4th Beast Kingdom of the Gentiles' ultimate goal is to do.

About the Authors

Simon Driscoll

Simon Driscoll grew up in the shadow of the Rocky Mountains. He is a graduate of Brigham Young University. He has been writing for the last three decades and minored in English in college, focused on creative writing. Writing has always been his first passion. His understanding of the Scriptures and Prophecy comes from a lifelong study of the written word. These two passions are combined in this series.

You can connect with Simon in the following ways:
Email: simon@grendelmen.com
Website: http://www.grendelmen.com/
Twitter: @AuthorSDriscoll
Facebook: https://www.facebook.com/Driscoll.Books/

Simon Driscoll and James T. Prout

Other Works by Simon Driscoll

The Dragons' Bane Chronicles
(YA Fantasy Adventure)

The Dragons' Bane

Two people with broken hearts enter the Forgotten Forest, a place people go to forget their troubles, and themselves. Each of them has a story of their own, but Zanima, the dragon who rules the forest is looking for a champion to wield a very dangerous sword against her greatest foe. Can these three help each other, before they all lose everything?

Orphan Dani

Dani is a young orphan girl, living on the streets of a medium-sized border town. Her only friend in the world is a dragon. At fourteen years of age, she should be starting her apprenticeship, but all her schooling has come from a dragon. The same day he promises she can someday become a dragon herself, a Mage finally comes looking for her. But is he there to help her, or control her?

Traveler Dani

Dani's journey to become a dragon has finally begun. But it means leaving behind the only town she's ever known, just as she was finding a place for herself within the community. Bixby, the Mage who helped her, is still looking for her, but he isn't the only one. One year ago, she was an orphan girl with no past. Now she must hide from those who fear her future if she is to complete her quest to find the crystals of Kaldonia and learn their secrets.

Joining her on this journey is a young man named Mervad, who is also hopeful of becoming a dragon himself. But as Dani begins to develop feelings for Mervad, she learns she may have to choose between being with Mervad and becoming a dragon. Will she find the crystals, fall in love, or be caught by those who are hunting her?

Princess Dani

Dani's year-long journey to reach the cave is finally over, but her reunion with Miazan, the green dragon, is interrupted by Gwrana, an orange dragon sent by the Dragon King himself. Just when all seems lost, Dani is rescued by Prince Eyroc, to whom she was betrothed at the age of two. Now Dani is trapped in the gilded cage of Bimtor Castle, with the title of princess, and so many secrets to keep. Can she escape the castle and be reunited with Miazan? Or will her new fiancé condemn her as a Thrall?

Dani's Choice

Dani's quest began when she had nothing to live for, and no one to love her. Now she has an entire kingdom looking to her as their future queen, and a young Prince who loves her. She could delay becoming a dragon for several decades and have a human life, as Queen of Nebo, or she could leave the castle, leave Eyroc, and become a dragon now. The choice is hers to make, and it seems an easy decision at first. But when Dani meets her grandparents, their knowledge of her true past and the future they had planned for her comes into full focus.

Apprentice Eyroc - Coming Soon

Eyroc has lost his title as Prince, his home in the castle, and the love of his life in a single day. Now he must embark on a new journey as a Mage's Apprentice.

Other Works by Simon Driscoll and James T. Prout

The Ruin & Restoration Series
(Near Future Apocalyptic Fiction)

The Dark Eagle

Scott Knox is a newlywed whose marriage is torn apart by natural and political disasters. Now he's taking out his wrath on the only target he can find, President Towers.

But is Scott really acting alone? Or is he a patsy?

Can the President be saved?

Or will prophecy be fulfilled?

Redeeming Evil

Scott Knox is on the run from the authorities and the people who hired him to kill the Vice President. He's a rich man, if he can figure out how to spend it without revealing his location. Now he knows only enough to be a threat.

Can Scott survive long enough to discover who is really pulling the strings?

James T. Prout
Author: The "Last Days" Timeline

James T. Prout is the author of the books: *The "Last Days" Timeline* and *Ezra's Eagle*. James is an expert on the specific last-days events and is the founder of www.LastDaysTimeline.com

Find out how you can prepare your family for the next event in the sequence. Prophecy is simply the future, shown to Prophets of God in advance. Why not help your family by knowing the signs-of-the-times before they happen?

James has spent 20 years studying the scriptures and other authors. He pulls out the nuggets of truth and cuts through the clutter that has been recorded surrounding prophecy of the end-times leading to the 2nd coming of Jesus Christ. Let him help you discover the next domino to fall; so you can prepare your family for the next event in the sequence.

See the Presentation: "What the Scriptures Say about Donald Trump – How Long Will He Last?"

Other Works by James T. Prout

The "Last Days Timeline"

Do You Know the Exact Events of the Last Days in Their Specific Order According to the Scriptures?

The primary purpose of this work is to demonstrate with precision, what the future holds for the Saints of God using the scriptures themselves.

This is so that you may know how to prepare your family physically and spiritually for the exact events directly ahead.

The "Last-Days" Timeline - Volume 2

The Prophecy of The Tame and Wild Olive Trees

This 2nd installment in the series is all about the detailed prophecy in Jacob Chapter 5 as first put to pen by Zenos. And recorded in the Book of Mormon by Jacob, brother of Nephi.

What happens when a fictional story becomes real?

Many believe that Zenos' Prophecy of The Tame and Wild Olive Trees is only a fictional allegory. One that has meaning with man's relationship to God, but nothing else.

I have found that there is much more to Jacob chapter 5 than meets the eye.

When the internal definitions of the prophecy are realized, the whole history of this earth opens to your gaze. And also, most importantly ... the future of the nations can be gleaned.

Ezra's Eagle - The Ancient Concealed Prophecy of America's Future

America is great.

This country has been the bulwark of individual liberty in the modern age. Why is that?

The principles given to the U.S. Constitution by the Founding Fathers are most choice and pure gifts. The gifts are the rediscovered God-given liberties of natural law written down and enshrined as the crowning law of the land.

The Ezra's Eagle Prophecy shows us exactly how the designed encroachments upon the U.S. Constitution happened **and** when the U.S. Constitution is to be re-animated to hold down the federal government to free the people forever.